"What's wrong? Aren't you hungry?"

"What's wrong?" Julianna tossed the remainder aside and jumped up to face him squarely. He was tall, but then so was she. Tilting her head back a fraction, she glared at him. "Oh, let me see...I'd intended to go shopping but instead interrupted a robbery. I had a gun held to my head. I was forced to ride for hours with a stranger to an undisclosed destination. To put it in simpler terms—you kidnapped me. Tackled me. Threatened me. Tore my favorite dress." She indicated the hem with a sweep of her hand. "And worst of all," she added, her voice wobbling, "you made me miss my mother's birthday."

One rogue tear slipped down her cheek, and she blinked fast to dry her eyes.

Before she could comprehend what he intended, he lifted his hand to her face and ever so gently wiped the tear away with the pad of his thumb. His touch was as delicate as a butterfly's wing.

It confused her. There was more to this outlaw than she had anticipated.

KAREN KIRST

currently lives in coastal North Carolina with her marine husband, three boys and Andy the parrot. When she's not writing or dreaming up characters, she likes to read, visit tearooms, play piano, watch romantic comedies and chat over coffee with friends. She's incredibly blessed to be able to do what she loves and gives God the glory.

The Reluctant Outlaw

KAREN KIRST

Love Inspired

Recycling programs
for this product may
not exist in your area.

™ LOVE INSPIRED BOOKS

ISBN-13: 978-0-373-82885-2

THE RELUCTANT OUTLAW

www.LoveInspiredBooks.com

Printed in U.S.A.

For God has not given us a spirit of fear,
but of power and of love and of a sound mind.
—*2 Timothy* 1:7

To my husband, Marek—
thank you for your endless support and
encouragement. You are my voice of reason.
Without you, there would be no laughter in my life.

To my parents, Richard and Dorothy Kirst—
thanks, Mom, for all those trips to the library.
I wouldn't be living this dream today had it not been
for you. And Dad, your generosity
is what I love most about you.

To my critique partners—
my sister Shelly Benson, niece Jessica Price,
and best friend, Danielle Mattson—thank you
for your insights and encouragement
on this journey to publication!

A big thanks to my editor Emily Rodmell!
You took a chance on me and I'm so thankful you did!

My ultimate thank-you goes to my Heavenly Father
God and His Son Jesus Christ!

Apart from Him, I can do nothing.

Chapter One

Gatlinburg, Tennessee
June 1880

Blocking the entrance to Clawson's Mercantile, Evan Harrison tried to blend in with the overhang's shadows. He'd dressed in head-to-toe black, his hat pulled low to shade his eyes. Leaning against the glass-paned door, arms crossed and one ankle slung carelessly over the other, he could've been waiting for someone or simply watching the morning rush of people. What passersby couldn't see was his heart's sharp tattoo against his rib cage and the sweat sliding between his shoulder blades to trickle down his spine.

His narrowed gaze flicked to and fro, his muscles bunched and ready to spring should anyone head his way. *Hurry up, Fitz.* He wondered how Art was doing in the back alley.

This wasn't his first holdup, so why the unease? He scanned the crowd again, and the burning in his gut grew worse. He was worried about Fitz. The outlaw inside the mercantile was a wild card. Lenny Fitzgerald had proven time and again that he wasn't afraid to spill innocent blood. And he wasn't particular about his victims.

Evan had done his best to prevent the violence, but he could only do so much without arousing suspicion. He couldn't take a chance of blowing his cover. He'd worked too hard and waited too long to have that happen now.

He closed his eyes, wishing he could put off the inevitable. Then he remembered the reason he was there and his resolve hardened. He was on a quest for justice, and he *would* get it. No matter what.

He snapped his eyes open at the sound of someone approaching. Shifting his head to the right, he caught sight of a young woman striding down the boardwalk in his direction, her boots clipping the weathered planks with determination. She was on a mission, it seemed.

Please let her be headed anywhere else but here, he thought.

As she neared, he couldn't help but notice her bold beauty. Sleek red hair peeked out from beneath a navy-and-cream floral-print bonnet framing an oval-shaped face. He admired her ivory complexion, so rare in redheads, and the pert nose, regal cheekbones and generous mouth. Her sturdy navy dress outlined a pleasing female form, tall yet graceful.

She must've noticed him staring, for she quirked a cinnamon eyebrow, her lips firming in disapproval. Her eyes raked him before meeting his gaze head-on. One jerk of her chin hinted of a stubborn streak.

"Excuse me." She speared him with her gaze. "You're blocking the entrance."

Her eyes were green, not the expected blue. Deep green, the color of spruce trees streaked with sunset gold.

Straightening, Evan plucked the hay from his mouth and tossed it to the ground.

"You can't go in there."

A line of confusion formed between her fine eyebrows. "Why not?"

"Mr. Clawson had to step out for a few minutes. He asked me to tell any customers who happened by that he'd be right back."

Annoyance flickered in those gorgeous eyes. "That's impossible. Mr. Clawson is dead. His son-in-law, Larry Moore, is the owner now."

Swallowing his frustration, he struggled to maintain an air of indifference. Could she see the vein throbbing at his temple? "My mistake. Guess I mixed up the names."

A loud shout, followed by a heavy thump, sounded through the door. Evan cringed, resisting the urge to turn and look. She craned her neck to peer beyond his shoulder, and he sidestepped to block her line of sight.

"Someone is in there," she snapped, her eyes narrowing. "What kind of game are you playing?"

"Trust me, I'm not playing—"

"Is there a problem, Miss O'Malley?" a male voice interrupted from the street.

This situation was going from bad to worse. Evan turned to see a well-dressed man observing them, his curious gaze shifting from the young woman to settle on him. As a stranger in town, Evan would naturally be regarded with a certain amount of suspicion. He had to fix this. Fast.

"Good morning, Lane," the young lady greeted the man with a slight smile. "This *gentleman* and I were just discussing—"

"How rude I was for not opening the door for her," Evan finished. Grabbing the door handle, he made a slight bow. Surprise flashed across her face. "I do apologize for the oversight, ma'am." Evan pulled the door open and with a light hand on her elbow ushered her inside, calling over his shoulder, "I apologize for the misunderstanding. Good day, sir."

"Yes, goodbye, Lane."

The door closed with a final whoosh, cutting off her farewell. Through the window, Evan watched the man hesitate a moment before planting his hat back on his head and walking away. One problem taken care of. One to go.

"What was that all about?" she demanded.

Evan scanned the room. Fitzgerald was nowhere to be seen, which meant he was probably in the back, tying up the owner.

He took hold of her arm, speaking in low, urgent tones. "You're in a situation way over your head, lady. I need you to walk back out that door and as far away from this mercantile as you can. Talk to no one. I can't guarantee your safety if you alert anyone to what's happening here."

She stared at him. "What—"

"No questions. There isn't time—"

"What's that girl doing in here?"

Evan stiffened at the sound of Fitzgerald's cold voice behind him. "Keep quiet," he murmured in her ear. Without releasing her, he faced the outlaw whose features were concealed by a red bandanna.

"She was determined to do her shopping," Evan drawled. "Looks like her impatience has earned her a stint in the storeroom with the owner. I'll tie her up."

"You will do no such thing!" she cried, attempting to pry his hand loose.

Fitzgerald shook his head. "Forget it. She'll have to come with us."

"No." Her chances of survival were slim to none if she went with them.

"She's seen your face. We can't leave her here."

"I thought we agreed—no hostages. I don't like this—"

"Then you should've done your job and kept her away," Fitzgerald snapped. "Let's go."

Evan hesitated in order to give Fitzgerald a few second's head start.

"A hostage will only slow you down, you know," she argued, her eyes large in her pale face. "Leave me here. I'll tell the sheriff I didn't get a good look at you. You have my word."

He didn't reply. What could he say at this point? His mind was whirling with too many scenarios—all of them unpleasant—to attempt rational conversation.

"You're making a huge mistake! As soon as people realize what's happened, they'll organize a posse and come looking for you."

He sensed her mounting desperation, but was helpless to do anything about it.

"Isn't the cash enough? Do you really want to add kidnapping to your list of crimes?"

Ignoring her questions, he forcibly led her past the stockroom and the floor-to-ceiling shelves overflowing with goods, past the storekeeper's office and, finally, to the private quarters. At the rear entrance, he warned her to keep quiet.

"Where's Mr. Moore?" she demanded. "Is he okay?"

He slipped the Colt Peacemaker out of his holster, making sure she got a good look at it. He wasn't above intimidation to keep her in line. Her life depended on it. "Whatever you do, stay close to me."

For once, she didn't utter a word. Evan hoped that she wasn't too strong-willed to do as he said. He didn't know what Fitz would do if she made a scene.

He grabbed the bandanna bunched around his neck and tugged it up to cover his face. Opening the door a crack, he checked the alleyway. Fitz and Art were already saddling up. He hurried her down the wooden stairs to where his horse, Lucky, was hitched, prodding her forward with a hand on her back.

"Get on the horse."

She dug her heels in the rocky dirt. "Uh-uh."

"Do it or I'll toss you up there myself," he growled from his position directly behind her, letting her feel the tip of the gun barrel near her shoulder. Her resistance irritated him—didn't she have the good sense to be scared?

With a huff, she grabbed the saddle horn, placed her foot in the stirrup and hauled herself up. He replaced his firearm and swung up behind her.

Art's eyes bulged when he spotted her. "Who's that?"

Fitz barked, "Never mind. Let's ride."

"Might as well relax," Evan told his hostage, signaling Lucky to head out. "It's gonna be a long ride."

Juliana O'Malley seethed with anger. As the miles between her and Gatlinburg stretched endlessly into the distance, she passed the time dreaming up ways to get even with the man holding her captive—everything from pushing him off a cliff to hog-tying him and leaving him at the mercy of wild animals.

It was either that or succumb to mind-numbing fear. She was familiar with firearms all right, but never in her life had she had one waved in her face.

Lord Jesus, please help me, she prayed. *I'm in a bit of a situation here.*

If only she'd heeded her instincts. The moment she became aware of the man in black's blatant scrutiny, she'd known that he was no gentleman. Her cheeks burned even now as she recalled how his intense gaze had taken in every inch of her. Scandalous!

She squirmed in the saddle. His muscled arms tightened in response, imprisoning her against his rock-hard chest. His warm breath stirred the hair at her nape and prickles of awareness danced along her skin.

Juliana squeezed her eyes tight and tried not to dwell on his disturbing nearness. At least he smelled pleasant enough, she consoled herself. Beneath the smell of horse and sweat, she detected the clean scent of soap.

They would have to stop soon, she reasoned. They'd ridden for what seemed like an eternity, yet her kidnappers had given no sign of slowing the horses. She was hot and thirsty, her mouth gritty from the dust clouds stirred by the horses' hooves.

As desperately as she wanted to get off the horse, however, she wasn't eager to find out what they planned to do with her once they reached their destination.

As she saw it, she had only one option. Escape. She'd have to try to outrun him, because she was no match for his physical strength. Luckily, she was a fast runner. Just two weeks earlier, her cousin Caleb had challenged her to a footrace and she'd won. Not by much, but she'd won fair and square. He'd been hoppin' mad—

She gasped. Her mother and sisters would be wondering why she hadn't returned with the supplies. It was her mother's birthday, and they had a full day of work to get ready for the big celebration dinner that night. They wouldn't worry too much at first, but with each passing hour their concern would grow until finally someone would go looking for her.

The horses in front slowed and their mount did the same, veering off the trail into the dense woods. She straightened, nerves taut, thoughts of home scattered.

What now? Would the brute release her? Here in the middle of nowhere to fend for herself? Or did he have something more sinister in mind?

"Where are we?" she demanded. They'd used the trail along Baskins Creek heading southeast out of Gatlinburg, but she was in unfamiliar surroundings now. "What are you going to do with me?"

The man dismounted without a word. Reaching up, his hands spanned her waist and swung her down as if she weighed no more than a sack of feathers. The imprints of his fingers against her rib cage were like branding irons.

Fear shot through her, leaving her dizzy and weak.

He stepped away long enough to take hold of the horse's bridle. He tugged his bandanna down and gestured toward the other men already entering the forest. "Now we walk."

Juliana resisted, unwilling to blindly follow him. "I'm not moving from this spot until you answer me."

He spun on his heel and brought his face close to hers, his grip on her arm firm but not bruising. She'd noticed his eyes right off. A brilliant shade—dark, almost purple-blue—put her in mind of the poisonous larkspur blooms that dotted the meadows each spring. Beautiful yet deadly.

"Do as I say, Miss O'Malley," he said in a near whisper, "and I just might be able to get you out of this mess."

"You need help, Harrison?" The man who'd robbed Mr. Moore had stopped and was watching them. Something about him disturbed her. "Looks like a handful to me."

Her captor, apparently named Harrison, didn't turn around. His eyes never wavering from her face, he drawled, "Good thing I like my women feisty."

Juliana stiffened. She opened her mouth to protest, but

faltered at the almost imperceptible shake of his head. Strangely, his suggestive words were at odds with the grim light in his eyes.

"Not me," the other man snorted. "I like mine submissive."

Harrison's mouth flattened, his features hardening to granite. He was angry, perhaps even disgusted, by the other man.

To Juliana, he said, "There's a stream straight ahead and some shade. We'll rest long enough to eat a bite before heading back out."

Juliana felt a spark of hope. "You can leave me here. We're not so far from Gatlinburg, after all. Might take me a while, but I can make it back before nightfall. I don't mind walking—"

He held up a hand. "That's not an option. Come on, I'm parched and so is my horse."

"But I want to go home! My mother and sisters will be desperate to find me!"

He glanced over his shoulder. The others had disappeared into the woods, leaving them alone. His eyes bored into hers. "Trust me. I'm going to think of a way to get you home."

Trust *him?* A common thief? He was the one who'd forced her from the mercantile and ordered her onto his horse. No, his words were empty, as substantial as a fistful of air.

This was her chance. It might be her only one.

Grateful that she'd chosen to wear her brand-new, hard-soled work boots, Juliana did what she'd done as a child tousling with her cousins—nailed him in the shin with the toe of her boot and with her free arm elbowed him in the ribs. He grunted in surprise and relaxed his hold.

Juliana slipped out of his grasp and sprinted away,

uncertain which direction to take. She found herself following the hard-packed dirt trail on which they'd just traveled.

Her bonnet hung by its strings around her neck, and her hair, loosened by the jarring ride on horseback, uncoiled now to stream down her back.

Heavy footsteps sounded close behind and a small scream escaped her lips.

Faster! She pushed her legs to take longer strides. Her temples throbbed. Her side ached. The chase was over as suddenly as it began.

Bands of steel encircled her waist and down she went. Her captor twisted beneath her and she landed on top of him, his body a cushion against the rocky ground. The wind was knocked from her lungs. His arms locked around her.

"That," he puffed angrily, "was a stupid stunt."

Using her hands on his chest as leverage, she arched away from him, trying to break free of his hold. Her struggles were useless against his brute strength. He held fast. With a grunt, he rolled over so that he hovered above her, hands pressing her shoulders into the dirt. His face was inches from her own, his breath mingling with hers.

"Listen to me," he warned through gritted teeth, "if you want to survive the night you'd better do *exactly* as I say."

His dark blue eyes turned stone-cold and the look on his rugged face bordered on menacing. She trembled involuntarily.

"*I'm* not the one you need to worry about. Fitzgerald and the others will not have patience with your antics. They would've shot you dead the instant you bolted. In fact, I'm going to have to do some fancy talkin' to explain why I didn't."

At her swift intake of breath, his voice gentled somewhat. "I'm not trying to scare you into cooperating. I'm trying to keep you out of trouble. Understand?"

Juliana nodded.

"No, I wanna hear you say it."

"I understand," she managed.

"No more stunts?"

"No more stunts."

"I sure hope you mean that, lady."

He stood and pulled her to her feet. Then he marched her back to where his horse stood grazing and guided them both into the woods.

Twigs cracked beneath their boots. Far above them, birds twittered a cheerful song in their nests. Juliana was grateful for the shade. Her neck was damp from the weight of her hair, and the bodice of her dress clung to her skin. Her heart thumped against her rib cage. He'd frightened her there at the last, more even than when he'd aimed a gun at her. His forbidding expression still burned in her mind.

When she finally saw the stream up ahead, she resisted the urge to run and lie down in it.

Two of the bandits turned to stare at them. The skinny one seemed nervous, his gaze shifting between her and the other two. The man she assumed was Fitzgerald looked hard at her. He was not an unattractive man, average really, and built like a bull.

Juliana resisted the urge to hide behind Harrison.

"I thought you said you could handle her." The words came out as an accusation.

"She didn't get away, did she?" Harrison shot back.

"We'll have to get rid of her at some point, you know. She knows too much."

The cruel words, spoken so casually, washed over her like a wave of icy water.

"Not yet." Harrison stole a glance at her. "I want some time alone with her first."

Juliana faltered, suddenly sick to her stomach. After all his promises to get her to safety, she hadn't expected *that*. She lowered her gaze to the ground.

Fitzgerald barked a laugh. "Good for you, Harrison. I was beginning to wonder about you. Six months on the trail and you never once joined us at the saloon."

"Yeah, well, I've always been a sucker for Irish beauties."

Juliana's head shot up, but he kept his face averted from her searching gaze. A red flush climbed up his neck, indicating what? Embarrassment? No, that would mean he possessed a conscience.

Moving to dig in his saddlebags, he brought out a small tin cup and held it out to her without sparing her a glance. It chafed to have to accept anything from him, but thirst drove her. Careful to avoid his fingers, she grabbed the cup and hurried to the water's edge to fill it. The cold, crisp water washed away the film of dirt coating her throat.

"Take this." He appeared beside her with a bulging handkerchief. "We're only going to be here about fifteen minutes, so if I were you I'd eat fast."

"I don't want it." She stood abruptly and stepped back, wary of his intentions.

"Take it." He closed the distance between them and loomed over her. "You'll need your strength."

She *was* hungry. Snatching the bundle from him, she marched over to the nearest tree and, moving beneath the branches into the shade, sank down in the soft grass and smoothed her dress to cover her pantaloons.

She watched Fitzgerald and the young outlaw, who were crouched downstream and cramming food into their mouths as if it were their last meal. Harrison didn't join them. With clean, precise movements, he crouched and dipped his canteen into the stream. Lifting it to his mouth, he swallowed long and deep, his corded neck muscles visible. After refilling and capping the canteen, he retrieved his lunch from his horse's saddlebag and ate standing up. His hat hung on the saddle horn, providing Juliana with a clear view of his profile.

She noted his strong jawline, stubborn chin and grim mouth.

He wore his sleek, ebony hair short. The conservative style suited him. His clothes weren't of the finest quality but were in good condition. No missing buttons in the black cotton shirt, no patches or holes in the black pants. The fact that he was dressed in black from head to toe seemed to fit his personality.

He was, in a word, formidable. Impenetrable. Hard. Callous.

He glanced her way and caught her studying him. Juliana felt her cheeks flame, and she immediately dropped her gaze to the food in her lap.

Her lavish breakfast seemed so long ago, although in reality it had only been about five hours. The sun was almost directly overhead, so she guessed it was nearing noon. Unexpected tears came to her eyes as she ate the slabs of ham and hard biscuits, and she had a difficult time swallowing.

Today was to have been a day of celebration. Instead, it was a nightmare!

Why, Lord? I don't understand. What is to become of me?

Her mother's birthday was ruined. Ruined!

Certainly there would be no celebration now. All that hard work wasted! Fifteen-year-old twins Jessica and Jane had put in more hours than anybody, preparing various meats, pies and, of course, the birthday cake. How disappointed they must be!

She wondered if Megan had gone into town to search for her. Of her four sisters, Juliana was closest to nineteen-year-old Megan. She was the quiet, thoughtful one. The bookworm, her head filled with all sorts of romantic notions Juliana liked to tease her about. Poor Megan. Even she'd have a hard time putting a romantic spin on this situation.

What if Sheriff Timmons had sent someone out to the O'Malley farm to relay the awful news? They would be frantic with worry!

If it hadn't been for this trio of wastrels, especially Harrison, the scoundrel...that greedy, no good—

Dusty black boots appeared in her line of vision, and she looked up to find the blackguard staring down at her, his brow furrowed in question.

"What's wrong? Aren't you hungry?"

"What's wrong?" She tossed the remainder aside and jumped up to face him squarely. He was tall, but then so was she. Tilting her head back a fraction, she glared at him. "Oh, let me see... I'd intended to go shopping but instead interrupted a robbery. I had a gun held to my head. I was forced to ride for *hours* with strangers to an undisclosed destination. To put it in simpler terms—you kidnapped me. Tackled me. Threatened me. Tore my favorite dress." She indicated the hem with a sweep of her hand. "And worst of all," her voice wobbled, "you made me miss my mother's birthday."

One rogue tear slipped down her cheek, and she blinked fast to dry her eyes.

Before she could comprehend what he intended, he lifted his hand to her face and ever so gently wiped the tear away with the pad of his thumb. His touch was as delicate as a butterfly's wing.

"I'm sorry."

Juliana couldn't move. Was that regret darkening his eyes? All coherent thought evaporated. She hadn't a clue what to think or say. Him? *Apologize?*

He didn't give her a chance to respond. The next moment he pivoted on his heel and strode away, making her wonder if she'd imagined the tender moment.

"Time to go," he called over his shoulder. Apparently he was confident she wasn't going to try to run away again. And why shouldn't he be? He'd already proved she didn't have a chance of escaping him.

She eyed his holster. Her cousin Josh had taught her a lot of useful skills, one of them being how to shoot.

With the gun in his possession, *he* had the upper hand. But if she should ever get her hands on it...

Juliana determined right then and there to stay alert and watch for her chance to get that gun. It was her only hope of escape.

Chapter Two

"I've never understood why some people choose to live on the wrong side of the law," Juliana said. "Doesn't it bother you that you're harming innocent people?"

Harrison didn't acknowledge the question. No surprise there. Her attempts at conversation had been met with stubborn silence all along.

They were moving deeper into the Smoky Mountains, in the opposite direction of Gatlinburg and the larger towns of Pigeon Forge and Sevierville. The foursome had traveled through lush forests and meadows, beauty she would've appreciated in other circumstances. The air here beneath the soaring canopy of tree branches was cooler than in the open countryside, and for that Juliana was thankful. Midsummer temperatures in East Tennessee could quickly become unbearable.

It was late now, though, and the sun's heat had lost its bite. A soft breeze teased her hair and cooled her skin, rustling leaves whispering secrets above her. The forest was darkening, the shadows lengthening as they trudged on.

Juliana was having a hard time keeping up with Harrison. The trail had long since disappeared, and they were dodging trees and gnarled roots poking out of the ground. Twice she'd stumbled but managed to catch herself before hitting the dirt face-first.

"Poor Mr. Moore," she said. "I can't imagine how he reacted to being robbed at gunpoint. I hope he doesn't have a heart attack."

"Has he had one before?"

"No, but he isn't well. Don't tell me you're actually concerned?" When he didn't respond, she continued, "You *did* steal all his money, you know. What if he's forced to close the mercantile? I know for a fact he doesn't have any living relatives, so there's nowhere for him to go. He's such a kind, generous man, too. I don't want to even *think* about what he would do if he lost the store."

"If he's such a fine human being, then I'm sure someone would be willing to take him in."

"That's it?" she demanded, her breath coming in puffs. "That's your solution? You take away a man's livelihood and the best you can come up with is to let someone else take care of it? What about all the other people you've hurt? Do you ever stop and think about the damage you've caused?"

The skinny outlaw, whom she now knew was called Art, slowed to match their pace. "I think about it all the time. Even see some of the folks' faces I've robbed in my dreams."

Harrison's lips turned down at this, but he remained silent. Juliana studied Art's features. "Aren't you a bit young to be keeping company with ruthless criminals?"

"I'm seventeen," he said matter-of-factly. "Old enough to make my own choices."

The same age as her sister, Nicole. "Don't you have a family? Brothers? Sisters?"

"Yes, ma'am, I do," he responded softly, resignedly. "But my momma ain't got no idea where I am. Better if she thinks I'm dead than knows the truth. She'd never forgive me…"

Her heart ached for him. "Oh, Art, I'm sure you don't mean that. Were you and your mother close?"

His chest puffed out. "Yeah. I'm her oldest boy. She always said how proud she was to have me for a son."

"You know what I think? Your mother won't care what you've done as long as you're home, living an honest life."

Art was silent a moment, his brown eyes troubled. "You really think she'd take me back? And forgive me for up and leaving and joining this gang?"

"Yes, I do. But more than your mother's forgiveness, you need God's."

"My momma believes in Jesus. She read aloud from her Bible every morning and prayed with me before bed. But I—" He shook his head in shame. "I didn't always listen. I daydreamed a lot. Thought I was too young for religious stuff."

"And what about now?"

His earnest expression startled her. Here was a young man searching for the truth.

"More than anything, I want peace. I haven't had that in a long time." He lowered his voice. "I hang with a dangerous crowd. Ain't no tellin' when a bullet might find me. I've been thinkin' a lot lately about death. Trouble is, I don't know where I'm headed when I die."

"Art, I—"

"Enough yakking." Fitzgerald scowled over his shoulder. "Harrison, if you don't shut her up, I will."

With a shrug, Art moved away. Beside her, Harrison shot her a warning glance.

Frustrated with the interruption, she prayed for another opportunity to speak with Art about Christ. She couldn't help thinking perhaps *he* was the reason she'd been placed in this situation.

"How much farther?" she whispered.

Harrison wiped his brow with a handkerchief. "A quarter of a mile. Maybe more."

Ugh. While her new boots were great for defense, their stiffness tortured her feet. Blisters were already forming. She sighed.

"Take a drink." He paused to lift a canteen from the saddle. "I don't want you passing out from dehydration."

He made it sound as if he was more worried about her possibly holding him back than her health. Scoundrel. Her thirst overrode her distaste at sharing a canteen with a stranger. She took a long swallow of the cool liquid and handed it back to him.

"Watch your step," he advised. "The last thing we need is a twisted ankle or worse."

Juliana noticed he slowed his pace after that. When full darkness enveloped them, he lit a lamp to light their path.

God, I don't understand why You've allowed this to happen. I know You love me, but I'm having a hard time believing I'll ever get home. Please keep me safe. And comfort poor Mr. Moore. Somehow give him his money back. And my family, Lord, give them peace.

In all likelihood, every person in Gatlinburg had heard the news of her abduction. No doubt many of the church members were even now gathered at the church to pray. The thought brought her a small measure of comfort.

Had Sheriff Timmons already organized a posse to pursue her kidnappers? Her uncle and cousins were surely taking a lead in the mission to rescue her. But how long had it taken for someone to discover Mr. Moore?

Since she had no way of knowing what was going on back home, she comforted herself with the fact that at some point her captors would let down their guard, and she would be ready to spring into action.

Time passed more slowly than a snail in a windstorm. Juliana tried not to dwell on her bruised toes or aching calves. Nor did she attempt to start another conversation. What was the point? She would only be rebuffed.

"We're here."

The sound of Harrison's deep, no-nonsense voice in the darkness startled her. In the distance a tiny yellow light flickered. The cabin?

Juliana's steps slowed as reality slammed into her. There would be more outlaws in that cabin. She was alone. A single, unprotected female at the mercy of a gang of hardened criminals. A relentless procession of unhappy scenarios flashed through her mind, churning up the acid in her stomach. Every cell in her body screamed at her to flee.

She glanced at the enigmatic man walking beside her, recalling his vow to get her to safety. Had he meant it? Or had he said that to keep her from running again?

Her face flamed as she remembered his comments about liking feisty women and being attracted to Irish beauties. What were his true intentions? She was having trouble deciding what to believe.

Harrison must've sensed her unease, because he curled his fingers around her wrist and held fast. She glared at him but didn't try to free herself. Her muscles were weak from fear.

Fitzgerald and Art reached the cabin first. After securing their horses beneath a nearby tree, they waited for her and Harrison.

"Art." Harrison stopped before the young man. "I want you to stay out here with the lady."

Art's eyes bulged, his mouth flopping open like a dead trout. "Me?" His Adam's apple bobbed up and down. "I don't know—"

"It's simple," Harrison interrupted, his tone meant to instill confidence. "Stand right here beside her and whatever you do, *do not* let her out of your sight."

He released her wrist but didn't move away. Tucking his thumb beneath her chin, he eased her face up. "I'll be back in a few minutes," he reassured her in a surprisingly gentle tone. "Don't try anything foolish."

Juliana stared mutely at his rugged face, wreathed in shadows. So immobilizing was her fear at this point that stringing two words together seemed like an impossible task.

The cabin door banged open then and half-a-dozen men spilled into the yard, their greetings tapering to a deafening silence when they caught sight of her.

Evan stepped in front of Miss O'Malley to shield her from the men's predatory gazes. Young, innocent and beautiful, she was a lamb amid ravenous wolves. As they strained to get a glimpse of her, he could almost see them salivating in anticipation.

God, please help me get her out of here.

He stilled, stunned by the spontaneous prayer. He hadn't prayed in months, not since the day his brother had been gunned down in cold blood.

"It's about time you boys got back." Cliff Roberts, the gang's leader, separated from the rest of the group. The middle-aged man held up his kerosene lamp, casting a muted circle of light about him. "Got the loot?"

"Right here, boss." Fitzgerald held up two bulging sacks.

"Good." His steely gaze bore into Evan. "Who's the girl?"

"There was a situation at the mercantile." Evan held the man's gaze.

Fitzgerald snorted. "Harrison wasn't doin' his job."

Roberts arched a brow in silent question.

Evan clenched his teeth. "It was either get her inside or risk a scene on the front steps. I figured the mission was more important."

He heard her sharp intake of breath and wished he hadn't phrased it quite that way. She didn't know it yet, but it was about to get worse.

"I'll take care of her, boss," Fitzgerald challenged, his leer making Evan's skin crawl.

"No," Evan's tone brooked no argument. "She's mine."

"I'll wager two dollars Harrison can best Fitz!" one of the men hollered.

Murmurs rumbled through the group. "Yeah, fight!"

"Winner gets the girl!"

Ignoring Miss O'Malley's outraged sputter, Evan settled a heavy hand on his weapon. "No contest. If any of you wants her, you'll have to kill me first."

Thick silence settled over the group. Crickets' buzzes swelled to fill it, as did the odd horse snuffle. His senses on high alert, Evan waited for someone to challenge his claim. He'd meant every single word. She was there through no fault of her own. He would guard her with his life.

John Hooper held up his hands. "Whoa, Harrison. No use gettin' touchy."

"Yeah, we didn't know ya done fell in love!" Another man snickered.

Roberts studied him. "Enough! Everyone inside. Now."

Mumbling and laughing, the men filed back through the door. Evan's breath left his lungs in a whoosh. He held back until he and Miss O'Malley were the only ones in the yard.

"You're not taking me in there, are you?" she demanded in a strangled whisper, her fingers clutching his forearm.

"Not for long, I promise."

"I'm supposed to believe you?" Her voice went shrill. "After all the foul—"

"Harrison!" someone inside called. "Let's go."

"Come on," Evan said.

Placing his palm against her lower back, he pressed her forward into the small, musty cabin. The smell of unwashed bodies and cigar smoke assaulted his senses, but he quickly masked his distaste.

Most of the men were seated at the table, and at their entrance, their bold gazes locked onto the lady at his side. She hung back, no doubt frightened out of her mind. And for good reason.

Fitzgerald stood in the corner near the door, his lips curled in a menacing smirk and his dark eyes challenging.

"Harrison." Roberts motioned him toward the cabin's only bedroom. "We need to talk."

Evan started forward with Miss O'Malley.

"No, she stays here."

No way was he leaving her side. Evan opened his mouth to protest. "But—"

"Ten minutes. Gauging from your proclamation just now, I figure she'll be safe enough."

Evan changed direction and, leading her to an overturned carton in front of the fireplace, motioned for her to sit. Her wide green eyes begged him not to abandon her, and he almost caved. But he couldn't defy the gang leader's wishes without placing her in even greater danger. With a light squeeze to her ice-cold hands, he crossed the room with leaden steps.

Juliana watched him walk away, her heart frozen in fear. Her only ally, if he was truly that—and she had serious misgivings—was leaving her to face the enemy alone. Suddenly she understood a fraction of what Daniel must've felt as the guards sealed him in that lions' den and he awaited the advance of roaring, ravenous lions.

She began to pray in earnest, and to her surprise, the men largely ignored her as they took up their poker game. She kept her eyes downcast, thinking to defer their attention by being as immobile as a statue.

When their conversation faltered a few minutes later, she lifted her head to find out why. All eyes were on Art as he approached and crouched down beside her.

"Oh, go on about your business." He gestured toward the group. "I just wanna chat with the lady."

One by one, they turned their attention back to the game.

Art spoke in low tones, and she had to incline her head to hear him clearly.

"You don't have to be afraid of Harrison, ya know." His brown eyes appealed to her. "He ain't like the others."

"Why are you telling me this?" she whispered. She half wished he'd go back to his corner and let her go back to being invisible.

"I know you must be terrible scared," his voice dipped even lower, "but if I know Harrison, he'll try to get you to safety."

Interesting. Here was one outlaw urging her to trust another outlaw.

"Why would he do that?"

"Can't rightly say. But I ain't never seen him harm a living soul. Goes out of his way to avoid bloodshed." He dipped his chin. "And he's real respectful of the ladies. Harrison's a gentleman through and through."

Juliana smothered an unlady-like snort of disbelief. Gentleman? Hah. Her kidnapper resembled no gentleman she'd ever known.

Thinking perhaps this might be her last chance to broach the subject of faith, she leaned in close. "Remember what you said earlier about peace? And about not knowing where you're headed when you die?"

His face grew solemn. "Yeah."

"Jesus loves you, Art. He wants to free you from this life of sin. All you have to do is ask for forgiveness."

"I ain't never gonna be perfect."

She placed a hand on his arm, willing him to understand. "He doesn't expect us to be. We're only human, after all." She rushed to add, "But if we put our trust in God, He'll help us when we're weak and forgive us when we mess up."

"What are you two whispering about?" a gruff voice interrupted. "Hatching an escape plan?"

Art clambered to his feet. "N-no, nothing like that."

Catching Fitzgerald's hot glare at the young man, Juliana's temper took hold and she bolted to her feet.

"Leave him alone," she cried, "he was just trying to be nice."

With his bear paw of a hand, Fitzgerald seized her arm

in a painful grip. "You watch how you speak to me, you good-for-nothing—"

"Don't, Fitz," Art protested. "Harrison won't like it if you roughhouse his girl."

Juliana could feel the bruises already starting to form where his fingers buried into her flesh. She winced in pain.

Where was Harrison?

Chapter Three

Evan was having trouble focusing on the conversation. He couldn't shake Miss O'Malley's stricken expression. He could only hope that with his challenge fresh in their minds, the men would think twice before approaching her. His ears strained for any sound of distress, but he could hear only the steady hum of voices and the occasional bark of laughter.

"What's the story with this girl? Why did you bring her here?" Roberts propped an arm on the windowsill.

"Things got out of hand. She was making a scene right there in plain view, and then a gentleman friend of hers approached us. I had to think fast. Defuse the situation."

"You like her," he accused.

Evan gave a noncommittal shrug. "I've always been partial to redheads."

Where was Roberts going with this line of questioning?

The older man's gray eyes narrowed slightly. "She's a witness. You know what that means."

Ah. Roberts was probing his motives and trying to decide if he had the stomach to do away with her. With a deep breath, Evan set out to convince his leader that he didn't have a conscience.

"I've been alone too long," he said, forcing a lusty sigh. "A man needs female companionship every now and then, if you know what I mean. A few nights with her are all I need."

"Like 'em unspoiled, I see." The other man straightened. "Just don't get attached, Harrison. You understand what you'll have to do before you head back?"

Swallowing back the bile rising in his throat, he spoke without emotion. "I remember. Dead witnesses can't testify."

A malicious grin split Roberts's bearded face. "Exactly."

A high-pitched scream pierced the air. Evan's heart plummeted to his knees. He jerked open the bedroom door in time to see Fitzgerald's fist connect with Miss O'Malley's cheek, the force of the blow knocking her to the floor.

White-hot fury shot through Evan, and he unsheathed his weapon. "Outside now," he growled. "Just you and me."

"Gladly." Fitz took a step toward the door.

"No." Roberts stepped between them. He threw Evan an exasperated glance. "Remember your job, Harrison. Or do I need to leave it to someone else?"

"No." Evan fought for control over his emotions. So much was riding on the next few moments. "I'll do it," he ground out.

Deciding that it was high time to get out of there, he strode to the corner and hauled her up, ignoring her whimpers when all he wanted to do was comfort her. When he spoke, he made sure everyone heard him.

"Come on, sweetheart," he forced himself to say in as lewd a tone he could manage, "Let's go have some fun."

She shivered at his words. Evan felt nauseated, but he kept his expression blank. He looked at Roberts. "Give me a few days. I plan on takin' my time."

"Remember, Harrison, don't come back until the matter's taken care of."

Evan tugged the brim of his hat in response, half dragging her out the door and down the steps. Sweat dotted his brow. Adrenaline surged through his body. He had to get her out of there before Fitz talked Roberts out of letting her go.

Her breaths were coming in pitiful gasps. Walking with her body tucked against his side, he kept one hand on each of her arms as he propelled her through the darkness. Her steps were halting, as if trying to slow their progress. He hoped she wouldn't try to bolt again.

When he heard the cabin door slam open, he urged her to go faster. He didn't waste a second glancing back. He would *not* fail her as he'd failed his brother, James. He would get her to safety or die trying.

Reaching his horse, he pushed her up into the saddle and swung up behind her, digging his heels into Lucky's sides to jolt the big black into action. One hand holding the reins, he wrapped his free arm around her middle and held her snugly against him. They rode out in the opposite direction of the way they'd come. He wasn't sure of their exact destination at this point. All he wanted was to put as many miles as possible between them and that cabin.

He felt her trembling. In response, he tightened his hold.

He despised what he'd had to do back there. He'd given his word that he wouldn't hurt her, and look what he'd done. No doubt she believed what he'd said to the others and was scared out of her mind.

As soon as he felt confident that no one was following them, he'd stop and explain everything.

Juliana couldn't stop shaking. The stark terror flowing through her body rendered her weak and limp. She had no power to fight her fate.

Her captor held her in a steel grip, as if afraid she'd jump from the horse's back.

She resolutely focused on the movement of the horse's muscles beneath her, the heavy night air rushing past her face, the sense of light and darkness as they moved between shadows and moonlight. She refused to let herself wonder where he was taking her.

He'd promised not to hurt her. Why had she thought for an instant that she could trust him to keep his word? He was a criminal, for goodness' sake. How naïve could she be?

He'd seemed to want to keep her out of harm's way, though. He'd hinted at the cruelty of the men he associated with and had warned her not to try and escape. Had that just been a sly ploy to get her to trust him? Maybe he'd wanted to keep her all to himself, so that after they dropped off the money he could sneak off and do whatever he wanted with her.

Her stomach clenched into a hard, tight ball. She wondered how she would survive the coming hours.

The entire right side of her face ached where Fitzgerald had hit her. The blow had been unexpected—she'd had no time to brace herself or move away. The pain was excruciating.

When he slowed the horse to a walk, she stiffened her back and tried to hold herself away from him. He didn't seem to notice. Pulling his arm away, he slid off the horse and tied the reins to a low-slung tree branch. Then he was standing there with one hand on the saddle horn, waiting for her to dismount.

"Please," she pleaded, unable to look at him, "don't do this." She was not above begging.

"Come here," he said in a voice as smooth as velvet.

"I can't." She stared straight ahead, refusing to go willingly.

He moved closer, his chest pressing against her thigh. "Look at me."

Angling her head down, she obeyed, fearing that if she didn't he'd yank her out of the saddle. Standing in a patch of moonlight, his face was clearly visible except his eyes.

"I'm not going to hurt you. I've never in my life laid a hand on a female, and I don't aim to start with you." He spoke each word slowly and distinctly, as if addressing a small child. "Please get down. We need to talk."

Juliana hesitated. She'd always thought of herself as a good judge of character. Now she wasn't so sure. His manner was straightforward enough. But he'd handled her roughly and had insinuated vulgar things in front of the other men.

"I know I scared you back there." He grimaced, his white teeth glinting in the pale light. "Please believe me—it was all for show. I had to convince them that I meant business. I didn't want to take the chance of one of them challenging my claim on you."

"Your *claim?*"

"I'm the new guy. They don't know me, and they don't trust me. They have seniority. If any one of those men had decided he wanted you, Roberts would've sided against me. I would've had no say in the matter." He watched her for a moment, then dropped his hand and stepped back. He held his palms up in front of his chest. "If I promise not to touch you and not to come within three feet of you, will you come down?"

He certainly seemed to be telling the truth. If not, he was an accomplished actor. There was the other matter of his weapon. He didn't have to waste his breath being polite. He could've pulled his gun on her and ordered her down.

Juliana dismounted. When her feet hit the ground, her knees buckled. He moved to steady her, only to freeze midstep when he remembered his promise. She sagged against the horse's side for support. To his credit, the large animal didn't sidestep or flinch, just swished his tail at her.

Harrison passed a weary hand down his face, drawing in a deep breath. "Can I at least help you sit down?"

She shook her head. "No."

Straightening, she managed to walk, albeit unsteadily, to what looked like a good spot before sinking to her knees. She didn't take her eyes off him as he kneeled in the grass opposite her, his forearm resting across one bent knee.

She clasped her hands and remained silent, her eyes lowered to her lap. Her heartbeat was beginning to settle into a more natural rhythm. Surely if he intended to hurt her, he would've done so by now.

"This is going to sound dumb, but how is your face? I can't see it—that's why I'm asking."

Her first instinct was to examine the area with her fingers, but she was afraid to touch it. "I don't think my jaw is dislocated, though it hurts when I talk."

"And the pain? Is it bearable? Unfortunately, I don't

travel with whiskey, but I can make a poultice in the morning that will draw out some of the sting."

At this point, the pain was so great that Juliana would've gladly accepted whiskey if he'd had any. Her cheek throbbed in time with her heartbeat, and each time she opened her mouth to speak, it felt as if she was being punched all over again.

He spoke before she had a chance to respond. "It's that bad, huh?" He dropped his head. "This wasn't supposed to happen." Then he looked at her. "I'm sorry. If I'd known—" He broke off midsentence, standing to his feet in one fluid motion. He began to pace.

"What happened with Fitzgerald? Why did he hit you?"

"You mean, what did I do to provoke him? You think I deserved this, don't you?"

Juliana gasped when he dropped to his knees before her. "Never." He raised his hand as if to touch her. Instead, he let it drop back to his lap. "You are not to blame for what happened."

Staring at the man before her, she struggled to reconcile his gentle concern with the harsh intensity he'd displayed earlier in the day. Her mind flashed back to the moments before the other outlaws tumbled out of the cabin, and she remembered his reassuring words, his tender touch. Who was he, really?

"Art and I were talking," she said softly. "Fitzgerald didn't like it."

His jaw hardened, his hand curling into a tight fist. "He tends to lose his temper on a whim."

"Actually, I lost my temper first."

"What?" Harrison's gaze sharpened. "Why?"

"He was bullying Art. I couldn't sit by and watch

him do it when Art had done nothing wrong except befriend me."

He said nothing. Just stared at her as if she had suddenly sprouted an extra head.

"Aren't you going to say anything?" she queried at last.

"Frankly, I'm at a loss for words. I don't know whether to compliment you or give you a good scolding. Standing up for Art was a sweet gesture, Miss O'Malley." He cocked his head to one side. "On the other hand, it was an extremely foolish thing to do, given your situation."

Juliana couldn't argue with that. Still, she wasn't sure she'd do anything differently given the chance to do it all over again. Art struck her as an impressionable young man who'd been caught up with the wrong crowd.

"He's awfully young. How did he come to be with a gang of outlaws?"

"He's been with them longer than I have. Nearly a year, I believe. He was a good friend of Roberts's son, Randy."

"Was?"

"Yeah. About a month after I arrived, Randy and his father had an argument. A very loud, very contentious argument. Rumor has it Randy wanted Fitzgerald gone, but the old man wouldn't go for it. So Randy left."

"Why didn't Art go with him?"

"I can't answer that."

"Answer me this, then. Why are *you* with them?"

"Ah, that's a story for another time," he stood abruptly. "We need to get going."

Her heart lurched. "Where?"

He glanced away. "Home."

Home. How she longed to see her family, to feel their

comforting arms about her. She knew instinctively it would be a long time before she felt safe again.

"How do I know you're telling me the truth?"

His expression was unreadable. "I guess you'll just have to trust me."

Juliana realized she didn't have a choice. She didn't like it one bit that he was in total control of her fate.

No. That wasn't true. God was in control.

Evan appeared uncertain as he stood next to the horse, waiting for her to approach. He was obviously debating whether or not he should help her up. His behavior led her to believe he'd been taught to treat women with respect and that, despite his descent into criminal activity, he adhered to some ingrained habits.

Juliana made the decision to accept his help. Holding out her hand, she didn't miss the way his black brows shot up as he boosted her into the saddle. After untying the reins, he swung up behind her and spoke to Lucky in encouraging tones.

At first, Juliana sat ramrod straight in the saddle. Then her shoulders began to ache. And the horse's gait over the uneven terrain kept knocking her into Harrison. When her head bumped his chin, he curled an arm around her waist and tugged her back against him.

"Relax, Miss O'Malley."

His low, mellow voice washed over her, and very slowly the tension left her body.

Her lids grew heavier with each swaying step, until they fluttered closed and she surrendered herself to sleep.

Relaxed now against his chest, her head tucked against his shoulder, Miss O'Malley was a warm weight in his arms. The heady scent of lavender tickled his nose. Captivated, Evan lowered his face to her hair and inhaled her sweet fragrance. He sighed. How long had it been since he'd been in the company of a female? He'd certainly never courted one.

After his parents' sudden deaths weeks after his nineteenth birthday, he'd funneled all his energy into running the farm. His brother, James, just seventeen at the time, had put in the same grueling hours as he had. Side by side, they'd worked long and hard, determined to make a go of their father's homestead. Then the day came that changed everything. The news of James's murder had driven all thoughts of the future from Evan's mind. At twenty-five, he was long past the typical marrying age. Still, settling down and starting a family seemed about as likely as a fish sprouting legs.

Evan shifted in the saddle. His neck and shoulder muscles burned from overuse, and his lower back was stiff. Knowing it was past time to give his body a break, Evan decided to stop for the night. They'd spent most of the day in the saddle or walking, and tomorrow would be no different. They both needed rest.

Heading off the trail, he searched for shelter. He settled on a protected spot tucked in the midst of a stand of mature trees. The night air was comfortable enough that he wouldn't need to build a fire. The blankets in his bedroll would provide ample warmth.

Careful to balance Miss O'Malley's sleeping form, Evan slid off the stocky horse's back. It wasn't easy, but he managed to get her off Lucky and into his arms. Stepping carefully through the low grass, he lowered her to the ground. Then he returned for the bedroll.

Tucking the thickest quilt he owned around her body, he made certain every inch of her was cocooned in the material. Crouched beside her, he paused when she began to mumble words he couldn't quite make out.

With unsure fingers, he smoothed the silky strands away from her forehead. The action caused her to smile in her sleep, and she turned into his touch. Evan sucked in a breath. Her cheek, soft and cool, rested against his open palm. What now?

He didn't dare move a muscle. What if she woke and found him like this?

She'd panic, that's what!

With the steadiness of a surgeon extracting a bullet, Evan slid his hand free.

Then he bolted.

Relief flooded him when, looking back over his shoulder, he saw that she remained oblivious to her surroundings. Great. He'd avoided an awful scene. If she'd awoken to find him hovering over her, well, she surely would've assumed the worst.

Evan crossed the meadow and sank down at the base of a tree. The nervous energy surging through his body made him restless, edgy. Jerking off his hat, he slapped it against his thigh.

His mission had hit a major snag. Ten months with the gang and he had nothing. No leads and no suspects. While his brother lay in a cold, lonely grave, his murderers were living full and fancy-free. Bitterness left a bad taste in his mouth.

A wave of loneliness washed over him. How he wished he could turn the clock back to that fatal night and force James to abandon the trip! Maybe if he'd been more convincing in his arguments or outright refused to let his brother leave, James would still be alive today.

Evan had made the decision last night to go through with the robbery and then head to Knoxville on his own. James had been killed near the Tennessee River, on the outskirts of downtown. He planned to visit each and every saloon and tavern until he found the information he sought. No matter how long it took, he would never stop searching.

He glanced at the beautiful lady asleep in his bedroll. For now, though, his plans would have to wait until she was back with her family.

He gripped the rifle lying across his lap. He'd get little sleep this night. If Fitz or any of the other outlaws intended on coming after them, he would be ready.

Juliana woke shortly after sunrise to the smell of frying salt pork and coffee. Disoriented, she stared up at the patchwork of green leaves and blue sky. Where was she? Her sisters' animated chatter had been replaced by birdcalls and her comfortable bed by dewy grass and unyielding earth.

Then it all came rushing back. The mercantile. The kidnapping. The cabin.

Her stomach rebelled, and she thought she might retch. Holding very still and taking even, shallow breaths, she waited until the sensation passed.

Her cheek throbbed. She gingerly probed the area with her fingertips and winced at the pain. She didn't need a mirror to tell her what it must look like.

Propping herself up on her elbows, her hair falling in waves about her shoulders, she surveyed her surroundings. Her gaze locked onto Harrison, so intent on his task of tending the fire, and apprehension skittered down her spine. Should she trust this enigmatic stranger to stand by his promise to see her safely home?

Watching him now, she had to admit that under ordinary circumstances she would be curious about him. He was one of those men who commanded attention based on his calm self-assurance, the unleashed power in his muscular form and his dark, forbidding good looks. He was like no other man she'd ever known.

He looked up then from the cast-iron skillet and caught her staring.

"Good morning," he said matter-of-factly, as if they were old acquaintances.

He loaded up two trenchers with the pork and hoecakes. He rose in one fluid movement and approached her with long strides. Crouching beside her, he offered her one. "Can you eat something?"

His nearness intensified the queasiness in her stomach. Still, they'd skipped supper last night. "I'll try."

Juliana sat up, self-conscious about her disheveled appearance. When he didn't move away, she lifted her head. She read the displeasure in his expression.

"What?"

"Your cheek," he stated darkly. "It looks pretty bad. Is the pain worse this morning?"

Was that remorse in his voice? Surely he hadn't developed a conscience overnight.

"Not very." She wasn't being exactly truthful, but she wasn't about to admit to him the pain she was in. What was the point?

His eyes narrowed. "I don't believe you."

"Believe what you want." She shrugged, lifting her trencher of untouched food. "Can we please eat now?"

"Be my guest." He hesitated a moment before turning to his own breakfast.

Stubble darkened his jaw, and his eyes were bloodshot. Had he not slept? She quelled the urge to ask. What did she care whether he'd slept or not?

They ate in silence. Juliana nibbled at the slightly sweet hoecake, thankful that her stomach didn't protest. One taste of the salty meat was one too many, however, and she tossed it back on the plate. Gulping down coffee to rid herself of the aftertaste, she grimaced. She didn't like black coffee. Her mom had made sure to always have cream and sugar on the table for Juliana, the only one of her five daughters who drank coffee.

"Is something wrong?" he asked midchew.

"I'm not used to the strong stuff."

He swallowed. "You'll get used to it."

"Considering I'll be home in a few hours, I doubt it matters."

He didn't meet her eyes as he stood to his feet. "I'm going to rinse these off," he said, gathering the dirty utensils. "If you're done eating, you can come with me. You'll have a chance to wash up if you'd like."

What a difference a day makes, she thought. She supposed he felt guilty for what had happened and that was the reason he was acting kind. Rising to her feet, she tried in vain to smooth her wrinkled dress. "I don't suppose you have a brush in those saddlebags, do you?"

"There's a comb." He rifled through the leather bags and produced a simple black comb. "Will this do?" he asked, his eyes raking her mass of auburn hair.

Her cheeks warmed at his inspection. "Yes."

Falling into step beside him, she ventured a side glance. "How long have you been living like this? I mean…have you always been a thief?"

One black brow quirked up. "Yeah, it all started when I was three. I just had to have that lemon drop at the mercantile, so I swiped it."

"Ah, a sense of humor. I'm surprised, Harrison."

"Harrison is my last name. Call me Evan."

"Oh. Okay…Evan."

Her gaze drifted down to where the top two buttons of his cotton shirt were undone. His tanned neck shone with a fine film of perspiration, his steady pulse visible in the hollows above his collarbone.

Juliana wondered at her absence of fear in his presence. His close proximity made her feel unsettled, even nervous. But she didn't believe he would harm her.

"And your name is…" he prompted. His blue eyes, so distinctive and intense, were fastened onto her face in open scrutiny. His dark hair and clothes only made his eyes seem brighter.

"I don't believe I'll tell you, Evan Harrison."

"Why not?" his brow furrowed. "*Miss O'Malley* is a bit formal, don't you think?"

"Why should I? You and I will never again clap eyes on each other after today."

Chapter Four

Bone-weary from passing the night drifting in and out of sleep, Evan was in no mood to argue. So he clamped his mouth shut and continued down the path.

Contrary woman! He could only imagine how she was going to react when he told her the bad news—that she wasn't going home today or any day soon. His mind was made up, though. She could get angry, cry or throw a fit. Didn't matter. She would not sway his decision.

Leaving the cool shade behind, he stepped out into the bright sunshine. A wide ribbon of shimmering green meandered through the clearing, the sound of rushing water filling his ears. While not deep enough to bathe in, the stream was adequate for a quick wash.

He glanced back at Miss O'Malley, his eyes drawn to her sleek red hair glinting in the sun. Then he caught sight of her discolored cheek and winced.

He reached into his back pocket and pulled out his bandanna. He rinsed the black material in the cool water, wrung out the excess and folded it in a neat square.

He went to stand before her and, lifting the compress, lightly placed it against her cheek. For a moment she didn't blink. He lost himself in her impossibly green eyes.

There was a flash of apprehension which she quickly masked. That he'd caused her unease made him feel ill. He pressed the compress into her hand and stepped back abruptly. Of course she would be wary of him. He was her kidnapper, after all.

"Keep that on for a few minutes," he murmured. "It probably won't help much with the swelling, but the cold will feel good. As soon as we get washed up, I'll make you a poultice."

His concern for her, a stranger whose name he hadn't bothered to ask until a minute ago, was a foreign emotion. He'd been consumed with his own needs for so long—his desire for revenge and his well-thought-out plans to get it.

Evan felt ashamed. Selfish. Hard-hearted. Almost like an entirely different person than he'd been before his brother's murder. His cousin certainly had tried to convince him to let the authorities handle it, had warned Evan of the hazards of settling old scores.

The faith he'd grown up with and cultivated as an adult—the same faith he'd considered the foundation of his existence—had splintered beneath him in the space of a day. He'd fallen into an abyss of suspicion and inner turmoil.

"How long will it take to get back to town?" she asked, interrupting his thoughts.

Evan weighed his words carefully. "We're not going to Gatlinburg. I've decided it's too risky to take you back there. For now, anyway."

"I don't understand." Although her voice remained calm, he sensed the brewing storm.

"I'd planned to take you straight home to your family, but since the men know about you…we can't risk it. I figure the safest spot for you right now is my place—"

The hand holding the compress against her cheek went limp, and she looked at him in horror. "*Your* place? The home of a thief and kidnapper? No! I am not sleeping one night under your roof!"

Goodness, but she was stunning when riled up. A faint blush stained her cheeks, her pink mouth puckered in disapproval and graceful hands propped on her slim hips. She looked eager for a fight.

"You'll be safe there. That's what matters."

"Safe?" Her expression turned disbelieving. "With the man who held a gun on me, forced me from my family and is currently planning to whisk me away to parts unknown?"

"Why don't you calm down so we can discuss this rationally?"

"When it comes to my freedom, I don't feel particularly rational!"

"I brought you here. It's my duty to get you home safe and sound—"

"Oh, I see…" she scoffed. "You've got it all planned out. The triumphant return! You deliver me to my front doorstep and my family will fall to their knees in gratitude—a true hero."

"I'm no one's hero," he shot back. "Remember that."

Bitter regret rose in his throat like bile. He'd failed to protect his only brother—tried and failed.

He lowered his voice. "The men go into town once or twice a week for supplies. With your flame-colored hair, you might as well wear a sign around your neck. If I take you back now, I'd be risking your life and mine."

"I'm not the only redhead in town, you know."

"Gatlinburg isn't exactly a big town." He paused, trying to think of a way to make her see reason. "What about your sisters?"

She stilled. "What about them?"

"Suppose one of the men—let's say Fitzgerald—spotted you in town and followed you home. You wouldn't be the only one in danger."

She looked away, evenly spaced white teeth worrying her lower lip. He could see that she was torn. At last, she crossed her arms. She didn't appear pleased with the change in plans.

"Do you realize the anguish my mother must be feeling right now? And my sisters? I'm the oldest. They depend on me."

"You haven't mentioned your father."

Her eyes darkened. "He died four years ago of a heart attack."

"I'm sorry." Evan understood the pain of losing a parent. "We can send a telegram from Cades Cove, let them know you're safe and will be home soon."

She closed her eyes, distress twisting her lovely features. "This is a nightmare."

"A nightmare that will soon be over."

Resigned, she sighed. "What do you have in mind?"

"We'll pass by Gatlinburg and make our way to Cades Cove. My farm is there. We can make the trip in about three days if the weather holds. You'll have the place to yourself while I ride back to the hideout and convince the men I got rid of you. They'll be heading out in a week or so. Then I'll come back for you and escort you home."

"Why would you do that? Why go to so much trouble on my behalf when you're partly responsible for my kidnapping?"

He deserved that. "That's right. I'm responsible." He jammed a thumb in his chest. "As I said before, I got you into this mess and I intend to get you out of it."

"Something's not right." She studied him, a speculative gleam in her eye. "Little details about you that don't quite add up."

Intrigued, he crossed his arms and waited. "Such as?"

"Well, for starters, you talk funny."

He hadn't expected that. "Excuse me?"

"No, no, that's not the right word." She began to pace, and he could practically see the wheels in her brain whirling. She snapped her fingers. "Educated! That's it! You don't use foul language. And you don't speak as if you were raised in a saloon, as one would expect from a common criminal."

"And you're acquainted with common criminals, I take it?"

"Thanks to you, I am now."

"Yes, that's unfortunate. I apologize."

"There." She pointed a finger at him. "That's the other thing. You shouldn't be apologizing to me."

"I shouldn't?" This woman was beginning to confuse him.

"You treat me as if I have value. Those other men..." She shuddered. "What I mean to say is that, for the most part, you've treated me with respect. A truly hardened criminal would've done as those men suggested and gotten rid of me."

"Wait just a minute—"

"Shh! Don't try to distract me. There's one more thing, and it's a doozy."

A no-nonsense expression stole across her face and, straightening to her full height, she focused her entire attention on him. He felt like a witness under cross-examination.

"Well? What is it?"

"Money."

"What about it?"

"Where is the money you risked your life *and* mine for? You walked out of that cabin without a moment's hesitation. Have you even given it a second thought?"

"I've been kinda busy plotting our next move."

"Exactly."

Uncomfortable with her astute observations, he sought to distract her. "Is that all, Irish?"

"Yes, that's all." Her eyes narrowed. "What did you call me?"

"Fits, doesn't it? Or would you prefer *Red?*"

"Absolutely not!"

"I suppose I could try to guess your name," Evan made a show of studying her, and he gained much satisfaction at seeing her squirm. "How about Matilda?"

Her finely arched eyebrows shot up. "You think I look like a Matilda?"

"Hmm...no, that's not quite right, is it?" He stroked his chin thoughtfully. "I know. Bertha."

"Bertha?"

"That's not it, either, huh? Okay, a Bible name. Rachel. I like that one."

"Me, too, but it's not mine."

"Can you give me a hint? Tell me what letter it starts with?"

She bit her lip, and he could tell that she was beginning to find some humor in the conversation. A thrill shot through him. Trying to make her smile could become addictive.

"That would make it too easy. Besides, you don't deserve the help."

"In the meantime, then, I'll stick with *Irish.*"

"What? That's not a proper name!"

"It's yours until you decide to quit being stubborn." He shrugged, tossing her a washcloth. "See those trees over there? I'll be right on the other side washing up while you do the same here. You'll have plenty of privacy, but if you need anything just call out."

Juliana watched him stride away, her eyes fixed on his broad back. She noted the way the smooth material stretched across his powerful shoulders and biceps. A wall of solid muscle, he moved with purpose and confidence. On the outside, he was every girl's dream.

A pity he spent his days terrorizing innocents and taking what didn't belong to him.

His horse moved into her line of vision, his majestic black head low to the ground as he nibbled a clump of red clover. He was a fine specimen. Glossy coat, firm flesh, strong legs. Probably a fast runner…

Juliana clapped a hand over her mouth. Lifting his head, Lucky stared at her blankly for a second or two before resuming his snacking. No…she couldn't. *Or could she?*

She spoke in low, soothing tones as she approached the animal and tried to convey an air of calm she didn't feel. What would Evan Harrison do if he came back and caught her trying to steal his horse?

"You're a fine-lookin' boy, aren't you?" she crooned softly, taking hold of his studded bridle and rubbing her palm down his side. He was already used to her scent, and he seemed to welcome the attention. "Would you care to give me a ride somewhere, Lucky?"

She'd have to ride bareback, since she wasn't strong enough to lift the saddle with all the gear attached to it. While she preferred a saddle, riding without one was doable. If Lucky would let her, that is.

"I have to try, right, boy?" She continued to rub his soft coat, her heart thumping in her chest. "I need my freedom." She laid her forehead against his neck. "Will you help me?"

Juliana searched the woods where Evan had disappeared. Nothing. Now was her chance. She prayed Lucky wouldn't throw her.

Still speaking soft words of encouragement, she led him to a fallen log, where she stepped up, grabbed hold and vaulted up and onto his back. Half lying on her stomach, she scooted closer to his neck, her inner thighs pressing into his sides for balance. She signaled for him to move out.

The big black obeyed without a moment's hesitation. She glanced over her shoulder and again saw no sign of Evan. She was sweating—not from exertion but from sheer nerves. Her stomach, already upset, was now a hard knot. Her hands shook.

As she got farther from the campsite, however, Juliana felt like shouting for joy. Freedom was in her sights. God had surely presented her with this chance at escape.

The going would be tough, no doubt. She had no supplies of any kind. Her cousins, she thanked God, had taught her many skills that would help her find food and shelter. The only problem, in her mind, was figuring out which direction to go. But even if she couldn't get all the way back to Gatlinburg, she figured she'd come across a town eventually where she could get help.

She took note of the sun's position and rode in the opposite direction. They'd been traveling east, so it made sense that home was to the west.

"Mr. Evan Harrison is in for one big surprise." She grinned, ignoring the nudge of conscience. He's strong and healthy, she reasoned. Wouldn't hurt him a bit to hike to civilization.

What she would do with the horse once she got

home, she hadn't a clue. She couldn't keep him—he didn't belong to her. She couldn't very well return him, either. Evan knew she lived in or near Gatlinburg, and it wouldn't be difficult for him to find her. Although her time with him had been brief, she had a gut feeling that he would come looking for what was rightfully his. The thought of meeting him face-to-face at this point unnerved Juliana.

Pushing that disturbing thought away, she focused on her surroundings. She couldn't afford to daydream. Not only did she need to keep Lucky headed in the right direction, she also had to keep a lookout for snakes or wild boars that might spook him.

She was vulnerable out here alone, she knew. If only she had a weapon.

I will never leave you, nor forsake you. The words from the book of Joshua reassured her. *I know, Father, and I thank You for reminding me.*

After a mile or so of the beautiful yet monotonous terrain—wide-spaced hickory, spruce and sugar maple trees—her thoughts strayed again to Evan Harrison and his concerns about Lenny Fitzgerald and the others. He didn't have her completely convinced of the danger. If they only planned to be in the vicinity for a week or two, all she had to do was stay home and not venture into town.

And of course she planned to give Sheriff Timmons a detailed description of Lenny Fitzgerald. Wanted posters would go up all over town. That should send the criminal running in the opposite direction!

But what about Mr. Harrison? Would she give a description of him, too? William Timmons would want the man who'd kidnapped Juliana. In the sheriff's eyes, she realized, tracking down Evan Harrison would take precedence over capturing any of the others.

Juliana wanted justice. Evan deserved to be punished for what he'd done, of course, but somehow she couldn't place him on the same level as those other men. There was something different about him…she just couldn't put her finger on what that something was.

She had a knack for puzzles, though. It might take a while, but she was confident she'd figure it out sooner or later.

Evan dried his face and neck and wondered if Miss O'Malley was finished. He'd decided on a whim to give her some privacy. She'd already endured enough on account of him, and to be honest, she was handling the situation with unusual grace. It wouldn't kill him to show her a little kindness.

Deciding he'd been gone long enough, he ambled back toward camp. The weather was fine for travel, he noted with relief. Not a cloud to be seen in the pale blue sky. The temperature was climbing—it would be a scorcher—so they would stick to the forest as long as possible. He hoped they made good time. The sooner this whole mess was behind him the better.

When he emerged from the trees into the clearing, it didn't at first register that anything was amiss. A few seconds was all it took for him to realize his grave error.

He stood there slack-jawed for the space of a full minute.

She was gone. Gone! And so was his horse!

"Why that—" He clamped his mouth shut. He'd learned his childhood lessons well, and his mother had taught him not to disrespect women. Still…the woman had stolen his horse!

What did she expect him to do? *Walk* to Cades Cove?

He let out a low growl. Who did she think she was? Didn't she know the punishment for stealing a horse was a hangman's noose?

He set about packing his gear, only what he couldn't live without. His eyes fell on the saddle. She was riding his horse bareback? How had she managed to mount him?

She couldn't have gotten far, he reasoned. Irritation warred with concern. This was mostly uninhabited country—no place for a woman alone. How did she plan to feed herself? He checked the canteens. They were all there, which meant that she was traveling without water. In the height of summer. In the heat of the day. Great. He kicked a tin cup and it arced through the air. Just great.

He'd promised to return her home safe. It was his attempt at righting a wrong. If he failed at this, it would be like losing James all over again. Maybe worse.

Chapter Five

Juliana was thirsty. And hot. Her throat was so dry it hurt to swallow. In her haste, she hadn't thought about the need for water or protection from the sun's rays. Her bonnet was probably where she'd left it—tossed on top of her blanket. Her fair skin felt tight and was sensitive to the touch, especially her cheeks and forehead.

Gauging the sun's position, she guessed it to be near eleven o'clock. She'd left the forest behind about two hours into the journey and had been traveling through open fields ever since. In the distance, she saw another forest and hoped it wouldn't take long to get there.

Her stomach was empty and urgently protesting that fact. If she didn't find a place to fish, she would stop and search for berries and nuts. An apple tree would go a long way toward filling her stomach. Lucky's, too.

In all likelihood, Evan would laugh at her situation. After what she'd done, there'd be no room in his heart for compassion. It was an unwritten rule of their society— a man simply didn't mess with another man's horse. She supposed that rule applied to women, too.

While Juliana was thankful that she'd been able to

escape her kidnapper, she couldn't deny that men came in handy sometimes. Especially out on the open trail.

At long last, when Juliana was near to the point of falling off the horse, she reached the trees. She heard the sound of rushing water and sagged with relief. Past the point of all care, she ran to the water, flopped down on her stomach and submerged her face. Her unbound auburn hair floated on the surface like an intricate spiderweb.

Rolling over on her back, she lay there half-in, half-out of the water, arms spread wide. Lucky was there nearby, noisily drinking his fill.

"What a sight we must be." She chuckled, reveling in the cold wetness and blessed relief from the relentless sun. *Thank You, Lord. I was about to suffer a sunstroke, I do believe.*

Reluctantly she sat up to survey her surroundings. Water sluiced down her back, but she didn't mind. It felt divine. Nothing about her surroundings triggered a memory. Of course she'd slept in the saddle last night, so it stood to reason that she wouldn't recognize the landmarks.

Butterflies filled her stomach at the memory of being held in Evan's strong embrace. She'd fought to keep her eyes open, but between Lucky's loping gait and Evan's warmth enveloping her it had been an impossible battle. The fact that he'd carried and settled her in for the night made her face flame with embarrassment. Disgusted at herself for letting the outlaw affect her, she addressed his horse.

"Are you hungry, Lucky?"

The black had already searched out a patch of green grass and was chomping away.

Juliana scanned the brook, disappointed to find only

minnows in the shallow depths. There weren't any frogs, either. Not even a turtle. A flash of white caught her eye, and she glanced up to see a cottontail hopping past. "You sure are a cute little guy. I hate to say this within your earshot, but if I had a gun I'd be having you for lunch."

Squeezing the excess moisture out of her hair, she used Evan's comb to smooth the long locks.

Lucky didn't protest when she led him deeper into the woods. He was such a sweet horse. A prize, really. Evan must be heartsick at having lost him.

Well, if he hadn't kidnapped her in the first place, she reasoned, he would still have the horse in his possession.

They came upon a blueberry patch, but someone or something had beaten them to it. Few berries remained, which only seemed to amplify her hunger. It also brought to mind her mother's birthday cake, piled high with blueberries and strawberries. She'd never gotten a taste of that magnificent dessert.

When I get home, she promised herself, *I'm gonna ask the twins to make another one just for me.*

Daydreaming about her homecoming, Juliana thought her mind was playing tricks on her when she caught the scent of meat roasting over an open flame. Her mouth watered. Someone was nearby—with food.

As much as she longed to go crashing through the underbrush and demand to be fed, she decided not to announce her presence before getting a look at whomever was out there. A woman alone had to be cautious or risk serious harm.

With Lucky following close behind, she ventured closer to where she believed the scent was coming from. Unexpectedly, a raucous male voice broke the silence. She halted midstep and goose bumps skimmed along her skin. He was singing a ditty unfit for a lady's ears.

Juliana continued her approach, however, determined to see for herself what he looked like. Dense weeds and bushes provided cover so that she could get close without him spotting her. Looping the reins around a tree limb and issuing a command for Lucky to stay, she crawled into the bushes.

The pop and sizzle of meat made her mouth water. A fat brown spider landed on her hand and, gasping aloud, she flung it away. She *detested* spiders. Once, when she was a little girl, she had been playing in the hayloft when she disturbed a whole nest of them. Tiny spiders—hundreds of them—scurried in all directions and, of course, some of them crawled over her shoes. Screaming at the top of her lungs, she ran to climb down the ladder and, in her haste, fell to the hard dirt floor below. She suffered a broken arm and spent half the summer confined to the house.

Juliana searched the branches above her head and the grass below for more of the wretched things. Satisfied that she was safe, she crept deeper into the bushes. A dark form was visible through the leaves, and as she neared she saw that his back was to her. Unfortunately, he was still singing in a loud, off-key voice, sitting cross-legged before the fire and guzzling whiskey from a half-empty bottle. His clothes were wrinkled and stained and the edges ragged.

He looked harmless enough. Probably a down-on-his-luck drifter. And the demands of her empty stomach were starting to override her hesitation. What could she offer him in exchange for a share of the meal? All she had was the comb in her pocket, and from the looks of him, he wouldn't be interested. Did she dare hope he would help her out of the goodness of his heart?

All he could do is say no, she supposed.

Her mind made up, she retraced her steps and approached the campsite.

Rounding the bushes, she collided with a tall, thin body. She jumped back with a startled gasp.

"Miss O'Malley!"

Juliana glanced up into Art's shocked face. "Art! What are you doing here?"

"The boss sent us. Didn't trust Harrison—" His gaze skittered away for a brief second before returning to her face. "I'm mighty glad you're okay, miss. 'Course, I never believed any of that stuff Harrison said. Where is he anyhow?" He glanced over her shoulder at Evan's horse.

"He, um..." She stalled, racking her brain for a plausible story.

"Oh, miss." Art groaned, brown eyes going wide, "You didn't give him the slip, did ya?"

"Well, I—"

He slapped his head. "This ain't good at all! He'll be hoppin' mad! And there's no telling what Fitzgerald will do."

Juliana took an automatic step back. "Fitzgerald? He's here? With you?"

"Yep, that's him singin' like a drunk bullfrog."

Oh, no. What now? Harrison was right!

Her pulse skyrocketing, she pivoted on her heel and strode toward Lucky. "I have to find Evan!"

She had one foot in the stirrup when she heard the click of a gun hammer.

"Stop right there."

Juliana froze. Dread settled like a leaden weight on her shoulders.

"Step away from the horse," Fitzgerald ordered with a wave of his pistol.

She was in big trouble, and Evan was miles away. Too

far to rescue her this time. Not that he would after what she'd done to him. Silently, she did as she was told.

"Where's Harrison?" he demanded, all joviality of a few moments ago gone.

"He's not here." She looked him straight in the eye, refusing to give him the satisfaction of seeing her fear.

"I can see that," he snapped. "Where is he?"

"A few miles back at camp."

Juliana jerked when he barked a harsh laugh.

"Harrison underestimated you, I see. I'm beginning to understand his preference for spirited women. Maybe I'll keep you around for a while." His full lips curled into an insolent sneer. "See for myself what all the fuss is about."

Art spoke up. "What are you planning, Fitz?"

Juliana squelched the urge to squirm beneath the outlaw's lewd stare. She clasped her hands together to stop them from shaking.

"Give me time." He looked over at the young man. "I'll come up with something. For now, nature calls. Make sure she doesn't escape. Or else."

Art gulped. He watched Fitzgerald disappear into the woods. Then he approached with eager strides.

"You have to go *now!*" He urged her in Lucky's direction.

Staring up at his boyish face, years away from manhood, Juliana felt like weeping. Here was her chance at escape, and she couldn't take it.

She placed a restraining hand on his arm. "I can't," she whispered. "Who knows what he'll do to you?"

Art shook his head, his fine blond hair sliding into his eyes. "Don't you worry about me. Go back to Harrison. He'll help you—I just know it."

Evan's handsome face swam before her eyes, and she wished with all her being that she'd trusted him.

"I'm not so sure about that," she choked out. "In any case, I can't leave on your watch."

Straightening to his full height, Art gave her a stubborn glare. "And I say you *can*. And you will."

Unaccustomed to seeing the awkward teen so sure of himself, Juliana's jaw dropped. He was maturing before her very eyes. Too bad it was a wasted effort. She could not in good conscience leave him to the mercy of Fitzgerald's wrath.

"I appreciate what you're trying to do, Art. But I just can't do it."

"Do you know what Harrison will do when he finds out Fitz has you?" he demanded. "I'd almost rather face Fitz. Please. Go."

A loud whistle threaded through the trees, and they jumped apart as Fitz strolled back into the clearing. He looked from one to the other.

"I'm starved. Let's eat."

Evan hated to admit he'd been outsmarted by a female. He'd gone over the morning's events a couple of times, drawing the conclusion that he'd gone soft. Give her some privacy, he'd told himself. Be a gentleman!

The kicker was he'd left his horse in the care of a stranger. When was that ever a smart thing to do? He had let his guard down, and now he was minus one first-rate horse. It was a costly mistake in more ways than one.

Where was she?

He'd seen horse droppings and broken shrubs, even spotted some fresh tracks in the soft earth. He was confident he was on their trail, so why hadn't he found them yet?

He'd been walking for hours. What he needed was a cup of coffee to perk him up. With the little sleep he had to go on, he was dragging. His feet hurt. There was a permanent dent in his shoulder from the saddlebag strap. He had every right to be irate. Somehow…he wasn't. Not at her. If anything, he blamed himself for getting her into this situation in the first place.

If only she had waited a little longer to do her shopping yesterday.

If only he hadn't been too ill to take his brother to Knoxville ten months ago.

There were too many twists and turns in life that could lead a man down the wrong path.

Especially when the man was doing the leading and not God.

Evan stopped walking, one hand on his hip and the other hanging on to the strap. Where had that thought come from? He'd been running from the Lord for a while now—since James's death. Evan's faith had shattered the moment he heard the news. Guilt was his constant companion these days, not the Lord.

Tilting his head back, he watched tiny robins hop from branch to branch, singing merrily to each other. Squirrels darted up the broad, grooved tree trunks, searching for acorns. Buttercups and dandelions dotted the forest floor.

God's touch was evident in every insect, every petal, every leaf.

Oh, Father, I miss You so much sometimes it hurts.

Evan shook his head, wondering how much longer he could take living like this.

He scanned the forest, noting that the trees were beginning to thin and that it appeared brighter in the distance. He was headed for a clearing. Lifting his hat, he wiped his forehead with his sleeve, too lazy at this point to dig in his pocket for a hanky.

Where was she?

He took a long swallow from his canteen, screwed the lid back on, and started walking again.

Ignoring Art's sidelong glances, Juliana stared into the fire. What now?

"Sit down." Fitz motioned with his half-empty whiskey bottle.

Her appetite had fled at the sight of him. Now bile rose up in her throat at the thought of having to share a meal with the outlaw.

When she hesitated, he leaned over and seized her upper arm, forcing her to sit down hard. Ducking her head, Juliana swallowed an anguished groan. Surely any sign of weakness would only stir his anger.

Art was silent. Still, she sensed his frustration as he plopped down beside her.

Fitz sat opposite her. With his bare fingers, he snatched the meat from the still-sizzling skillet, tore off a big hunk and dropped it on a flat green leaf. "Enjoy it." He leered viciously. "Might be your last."

Juliana ignored him. She pulled off tiny bits and somehow managed to swallow without choking. Nauseous from the rush of adrenaline, her stomach protested but she managed to keep it down.

Lord Jesus, please help me think of a way out of this mess. Give me wisdom and courage. I need You desperately.

"Did you leave Harrison alive or dead?" Fitz grunted, wiping his sleeve across his greasy mouth.

She lifted her eyes to his and was shocked by the coldness and hatred there. This was a person with absolutely no morals, a person who wouldn't think twice about hurting or even killing another human being.

How foolish she'd been to leave Evan Harrison's protection! He was an outlaw, yes, but he hadn't harmed her. He had even promised to escort her home!

With Lenny Fitzgerald calling the shots, her life could be over in the blink of an eye.

"Last I saw him, he was alive and well," she said.

"How did you manage to steal his horse?"

"He let his guard down."

"We won't do that, will we, Art?" Fitzgerald shot Art a warning glare.

Juliana swallowed hard. This conversation was going nowhere fast. Her gaze darted around, looking for a weapon of some kind. If she could delay him just long enough for her to get a head start, she was sure Lucky could outrun his mount. Besides, the man was half-drunk. He'd be slower than normal.

Her gaze landed on the cast-iron skillet resting above the flames. Melted fatback popped and hissed. An idea seized her, and she acted on it before she could change her mind.

Leaning forward, she reached out a hand. "Mind if I help myself to some more meat?"

He eyed her a moment, then shrugged his beefy shoulders.

Inhaling deeply, she grabbed the handle and slung the skillet upwards, the burning hot liquid spilling out to splatter across his face and neck. He yelped in pain, his hands clawing at his face.

Panicked, Juliana let the skillet fall to the ground. She jumped to her feet and sprinted to Lucky's side, vaulting onto his back with more speed than she knew she possessed.

"You'll pay for this!" he bellowed in a fit of rage. "You won't get away—"

Hearing him hollering for Art to follow her, she glanced back and saw him pretend to stumble and twist his ankle.

She silently praised Art's quick thinking.

Juliana urged Lucky into an all-out gallop. Her heart throbbed in time to the horse's hoofbeats against the hard earth as they dodged trees and fallen logs. Within moments, they left the forest behind for the wide, open plain. Juliana held on tight as the black lengthened his stride— heading back the way they'd come, back to where she'd started from, back to Evan Harrison.

Chapter Six

Finally emerging from the trees, Evan paused to take in his surroundings. Before him lay miles and miles of grassland. The forest behind him covered the hills to the right and curved around in front of him far in the distance. It would've made sense for her to have stayed with the tree line, but he could clearly see the trampled grass leading into the empty field.

He thought of the bonnet she'd forgotten back at camp, now tucked safely in his pack. He could only imagine her discomfort traveling in the direct sunlight without the benefit of shade. If she hadn't found water… No, he wouldn't allow his thoughts to go there. She was smart. Resourceful.

About a quarter of a mile later, he caught sight of what looked to be a horse and rider. To be safe, he unsheathed his gun. Too slow for his liking, the figure neared, and he saw that the animal was dark in color, although whether brown or black he couldn't tell. The rider was slumped over, using the horse's neck for support.

Evan stiffened, his muscles primed to spring into action. Something was wrong. In the instant he realized that it was *his* horse carrying Miss O'Malley, he slid his gun back into the holster and started running.

When he came alongside Lucky, she fell into his arms, her unexpected weight and forward motion knocking him to the ground. Evan pushed up into a sitting position, his arms locked around her slender form.

"Irish! What happened?"

"Oh, Evan." She sobbed into his chest, her fingers clutching his shirt. "I'm so s-sorry—"

His anger evaporated at the sight of her tears. "Are you injured? Ill?"

"N-no."

Relief filtered through his soul like soothing rain. She was safe.

"Shh," he murmured, resting his chin against her head. "Everything's all right now."

Comforting her, holding her, felt so right. His eyes drifting closed, he inhaled her sweet lavender scent and smoothed her hair with gentle strokes. The strands felt like pure bliss to his fingertips…thick and heavy and silken. His hands drifted lower to rub circles along her back. He felt her sigh as she settled her weight more firmly against him, the wetness from her cheeks seeping into his shirt. He didn't mind.

He tightened his hold, aware of the need she was stirring within him. The need to connect, to *matter*. To share life's joys and burdens. To love and be loved.

Irish lifted her face to gaze at him, her tear-filled eyes looking like forest ferns sparkling with dewdrops. His eyes dropped to her pink lips, the lower one full and inviting. It would be so easy to angle his head down and—

"Evan, I stole your horse. And Fitzgerald found out—" She broke off, a shudder racking her body.

"What?" His heart skidded to a halt, and his gaze

jerked upwards to meet hers. Evan gripped her shoulders and held her away from him. "You saw Fitzgerald? Where? What happened? Did he hurt you?"

"No, but he threatened me. And after what I did to him—" She clutched his biceps, "Evan, we have to go! We have to get out of here before he catches up to us."

"What did you do, Irish?" He tensed.

"I threw hot grease in his face."

"You *what?*"

"It was my only option at the time." Her chin came up in defense, a spark of her usual spirit flaring in her eyes. "I had to distract him…somehow get a head start. It worked, didn't it?"

Evan dropped his hands and sat back, his mind numb with the implications. There was no question now as to whether or not Fitzgerald would follow them and watch for a chance to strike. After what she did to him, he would be out for blood.

"Art was with him."

"Art?" Evan repeated. "Did he say why?"

Her eyes dulled. "Your boss sent him and Fitzgerald to make sure you held up your end of the bargain."

He couldn't say he was surprised. After the way he'd reacted to Fitz's treatment of her, Roberts was bound to have his doubts.

"I didn't mean a word of it, remember?" he said softly, reaching out to stroke her cheek. She looked so lost just then. And vulnerable. It made him all the more determined to get her home safe.

"You realize, don't you, that you absolutely can *not* go back to Gatlinburg until he leaves the area."

A worried crease appeared between her brows. Her hair was tousled, her skin sunburned, her dark dress streaked with dirt and grass stains. In his opinion, she couldn't have looked more beautiful.

"I should've stayed with you." She swallowed hard. "I didn't believe you when you said he might be following us. I'm sorry I abandoned you."

After her run-in with Fitzgerald, Evan was confident she wouldn't try another stunt like that again. No reason to make her feel worse than she already did.

"Would you have kept Lucky?" he said.

"I figured you'd come looking for him. I planned to take good care of him until you found us."

"Good answer." He stood and helped her up, resisting the urge to pull her close. He couldn't believe he'd almost kissed her a moment ago. Bad idea. The worst. No matter how beautiful or alluring she was, he could not allow himself to be distracted from his mission. Nor could he afford to forget the immeasurable pain that love ultimately cost a man. He was better off alone.

"Come on. Let's go back to camp and get the rest of my stuff."

She placed a hand on his forearm, her expression somber. "Can you forgive me?"

Her humble request shamed him. Brushing her aside, he picked his hat off the ground and thumped it against his thigh to dislodge the dirt. "You kidnapped my horse—an animal that's happy as long as he has food and a kind word now and then. I had a part in kidnapping you—a woman with feelings and needs and family you care about." He put on his hat and pulled the brim down low. "Think on that and then tell me who needs to ask for forgiveness." He turned his back. "It's time to go."

Irish appeared to sense his need to be alone with his thoughts because she didn't say anything else. He helped her mount before hauling himself up behind her.

He pulled her bonnet out of his bag and handed it to her, waiting until she put it on to signal Lucky. He would've liked to urge him into a full gallop, but he knew his horse's limits. They traveled instead at a moderate pace, stopping now and then for a drink of water and a short rest.

Evan could tell that she was nervous. She searched the woods continually, as if expecting Fitzgerald to jump out from behind the nearest tree.

He gave her arm a squeeze. "Relax, Irish. You have my word that I'll do everything in my power to keep you safe."

She responded by resting against him. "I'm glad I have you to protect me."

Again her words hit him like a punch in the gut. Guilt gnawed at his insides. He certainly didn't feel like a hero in all this.

Evan tried to recall what life had been like before James's murder. Plowing the fields, feeding the animals, repairing tools and broken-down equipment. Hard work that brought satisfaction at the end of the day. Going to church on Sundays. Attending town picnics.

Those days of normalcy were long gone. He was living a nightmare…forced to do things he'd never dreamed he'd do. If someone had told him a year ago that he'd be robbing banks and keeping company with a nest of vipers, he would've laughed his head off. If someone had told him that he would kidnap an innocent young lady, Evan would've punched him square in the face and spit on him to boot.

Goodness, but how life could take twisted turns.

By the time they arrived back at camp, the brilliant yellow-orange sun hung low in the sky. The intense rays blended into the horizon, painting the pale expanse in swirls of pastel pink and orange.

Evan was eager to dismount and put some much-needed space between himself and his lovely riding companion. She filled his senses with her scent and softness. He was aware of her every sigh. He imagined that he could even detect her heartbeat pulsating in the creamy skin near the base of her throat.

Get a grip, Harrison. Yanking on the reins, he slipped to the ground before Lucky could come to a complete stop. He helped her down, breaking contact as soon as her boots touched the ground. "Why don't you rest a spell? I'll rustle up something for us to eat."

"I'd actually prefer to help if you have something for me to do."

He hesitated. "You can gather wood for the fire, if you'd like, but I don't want you to overdo it."

"I'm fine."

"Okay." He stepped away, only to halt midstep to glance back at her. "Oh, and Irish?"

She met his gaze with an unreadable expression, cinnamon eyebrows raised in question.

"Don't disappear on me this time."

A ghost of a smile crossed her lips. "I'll be here, I promise."

"Good."

As Evan tended to Lucky, he reminded himself that he was better off alone. Loving someone left a man vulnerable and open to heartache. God had seen fit to take away everyone who'd ever mattered in his life—first his parents, then his only brother. No way was he going to let anyone else get close. He simply could not face another loss.

Feeling irritable, he went in search of his saddle and

other belongings. They were exactly as he'd left them, which should've pleased him. Walking back and seeing Irish's flushed countenance as she worked sparked his ire. He strode to her side and took the bundle of wood from her arms.

"I thought I told you not to overdo it," he growled. "Go sit down."

"And I told you, I'm fine. I think I'm smart enough to know my own limitations." Her glare dared him to challenge her assertion.

His gaze took in the damp tendrils clinging to her temple and nape and the fine sheen of moisture on her forehead. "You're short of breath, and your face is redder than a strawberry patch. With all the layers you're wearing, it's a wonder you haven't passed out standing still in this heat."

Her mouth fell open. "Gentlemen do not discuss ladies' undergarments."

Oddly amused by her discomfiture, he smirked. "I never claimed to be one." He placed a hand on her shoulder and gently turned her in the direction of the nearest shade tree on the bank. "Humor me. Go sit down."

Shifting the wood, he watched as she did his bidding. Once settled, her skirts arranged about her just so, she speared him with her dark gaze. "Happy now?"

"Yes, thank you. Rest while I fetch you some cold water."

She was silent, offering only a simple thank-you when he handed her the cup. Evan gathered his fishing gear and settled on the bank beside her.

His gaze on the shimmering water, he asked, "So who taught you to ride bareback?"

"My cousin, Joshua."

He glanced over at her. She appeared at ease, her legs

tucked to one side and her graceful hands clasped in her lap. Her green eyes seemed to miss nothing.

"And he thought that was necessary because…" Evan prompted.

"Oh, I don't think he had any particular reason. We did it for fun and, like everything else, it turned into a competition. He's two years older than me and more like a big brother than a cousin. He lives next door with his folks and two younger brothers, Nathan and Caleb. We see each other almost every day."

"Did he teach you how to shoot a bow and arrow, too?"

"Now you're teasing me." Her lips curved in a most intriguing smile.

An answering smile on his face, he held up his hands. "No, honest. I'd like to know what else your talented cousin taught you."

"Let's just say that because of his patient instruction, I'm more skilled in manly pursuits than the average woman. And severely lacking in those skills necessary to make a comfortable home."

Evan felt a tug on his line. He eased it up out of the water, pleased to see a medium-weight trout dangling on the end. He made quick work of unhooking the fish and getting his line back in the water. "So let me guess, while your sisters were learning to make biscuits and crochet, you were gallivanting about the countryside with your cousins."

Her soft trill of laughter warmed his insides. "That about it sums it up, yes. I do my share of chores, of course. I like to work in the garden and oversee the care of the animals."

"You don't look like a tomboy," he offered over the rim of his cup.

He was rewarded with a soft pink blush along her

cheekbones. She shot him a wry glance. "I'm not as particular about my appearance as some of my sisters, but I do like nice clothes. Of course, this dress is sadly ruined."

"I'll replace it."

Irish shook her head. "I could never accept such a personal gift from a stranger."

He lowered his gaze to the creek. Odd, he didn't consider them strangers. Not friends, certainly. What then? Two people whose lives intersect for a fleeting moment, like two leaves floating on the breeze, colliding, twirling together in a delicate spiral, only to drift apart and land in separate spots?

He sighed. This line of thinking could only lead to trouble.

"You must be tired after all that walking," she said, obviously interpreting his sigh as a sign of physical exhaustion instead of the emotional upheaval it reflected. "Am I allowed to help at all? I can get the fire going and make coffee, at least."

"Can you fish?"

"Yes, of course."

He handed her his pole and a small collection of worms. "These don't bother you?"

"Nah."

"Okay, then. You catch our dinner, and I'll cook it. Deal?"

"I think that's a wise solution." She laughed again, a delightful, enchanting music that washed over him and made him long for impossible dreams. He bolted to his feet to keep from doing something rash, like kissing her sweet mouth.

"I'll leave you to it then."

As Evan lit the fire and set the coffee to boiling, he

forced all thoughts of Irish from his mind. He had to get a grip. Focus. Fitzgerald was out there somewhere. Evan couldn't afford to let down his guard, not even for a second.

When she presented him with four fish half an hour later, he praised her efforts but didn't attempt conversation. He cleaned, gutted and cooked them in silence while Irish stowed his fishing rod and spread out a blanket for them to sit on.

Evan noticed that she bowed her head to pray silently before eating and found himself doing the same. As they ate, darkness slowly swallowed the last fingers of light. A soft breeze rustled the leaves and water trickled over mossy stones.

"I can't recall the last time I ate a meal outside." Her honeyed voice was subdued. "There's a spot on our land similar to this." She gestured to the surrounding meadow. "It's so peaceful. Reminds me of the Psalm, 'He makes me lie down in green pastures, He leads me beside still waters.'"

"He restores my soul," he finished almost without thought.

Her head came up. "Evan, is God a part of your life?"

Evan hesitated. "He used to be, but now…let's just say I've long since lost sight of Him."

"I'm sorry to hear that." She was quiet, absently plucking blades of grass. "You know, He hasn't lost sight of *you*. His Word says that *nothing* can separate us from the love He has for us."

His mood turned somber. "I remember. It's just that there's some things I need to do before I can fix my relationship with Him."

"I think you've got that backward, Evan. Think about

it." She stood and gathered the dishes. "I'm going to wash these and repack them."

He watched her walk to the water's edge, relieved that she'd dropped the subject. He wasn't eager to talk to her or anyone else about his failures.

By the time she returned, he had the bedroll laid out near the fire. "You'll sleep here." He pointed to a cluster of trees across the way. "I'll be over there standing watch. If you need anything just call out."

"You don't plan on sleeping at all?"

He held his cup of steaming coffee aloft, his third since supper. "Not if I can help it."

"But," she hesitated, "you need rest just as much as I do."

"I'm used to living on little sleep."

"I've slept outside a number of times, but always close to home." Her voice was hushed in the darkness. "Do you think we're safe here?"

Evan wondered if her mind was on the wildlife or their pursuer. In his opinion, Fitzgerald would've had to tend to his injuries before setting off after them. Animals were another matter.

"Yes, I do. Try not to worry."

He couldn't see her features, but he caught the slight shake of her head. "Fear is a foreign emotion for me. I hadn't realized until this moment how predictable my life is. Since every day is much the same, there's never any reason to feel insecure or frightened. If my sister, Megan, were here, she'd know just the right verse to make me feel better. She's memorized the most of any of us."

He was quiet a long time. Finally, he spoke. "I will lie down and sleep in peace, for You alone, O Lord, make me dwell in safety. Psalm 4:8."

"Thank you, Evan," she whispered softly. "I needed that."

"Sweet dreams, Irish."

Evan tried to get comfortable, but it was next to impossible. He gazed up at the velvet black sky, his thoughts on the lady across the way. He hoped she was able to get some rest.

He'd never met anyone like her. She was sweetness and spice. Unafraid to speak her mind, yet wise enough to know when not to. With her to worry about, thoughts of James's death and the need for revenge no longer dominated his every waking moment.

He found himself longing to be in his own cabin, sleeping in his own bed. Longing to live simply once again—tending his crops and cows and goats and chickens—not living in the shadow of danger, keeping company with amoral, ruthless outlaws.

Evan wondered what Irish would think about his spread. It certainly was no stretch to picture her on his front porch, rocking in the chair he'd carved with his own hands, her red-gold hair fluttering in the breeze.

He didn't even know her name. On impulse, he left his post and went to crouch beside her sleeping form.

"Irish?" He placed a hand on her shoulder and squeezed.

"Mmm?" Eyes closed, she smiled in her sleep.

"Irish, what's your real name?"

"Mmm?"

"Your name."

"Juliana, silly," she mumbled before turning on her side, her back to him.

"Juliana," he breathed softly, testing her name on his lips. "Beautiful, just like you."

Chapter Seven

A heavy hand covered her mouth, startling her out of a deep sleep. Her foggy brain couldn't make sense of the rapid-fire words assailing her ear. Panic swelled in her chest. Whimpering, she tried to pry the fingers away.

"Hush," a low, familiar voice murmured against her ear. "It's me, Evan."

His clean scent reached her nose, and the tension left her body. He dropped his hand and helped her sit up.

"There's something out there. Follow me and be quiet."

She stuffed her feet into her boots without bothering to tie the laces. She took hold of his outstretched hand, taking comfort in the warmth of his touch. That connection was her lifeline as he pulled her quickly through the darkness. She was breathless by the time he stopped.

He settled both hands on her shoulders and leaned in close. "Stay here. I'm going after Lucky."

All she could think was that Fitzgerald had found them, and the possibility struck terror in her heart. He would surely kill her after what she'd done. "Do you think he's found us?"

"I don't know," he said. "But I want you to promise me you'll stay right here."

"I promise."

"Right here," he reiterated, "in this very spot."

"I won't move an inch."

He hesitated. Was he wondering whether or not he could trust her?

"Do you know how to shoot a gun?"

Juliana hid a smile. If he only knew. "As a matter of fact, I do."

He dropped his hands and reached for his holster. Then he pressed a gun into her hands. "Here. Whatever you do, take care where you aim this thing."

She took it, oddly touched by his gesture. "Why are you doing this? Considering that I stole your horse, how can you trust me with a weapon?"

"Am I wrong to trust you, Juliana?"

Her name on his lips was a soft caress. It had a strange effect on her. "How do you know my name?"

"Simple. I waited until you were half-asleep to ask. You gave it up readily."

"You don't play fair," she said, heat rushing to her face. What else had he learned?

"And you do?" His black brows winged up.

He had a point. He'd been very forgiving yesterday when he met up with her and Lucky. Why, he hadn't even scolded her for stealing his horse and stranding him in the middle of nowhere! She'd deserved a good tongue lashing at the very least. Instead he'd been gentle, soothing her as she wept in his arms.

A high-pitched whinny pierced the night air.

Evan flinched. "I have to go."

"Be careful."

His gave a brief nod. Then he was gone.

Juliana watched the dark path where he'd disappeared, her fists clenched so tightly her nails pinched her palms. *Maybe it's just a deer,* she told herself. *Or a razorback.*

She looked down at the gun he'd given her, turning it over in her hands. With this one act, he'd made it clear that he no longer saw her as his hostage but an equal. He trusted her not to turn on him or, worse, shoot him.

After yesterday, Juliana wouldn't even consider using his weapon against him. Lenny Fitzgerald's presence had changed everything. With that madman in pursuit, she wasn't about to try to make it on her own.

She flipped open the chamber to check for bullets. Five and an empty. But wait. There was something jammed into the empty chamber. A small piece of paper. A banknote, perhaps? She'd heard of men doing that. After all, no one was going to get to it unless you were dead.

Juliana bit her lip. Should she or shouldn't she? It wasn't like she was going to steal it. She just wanted a peek.

Unfurling the paper, she moved into a patch of moonlight in order to read the bold words:

WANTED:
← $100 REWARD →
FOR THE ARREST AND
CONVICTION OF EVAN TREY HARRISON.
SHERIFF AARON TATE
CADES COVE, TENNESSEE

She gasped and clapped a hand over her mouth. It couldn't be!

Why was she so shocked? He'd never denied being an outlaw. Now she held the hard evidence in her hands. Her disappointment felt like a dull blade jabbing her skin.

She'd glimpsed tenderness in Evan. And goodness. He was responsible, intelligent, and, yes, even charming when it suited his purposes. The crazy part was that she was attracted to him.

Face it, Juliana. Deep down inside you wanted this whole thing to be a mistake. You wanted him to be a normal man with a reasonable explanation for kidnapping you.

Lucky's protests reached her ears, reminding her that Evan could return at any moment. No way did she want him to find her with this. She rolled it up with unsteady fingers and shoved it back in place.

Her promise not to move forgotten, she crept through the darkness toward higher ground. She needed to see what was happening. Spying a fallen log at the base of a sycamore tree, she stepped up and braced herself against the trunk. The extra height gave her a clear view of camp. The flames had died down, but there was enough light for her to make out Evan's tall form and that of his horse.

Evan was trying to calm him and lead him in her direction. He wasn't having much success—whatever was out there had Lucky spooked. The horse pranced sideways, the whites of his eyes showing. Not a good sign.

Watching Evan, Juliana couldn't help but admire his ability to control the large animal. His shoulder and arm muscles bunched as he held firm to the bridle. He didn't get angry and lash out. Instead, he held his ground and used quiet tones to soothe the horse's nerves.

The wanted poster fresh in her mind, she reminded herself not to forget that he was a common thief. And kidnapper. She couldn't stop the sigh of relief, however, when they finally began to walk in her direction.

Backtracking, she reached her prior spot just as Evan

and Lucky rounded the corner. He gave her a measuring look but said nothing.

"What now?" she said, adrenaline pumping. Would her nervousness give her away? He knew, after all, what was hidden in his gun.

"We find a place where we can watch the campsite without being detected."

"How about up there?" She pointed to the place she'd just been, trying for an even tone of voice. "Looks like a good place."

Again, he studied her. Then he dipped his head. "Let's go check it out."

He led the way, guiding Lucky. Juliana followed at a close distance. Within minutes they were standing side by side, sheltered by the thick foliage.

While she felt protected in his presence, she wasn't entirely at ease. Standing so close to him, she was aware of the hardness of his body, the unleashed power of his muscles. When his shoulder brushed hers, her skin heated. The darkness cloaking them only added to the sense of intimacy.

He stiffened and sucked in a breath.

Juliana scanned the forest, but didn't see a thing. "What is it?" she whispered.

"Bear."

Her heart sped up. Hopefully it was a male. There was nothing more dangerous than to come between a momma bear and her cubs. She searched the area again, paying attention to the dark shadows near the fire. One of the shadows separated from the rest.

Even from this distance, the black bear looked menacing. On all fours, the animal was short but stout with a wide block-shaped head, massive shoulders, rounded stomach and legs the size of tree trunks. The bear's long snout swayed to and fro, sniffing the air.

When Evan lifted his rifle and took aim, she seized his forearm. "Don't shoot him!" she hissed. "He'll leave as soon as he doesn't find what he's looking for."

"I'm not going to shoot him," he said without taking his eye off the bear. "I'm going to shoot *at* him. There's a difference."

"Why?"

"I don't want him coming back."

"We're not staying here, are we? I won't be going back to sleep, I assure you."

He was silent. Then he said, "It's nearly dawn anyway. We can head out once I retrieve our things. Still, I want to know for sure he's long gone while I do that."

The blast of the firearm startled her, and she almost lost her footing on the log. She glared over at him. He could've given her a warning! He didn't seem to notice her irritation.

The bear lumbered back in the direction from which he'd come. Evan lowered his rifle and, curling his fingers around her upper arm, helped her down. "Let's get out of here."

She waited until he'd strapped the rifle onto the back of the saddle to return his six-shooter.

"Here." She held it out to him.

He didn't immediately take it. "You can hold on to it if you want."

Didn't he remember the wanted poster? "No, thanks."

He swept off his hat and plunged his fingers in his hair. "Juliana, you realize I'm not holding you here, don't you? All I want is to get you home safe and sound. Do you believe me?"

The logical part of her urged her to remember that

he was a crook. A man unworthy of her trust. Her heart sent out a different message—*trust him*. Straightening her shoulders, she looked him square in the eyes. "I do."

"Good. I'm glad." He looked relieved.

Again she held out the gun. This time he took it and slid it in his holster. They walked back in silence. As they gathered the bedroll and saddlebags, Juliana kept glancing over her shoulder to check the woods. She couldn't help but be glad when they were finally back in the saddle.

It didn't occur to Juliana to wonder why she wasn't bothered by the fact they were heading in the opposite direction as her home, putting more miles between herself and her family. Or perhaps it did, and she just wasn't brave enough to face the truth.

By midmorning, Juliana was famished. Last night's fish was a distant memory, and she'd been up since before dawn. She wondered if Evan was planning to skip breakfast altogether. Surely he craved his coffee.

Her mouth watered in anticipation at the sight of a berry patch not far off the trail. "Evan, look! Can we stop?"

He tugged on the reins. "Are you a fan of blackberries?"

"I am. What about you?" She shouldn't care about his likes and dislikes. Remember the wanted sign!

"I prefer blueberries," he said, dismounting, "but these are good, too." He helped her down. "Sorry I didn't stop sooner. I was trying to put as much distance between us and that bear as possible."

Juliana figured he was more concerned about Fitzgerald than the bear, but didn't want to worry her by saying so.

"Would you mind if I left the picking to you while I

get a fire going? I can't wait a minute longer for a cup of coffee."

She couldn't hold back her grin. "Not at all."

He cocked his head to the side. "What's so funny?"

"You're addicted to that stuff," she said with a soft laugh.

"I admit it. I am," he said in all seriousness. "Are you gonna join me?"

Juliana realized that they were becoming familiar with each other's habits. She wasn't sure if that was a good thing or not.

"Yeah, sure."

"That's what I thought." He arched a brow at her, a hint of a smile playing around his mouth, before turning on his heel and striding away to gather firewood.

Her grin widened, pleasure rippling through her.

She instantly quashed it. Why did the first man to stir her interest have to be a criminal? With a sigh, she bent to pluck enough ripe berries for the both of them. For every handful she dropped into the empty tin, two went into her mouth. She couldn't help it. Fresh fruit was a rare treat. Besides, she was starving!

When she'd filled the tin, she walked over to where Evan was crouched beside the small fire. The brim of his hat hid his face.

"Want some?" she said, extending the tin to him.

He lifted his head, his gaze shifting from the fruit to her face. His eyes went wide, and his mouth went slack.

Juliana was instantly on guard. "What is it?" she demanded, her hand going to her hair. "Is there a bug on me?"

Clamping his lips together, he shook his head. A merry twinkle entered his eyes, and she guessed that he was trying not to laugh.

"Have you been snacking on the job?" He couldn't disguise the tremor of amusement in his voice.

Planting one fist on her hip, she retorted, "What if I have?"

Unable to contain his mirth, Evan threw back his head and laughed—a deep, hearty sound that rumbled through his chest. She would've appreciated the sound of it if she wasn't so irritated.

"Oh, Juliana," he breathed, his hand splayed across his flat stomach. "You should see yourself. Your lips are stained dark red! Your teeth, too."

"What?" Mortified, she covered her mouth with her hand.

He popped one of the berries in his mouth. Then he flashed her an impish grin. "Mmm. I can see why you couldn't wait. Very tasty."

Indignation rose in her chest. "You've been out of polite society far too long, Evan Harrison. A true gentleman wouldn't dare make fun of a lady."

His expression sobered, but his eyes continued to dance. "You're right. I'm sorry." Scooping up a few more berries, he chewed slowly as if to savor the taste. His smile was a mile wide. "Are my teeth red now?"

Juliana didn't want to let go of her irritation, but it was hard not to in light of his good-natured teasing. Seeing him this way was a welcome change from his normally serious manner.

She dropped her hand from her waist. "Not as red as mine, I imagine."

"Hey." He caught her wrist. "I didn't mean to insult you."

A small smile touched her lips. "I know. I shouldn't have gotten so riled up. Guess I'm a bit touchy about my appearance right now. I don't remember ever going without a bath and a change of clothes before."

She could only imagine what she must look like. Wisps of hair had escaped her untidy braid to trail down her neck. Her injured cheek was no doubt a mottled purple and yellow, and now her lips and teeth were red. Her dress was torn and stained and missing a button. Her new boots were scuffed and dirty.

She was a mess! While she wasn't fashion crazy, like her sister, Nicole, she liked to look nice and neat. That Evan should see her like this bothered her. That she cared bothered her even more.

His indigo eyes bored into hers. "Let me be frank, Irish. You are the most beautiful woman I've ever met. A little dirt can't hide that fact."

Juliana's lips parted in disbelief. Her knees went weak. The heat of his fingers burned into her wrist and moved up her arm.

She couldn't speak. Evan thought she was beautiful? Did that mean he was as affected by her nearness as she was his?

Gazes locked, silence stretched between them.

When he released her and turned back toward the fire, she swallowed back regret.

Admit it. You want him to kiss you.

No! It was wrong to want anything from this man. He made a living stealing from honest people. His friends were thieves and possibly murderers. And while he admitted that he was once close to God, he certainly wasn't now. Everything he stood for went against her beliefs.

"Evan."

He looked up at her, his expression guarded.

"Have you ever killed a man?"

A veil came down over his eyes, but not before she glimpsed a spark of anger. "No, I have not."

"Have you shot a man?"

His lips thinned. "No," he ground out, "I have not."

He was angry, but her questions were legitimate. She simply *had* to know.

"I guess your next question is whether or not I've kidnapped a person before. The answer is, no, I have not. You're the first. Anything else you'd like to ask?"

Actually, yes. But she wasn't about to push her luck. "No."

"Good," he said in a clipped voice. "Let's eat and get back on the trail. We've wasted enough time here already."

Chapter Eight

He was wet, cold and miserable. Exhausted, too.

Gray clouds had rolled in about an hour earlier, spitting rain off and on. In the last twenty minutes the rain had come down more steadily. Didn't look like it was going to stop anytime soon. He'd kept his eye open for shelter, but hadn't spotted anything.

He was getting desperate.

His hat kept his head and face dry, but water dripped off the brim to slide down the back of his neck and under his shirt collar. Juliana's bonnet, made of less sturdy material, was saturated and provided little, if any, cover from the rain.

She shivered and his arms tightened around her.

"What's that?"

His gaze followed the direction of her outstretched finger to a dark structure nearly covered by vines. Whatever it was, it was old and had probably been abandoned a long time ago. But with the storm nearing, it wasn't as if he had much choice.

He leaned in close, his face pressed close to her cheek. "Good eyes, Irish. With a little work, it might be just the thing we need."

Evan dismounted and turned to help her down. He noticed that her face and lips were pale, and beneath the bonnet her hair was plastered to her head.

"I'll work as fast as I can," he promised, determined to get her warm and dry as quickly as possible.

He searched for the oversize knife he packed for emergencies and began cutting away the vines and undergrowth. It was muddy, backbreaking work. He kept his eye out for snakes and others critters. Of course, he was more concerned about the condition of the inside of the cabin. No telling what he'd find there.

A bolt of lightning split the sky, followed by a deafening crack of thunder. Juliana let out a small cry, but had the peace of mind to grab his horse's bridle and calm him with soft strokes. Evan worked faster.

Fifteen minutes later, sweating and out of breath, he stood back to survey what he'd uncovered. "What do you think?" he called over the noise of the rain.

"Great job." The admiration on her face made all the hard work worthwhile.

"Thanks. Wait on the porch while I check the inside."

She followed him up the steps and onto the porch, standing off to the side as he pushed on the door. It didn't budge, so he threw his shoulder against the weathered wood. It scraped along the floorboards. An unpleasant musty odor hit him in the face and he drew back, giving his eyes time to adjust to the dim interior. As he scanned the square room, he noted a rough wooden table and four chairs in one corner and a cot along the far wall. A large stone fireplace took up the wall opposite the door.

He shoved the door open wider to let in more light. Vines had squeezed through the floorboards and climbed up the walls, and spiderwebs hung suspended in the corners. He tested the floorboards with his weight as he went farther inside. There were a couple of soft spots, but all in all he thought it was sound.

"Not the best of accommodations, but it'll do," he told Juliana, who stood in the open doorway. "Come in. I'm going for my bags."

She scooted past him, her eyes wide as she looked around the small space. "Please don't let there be any spiders in those webs."

"That's what I'm here for, remember?"

She shivered again.

"I'll be right back." He bounded down the steps. His boots splashed through the mud as he ran to retrieve the saddlebags.

Back inside, he held up one of the bags. "There's a shirt and pants in here. Put them on. They're clean and dry."

"I couldn't possibly—"

"You're soaked to the skin. Trust me—you don't want to catch pneumonia."

Sighing, she reluctantly accepted the clothes. The bill of her bonnet drooped over her eyes and she pushed it back up with one finger. "What about you?"

"I've got another change in this one."

"I don't have any other choice, do I?"

"Not if you want to stay well. I'll be outside working on some sort of shelter for Lucky."

He tugged the door closed behind him and went to work hacking out an overhang. By the time he was finished, his palms were raw and bruised. His shirt and pants were plastered to his skin. Although it was the middle of July, he was beginning to feel chilled. He longed for hot coffee and a fire, but at least he had a change of clothes. With the big horse blocking him, Evan peeled off the wet garments and slipped into the dry clothes. Holding the satchel over his head, he sprinted to the cabin.

Juliana was perched on one of the chairs, her arms wrapped around her middle to ward off the cold. She looked like a young girl with her wet hair hanging loose around her shoulders. She was clearly uncomfortable wearing his clothing, but trying to make the best of it.

He moved closer, removed his hat and placed it on the table. Staring at her in the faint light, he noticed the swelling in her cheek hadn't gone down.

"Does it hurt worse?"

She lightly trailed her fingertips across the purplish-yellow skin. "About the same."

When she didn't elaborate, he got the feeling she was trying to spare him more guilt. He had no idea why she would do such a thing. She owed him nothing. After all he'd done, he deserved nothing less than her contempt.

"I was afraid of that," he murmured, frustrated at his inability to help ease her discomfort. If only he had some alcohol on hand... He kept some at home for medicinal reasons, of course, but he didn't travel with the stuff. "A poultice would help, but with this rain it will be a while before I can make one."

A shiver coursed through her body. She began to briskly rub her hands up and down her arms. No doubt her wet hair wasn't helping. He was cold, too.

"Do you have a ribbon or string to tie your hair back with?"

"No. And in my haste last night, I misplaced the last of my hairpins."

Evan thought for a moment. "Let me braid it for you, and I'll tie it with a strip of cloth." He rifled through his bag for a cloth and his knife.

"I can braid my own hair," she protested.

"Oh, really?" He paused in what he was doing to look at her. "Hold out your hands."

She stopped rubbing her arms and held them out. "So?"

"So?" He closed his hands over hers, resolutely ignoring the pleasure he felt at the simple touch. "You're trembling. And your fingers are like ice."

She dropped her gaze and gasped. "Evan, you're bleeding!"

He looked down and noticed the angry red scratches crisscrossing the tops of his hands. One in particular was deep and oozing blood. Only after he spotted it did the stinging set in. He pulled his hands away.

"It's nothing."

"It isn't nothing," she countered. "We have to wrap this up tight. Give me that clean cloth."

"Hang on." With one quick movement he cut a long strip from the cloth and laid it on the table. "That's for your hair."

She gave him a look but didn't comment, only motioned for him to sit next to her. She cradled his injured hand in her lap and pressed the material against the wound to stanch the flow. Her touch was gentle, calming. Evan stared at her bent head. He wondered what she was thinking as she wrapped the material around his hand and secured it with a knot.

"There. It's the best I can do."

"Thank you." He didn't know why, but Juliana's fussing over him made him feel lonely. "Now for your hair."

"What about your hand?"

"I can still move my fingers, see?" He wiggled his fingers.

"Don't tell me you've done this before." Her eyes searched his expectantly.

"No, but it can't be that hard, can it? Face the other direction so I can reach." When she only stared at him, he leaned forward. "Don't be stubborn, Irish." He deliberately kept his tone light so as to put her at ease. "I'll be quick, I promise."

With a doubtful expression, she presented him with her back. He realized his mistake the moment he plunged his fingers in the silky tresses. Her scent enveloped him, awakening his senses to her sweetness. The warmth of her body beckoned him. He wanted to hold her, to discover if her graceful form would fit against his as well as he suspected. When his fingertips raked across her nape, he heard her swift intake of air. His hands stilled.

He spotted the blush staining her cheek and leaned forward an inch. He would press a kiss against her smooth skin.

"Evan?"

The uncertainty in her voice stopped him. Juliana would not welcome his attentions. Of course she wouldn't. And why was he thinking such thoughts, anyway? He wouldn't allow himself to feel anything for her.

He straightened. He made quick work of her hair, then moved back to put as much space between them as possible. When she reached up to touch her hair, he noticed her fingers trembling. So. She was not unaffected by him. Evan tried not to be pleased, but failed.

Clearing his throat, he pulled a compact tin can out of his bags. "Have you ever eaten smoked oysters?"

"N-no, not that I recall."

"Hooper couldn't get enough of these, so he swiped a few cans from each mercantile we came to. I'd forgotten I had it, actually, but it's our good fortune. Without a fire, I've little to offer in the way of food." He worked to get the lid open.

"I'm hungry enough to overlook the fact I'm eating stolen property," she said dryly, the tension between them easing.

"You first."

Scooping one up with her fingers, she popped one in her mouth and chewed. "It's good."

"Yeah? I think so, too." He ate slowly, savoring the taste.

The rain intensified suddenly. It sounded like a hundred men stomping on the roof. Juliana looked around him to peer out the one dirt-caked window. "Do you think we'll be able to travel tomorrow?"

"Hard to say." He shrugged. "I know you're eager to get to Cades Cove and send that telegram. I'll do my best to get you there as quickly as possible."

Her expression grew troubled. "The longer my family has to wait for news, the tougher it will be. If I can't be there in person, I can at least put their minds at ease…" Her words trailed off, her lashes lowering to hide her eyes. She plucked absently at her sleeve.

She was obviously thinking of her family, missing them, and he felt awful about what he put her through. Maybe talking about them would lift her spirits. Besides, he was curious about Juliana and her life back in Gatlinburg.

"Why don't you tell me about your sisters?"

Her expression turned affectionate. "Megan is nineteen, two years younger than me. She's the bookworm."

So Juliana was twenty-one. He couldn't imagine why she was still unmarried. Were the men of Gatlinburg blind?

"Some nights we gather around the fire and listen to

Megan read aloud. All sorts of books...poetry, historical documents, adventure novels. And after Megan is Nicole." An indulgent smile lifted her lips. "She's seventeen. Ah, it seems that Nicole's sole purpose in life is to be beautiful. I'm not certain which she deems more important—bonnets or ribbons. Momma still holds out hope that she will turn her attention to more worthwhile matters, but I'm not convinced."

"Give her time."

"I'm afraid it will take something drastic to change her ways." She pushed the too-long sleeves back up. "After Nicole are fifteen-year-old twins, Jessica and Jane. And, before you ask, yes, they're identical." It was obvious that she adored her sisters, and that they all shared a special bond.

"Do all your sisters have red hair?"

She touched a hand to her hair. "I'm the only one, although the twins' hair does have an auburn tint. Mother says I inherited this hair from my father's side. A great-grandmother, I believe."

"Were you teased a lot growing up?"

"Actually, no. There may have been a few comments, but I didn't let it bother me. I was happy to be different."

"It's beautiful," Evan blurted, his voice hushed in the still air.

She ducked her head. "Thank you."

"I'm glad you told me about your family. You're lucky to have them."

Her gaze searched his face. "What about you? Don't you have any family?"

The question sparked sad, bittersweet memories. No, he didn't have family. Not anymore.

"My parents died six years ago," he admitted. "I was nineteen, old enough to be on my own but still a kid in many ways. I was devastated. Lost. Confused...but I had James—" He stopped, unwilling to continue lest he spill the whole sordid story. Juliana was too easy to talk to.

"How did they die?"

"Hmm?"

"Your parents?"

"Cholera outbreak. It happened so fast there wasn't time to say goodbye."

He remembered the shock of it all, how his mother and father fell ill that fateful spring morning. By nightfall they were dead. In a flash, responsibility for the homestead—their very livelihood—was thrust upon him. And his brother...

"I'm so sorry." Her voice, soothing and heavy with compassion, interrupted his thoughts. "I know what it's like to lose someone you love dearly. My father died when I was ten. He and I were close."

Evan was silent, not trusting himself to speak just then. How long had it been since someone, *anyone,* had cared how he felt? Had showed him an ounce of compassion?

"Who is James?"

"My brother."

"And he's where now?"

Gone. Dead. "He died almost a year ago. I'm alone now."

"Evan." She leaned closer and placed a cool hand on his arm. "Are you familiar with the verse promising that God will never leave us nor forsake us?"

"Yes, of course." At his mother's insistence, he and his brother had memorized many verses from the Holy Scriptures.

"God's Word tells us Jesus is a friend who sticks closer

than a brother. If you have Jesus, rest assured that you are *never* alone."

"I appreciate your kind words, Juliana. After what I've put you through, I don't deserve your compassion."

"I'm simply speaking the truth. All you have to do is trust Him."

"I'm not ready," he admitted with regret. The grief inside him was too fresh, too deep to ignore. Suddenly he was exhausted, both physically and mentally. Unfortunately, he doubted that he'd get much sleep that night.

He rose to his feet. "Would you mind if I turned in early?"

"Where exactly do you plan on sleeping?"

"The front porch."

Her gaze slid to the cot with its ratted cover. "How about I take the porch and you take that thing?"

A smile touched his lips. "Sorry."

"How do you expect me to sleep with spiderwebs hanging above my head? And who knows what sort of filth is embedded in that blanket? I'd rather sleep standing up!"

"I would make you a pallet on the floor, but the bedroll is soaked."

"Whatever. I'll think of something."

Lightning flashed, illuminating the room for a brief second, followed by a low growl of thunder directly above them. The window glass shuddered. "It could be worse, ya know. We could be out in that."

Her brows drew together. "Are you sure you'll be okay on the porch?"

Her worry about his safety touched him. "I'll be fine." If he didn't get struck by lightning. "Try to get some rest."

He'd opened the door when her voice halted him. "Good night, Evan."

He didn't turn around. "Good night, Juliana."

Chapter Nine

The quiet woke her. The storm had raged through the night, gusts of wind shaking the walls of the little cabin until she feared they would collapse. Her thoughts never strayed from Evan, out there in the elements simply to give her privacy and protect her reputation. She doubted he got even a minute of sleep.

She was eager to see how he'd fared.

Lifting her arms above her head, she stretched, trying to loosen the kinks in her muscles. Her back and shoulders were in knots. In the end, she'd been unable to bring herself to sleep on the cot, so she'd chosen to sit in a chair and rest her arms and head on the table. It was a miserable way to sleep.

Juliana touched a hand to her hair, grimacing as her fingers encountered her untidy braid. She longed for a bar of soap, a tub of hot water and especially a clean dress. Reaching across the table, she checked to see if hers had dried overnight. The shirt and trousers Evan had loaned her billowed about her body like a tent, and she felt undone.

Her dress was still damp, so she turned her attention to her hair. As it had been braided wet, her hair now fell in soft waves about her shoulders. She pulled a comb through the strands and tied the mass back. It was the best she could do under the circumstances.

A glance out the window told her it was daylight. Time to check on Evan.

She hurried to the door and tugged it open, a little anxious about what she might find. What if he'd been struck by debris tossed about by the wind? Or, worse, struck by lightning? Breathing a little faster than normal, her gaze sought his familiar form.

What she saw melted her heart.

He was huddled on his side, his arm thrown over his head in a protective pose, his knees drawn up toward his chest. His breathing was deep and even. His clothes were wet, which she didn't like, and he wasn't wearing his boots. Odd.

She looked around and saw them at the edge of the porch, near the steps. Why would he take them off, she wondered. Maybe they were new, like hers, and rubbing his feet raw in places.

Noticing water from the roof splattering down, she reached for them. Her fingers brushed against a rigid bulge beneath the lining in one of them and she paused. What in the world? Curious, she picked it up for a closer inspection.

The material was smooth all around the top of the boot except for that one spot. Raised bumps felt like tiny stitches of thread, as if someone had made a small slit in the lining and later sewed it closed.

She glanced at Evan, relieved to see that he hadn't stirred. Had he hidden something in his boot? After finding the wanted sign stashed in his gun, she wouldn't be surprised.

Prodding the area, she felt a small, round object with

ragged edges. What could it be? Not a gold or silver coin. The edges weren't smooth. She racked her brain for clues but couldn't imagine what he would want to hide.

Too bad she didn't remember where he put his knife.

She put the boots back where they'd been, and with another glance at Evan, tiptoed back inside and shut the door as quietly as possible. She sat back down at the table and plotted her next move. One way or another, she would eventually uncover his secrets.

One very long hour later, she heard him stirring. He jerked his head up in surprise when she threw open the door.

"Morning," he greeted, his voice husky from disuse. His brilliant blue eyes fastened on her face. In her mind, he looked much too fresh for just having spent a cold and miserable night in the rain. "Did you get any rest?" he asked, bending to tug on his boots.

She watched closely, noting their snug fit. Surely the hard object would chafe against his leg.

"Juliana?"

He straightened, his expression questioning.

"Oh." She realized that she hadn't answered him. "Yes, well, I managed to get a little. What about you? Was it awful?"

He folded his arms across his chest and stared at her. "I've slept in worse conditions."

"Worse than this?" Her brows shot up to her hairline. "I don't think I want to hear about it."

He smiled then. "No, you don't."

She glanced beyond his shoulder. The sky was a clear, robin's-egg blue this morning, the greens and browns of the forest crisp and vibrant as if the rain had washed away a film of dust from the tree leaves, the grass, the flower petals, the rocks.

"Is it too muddy to travel?"

He twisted around to look over his shoulder. "Not if we're extra careful." He turned back. "I want coffee first, though. And breakfast. The first order of business is finding dry wood for a fire. I'll probably have to break apart one of the chairs. Maybe two."

Juliana's stomach rumbled at the mention of food. She held out her hand. "Give me a gun and I'll rustle up breakfast."

His mouth went slack. "What?"

She grinned at his dumbfounded expression. "You heard me."

His dark brows slashed together. "Let me get this straight—you can't cook but you can shoot small animals?"

"I thought I explained about my cousins. They taught me a lot of things, one of them being how to shoot a gun."

He studied her a moment, then shook his head no. "I'll do it. I'll get a fire going and you can be in charge of the coffee." He brushed past her on his way inside.

"Which is it?" she demanded, her humor fading. "You don't trust me with a weapon or you don't believe I have enough skill to bag our breakfast?"

Evan shot her that look of his that said he thought she was acting foolish. "If I didn't trust you, I wouldn't have given you my gun the other night. And I believe you can do whatever you set your mind to. You're a very resourceful woman."

His words erased her irritation. All that was left was bewilderment. "Then why?"

He paused with his hand on the chair back, his mouth set in a stubborn line. "I can't let you go alone. Fitzgerald is still out there. He won't give up until he gets his revenge."

Her stomach quivered at the thought. "It's because of what I did back there, isn't it? I mean, he despised me before—"

Evan was suddenly right in front of her, his fingers gently tipping up her chin, forcing her to look at him. His blue eyes blazed at her. "None of this is your doing, Juliana. You're in this situation because of a decision I made—a foolish one. Fitz hates my guts. That hatred extends to anyone associated with me. Understand?"

Juliana simply nodded. He held her gaze a moment more before dropping his hand and taking a step back.

"What does he have against you?"

Evan was quiet, weighing her question. "He considers me a threat because I'm not afraid of him. I don't cower at his rantings and ravings. And Roberts likes me, which makes Fitz worry that someday I could become the second in command instead of him."

Juliana stared at Evan. The words coming out of his mouth did not accord with the man she knew him to be. No, she corrected herself, the man she desperately *wanted* him to be. Frustration bubbling up inside, she fisted her hands at her sides. She decided that she did not want to hear anymore about his lawless life. If by that she was hiding her head in the sand and ignoring reality, so be it.

"I'm going outside," she announced. At his intake of breath, she added sardonically, "to answer the call of nature."

"Fine. Take this with you." He pressed a gun in her hand. "And keep your eyes open."

"Yes, sir."

He cocked an eyebrow. Before he could respond, she whirled around and stalked out.

Evan watched her hasty retreat, hoping she'd calm down and pay attention to her surroundings. He didn't have a clue what had sparked her ire. One minute she'd been cool as a cucumber and the next she'd looked as if she'd like to throttle him.

He couldn't stop the grin tugging at his mouth.

Juliana O'Malley was one amazing woman. One in a million. His initial instincts had been on the mark— she was no simpering wallflower. She was spirited. And brave. Smart. Witty. *Don't forget beautiful.*

"How can I?" he muttered to himself, pulling his small axe out and beginning to hack the chair into pieces.

Every time she turned those wide, luminous eyes his way, the cracks in the walls around his heart fractured another inch. And that smile…at times sweet, at times teasing, at all times harboring secrets he'd like to explore…made him want things he'd never have. Love. Laughter. Marriage.

He brought the axe down with more force than necessary. No. He couldn't afford to dream dreams. He'd made his decision to go it alone and he would stick by that.

Twenty minutes later, the fire was roaring and coffee was made, yet Juliana had not returned.

Evan wore a trampled trail in the grass, his gaze searching the woods for a glimpse of her fiery hair. He strained for any sound at all that might mean she was nearby or, God forbid, in trouble.

She has the gun, remember?

True, but if she'd been caught by surprise…

His gut twisted as his mind flashed back to the cabin and Fitz's assault, then to the moment she'd fallen into his arms after escaping the outlaw's clutches. The abject terror in her eyes had stirred within him a fury at the other man like nothing he'd experienced before. Not even the news of James's murder had evoked such a reaction.

Evan scanned the woods again. Surely she wouldn't have gone so far as to get lost.

What if Fitz had her even now? The thought made his blood run cold. If anything happened to her—

There. A rustling to his right. Unsheathing his weapon, he crept toward the sound, all senses on high alert.

The flash of red hair glinting in the sunlight made his limbs go limp with relief. It was her. Then he spotted what she carried in her hands, and his blood pressure skyrocketed. She'd blatantly disregarded his order to stay close. Stuffing his gun back into his holster, he marched back to the fire.

Juliana strolled back into camp feeling extremely satisfied with herself. She could only imagine Evan's surprise—

"Where have you been?"

She halted in her tracks, her gaze flying upward to find him standing near the fire, arms crossed across his chest and feet braced apart, the brim of his black hat shielding his eyes. Eyes she supposed were as blistering as the flames spitting and popping near his feet.

Holding up her bounty, she gave him a smile meant to cool his ire. "These two crossed my path, and I wasn't about to let them get away. I don't know about you, but I'm ravenous."

His gaze flicked to the rabbits dangling from her fingers then back up to her face. His expression remained inscrutable.

"One more minute and I was coming to look for you. From now on I'll be accompanying you on all your calls of nature."

Juliana opened her mouth to utter a retort, then bit her lip. Arguing wasn't going to improve his mood. She simply shrugged. "So are you going to ready them or shall I?"

Surprise registered, but he didn't comment. "I'll do it."

He held out his hand, and she crossed to where he stood. He took her burden from her without a word. When she started to move away, his hand shot out and imprisoned her wrist. Startled, she gasped at the severity of his expression.

"Promise me you won't do that again."

"Evan, I—"

"You've no clue what's been going through my mind the last half hour."

Frustration edged his generous lips. Worry was there in the line between his dark brows. Concern darkened his eyes to that beguiling purple-blue.

She sighed, truly repentant for causing him trouble. "I'm fine. Nothing happened."

"This time. Juliana, I don't think it's registered just how dangerous this man is. I've watched him gun down men for no other reason than the thrill of shedding blood. He has a reason to despise you now as much as he does me. If he catches you, he will kill you."

Her blood ran cold at the conviction in his statement. She'd seen the cold emptiness in Fitzgerald's eyes, had known instinctively that he wouldn't hesitate to hurt her.

"I'm sorry. You have my word I won't do it again."

With a terse nod, Evan turned away. She stood quietly by as he dressed the rabbits and readied the spits, unable to think of a single thing to do. By the time he had breakfast started, she couldn't handle the silence any longer.

Juliana settled herself on a fallen log near the fire, a cup of coffee cradled in her hands.

"How much farther until we reach Cades Cove?"

He glanced at the sky. "If the weather holds we should arrive late tomorrow."

"Tell me about your town. Is it large?"

The tension left his features as his thoughts turned to home. "What it lacks in size, it makes up for in charm. It's nestled in the most picturesque, most fertile valley in East Tennessee. You'll see for yourself soon enough."

"What about the people? Are they friendly?"

"Friendly enough, I suppose. Why do you ask?"

"Just curious." She shrugged. "I've never traveled outside of Gatlinburg."

His brows lifted in surprise. "You're in for a treat then. I guarantee you'll be impressed."

"How long have you lived there?"

"Since I was fifteen. We lived just over the mountains in North Carolina before that."

"I've heard that North Carolina rivals Tennessee in beauty."

"I'd agree with that." He turned the skewers so the meat would cook evenly. He propped his arm on one knee in a half-kneeling position. "We were happy there. Then one day my father met up with an old acquaintance who had traveled through East Tennessee. He filled my father's head with stories of rich farmland, rivers teeming with catfish and trout, forests and abundant wildlife. Land was selling for a fair price, so my father convinced my mother to leave her home for a new one."

It wasn't a new story. Hundreds, if not thousands, of families living in the East had given up everything in search of a new and better life in the West. So far, Evan Harrison's childhood sounded typical. What had gone wrong? Why had he chosen a life of crime?

"Was she difficult to convince?"

A rare grin crossed his lips, and Juliana's breath hitched. He was solemn so much of the time that when he smiled the effect was mesmerizing.

"At first she was adamant about staying in North Carolina, but when she realized how important it was to him she agreed to come."

"Do you think she ever regretted the move?"

"Mother loved the valley, but I think she was lonely. She missed her friends. Since she was an educated lady, she assumed responsibility for our lessons. Of course, James and I weren't too pleased. Neither one of us were that interested in learning."

Juliana watched as Evan's attention turned inward, obviously remembering better times. She tried to imagine him as a carefree and happy young teenager. His parents sounded like such nice people. Perhaps their untimely deaths, combined with the loss of his brother, were the reasons Evan had turned to a life of crime.

Rising to her feet, she approached the fire and sat across from him. His blue eyes, darkened with sorrow and regret, fastened onto her face. He seemed a million miles away.

"Evan, do you have any living relatives? Grandparents? Aunts or uncles?"

Her question brought him back to the present, and he nodded. "My aunt and uncle live in Raleigh, and their son Lucas owns the land that adjoins mine. He's watching over my place and tending to my animals while I'm gone."

Surprise rippled through her. "That's wonderful! Are the two of you close?"

"Yes, of course. He's a good man."

"You're not alone then, Evan. You should be thankful that he lives nearby. He sounds trustworthy, too, considering that you've left your home in his care."

"I am thankful," he retorted, removing the meat from the fire and setting it aside to cool. "We'll stop by his house on the way home."

She digested that information. Did he know about Evan's illegal activities? "And where does he think you've been all this time?"

"Luke respects my privacy," he said without meeting her gaze. There was an unspoken warning for her to do the same. She watched his nimble fingers carefully remove the meat and place it in their trenchers. She admired his strong, capable-looking hands.

Adding a couple of biscuits, he handed the plate to her. "Don't burn yourself. It's still hot."

"Thanks."

Sensing his reluctance to continue the conversation, she ate in silence.

When they finished, she wiped the grease from the trenchers and wrapped them in a towel while Evan cleared their belongings out of the shelter and readied the horse for travel. Determined not to wear his clothes any longer than necessary, Juliana went inside the cabin and changed into her damp dress.

His look was questioning when she stepped out. "Is it dry already?"

"Not completely, no."

He stood next to Lucky, watching her approach. "Are you sure you want to risk getting sick?"

She stopped in front of him. "In this heat and humidity, I'm sure it will dry soon enough."

He studied her before lifting a shoulder. "It's your decision."

He helped her into the saddle and, vaulting up behind her, grabbed the reins and signaled Lucky. Without conscious thought, Juliana leaned back against Evan. In response, his arms tightened around her waist. She could feel his heart beat through the thin material of her dress. It took all her concentration to keep her breathing even. She could not deny that she was thrilled to be close to him once again.

Juliana, a voice inside her head warned, *guard your heart. Evan Harrison may be attentive and attractive, but he's not for you. If he's ever captured, he could very well spend the rest of his life behind bars.*

The prospect sickened her, and she knew without a doubt that her heart was in danger. She had to wonder where her good sense had gone. Attracted to a criminal! What would her mother say?

Despite everything, he mattered to her. His future mattered.

"How long have you been living like this? And don't sidestep the question, as you did before."

A sigh rumbled through his chest, stirring her hair. "This isn't a career choice, if that's what you're worried about. It's simply a means to an end."

"I don't understand."

"I have no other choice," he asserted, his voice hard.

Juliana sensed the heaviness in his spirit. "Everyone has a choice—a choice to do right or to do wrong. There is no joy in a life of sin."

"I can't expect you to understand," he said, guiding Lucky around a rotten log blocking their path.

"Enlighten me," she implored, twisting her face around. "I want to understand."

"Why do you care?"

"Because I—" She hesitated, reluctant to admit her feelings. "I don't want to see you spend the rest of your life in jail."

"I don't plan to."

His complacency stirred her irritation. "Surely you don't believe that you can dodge the law forever! Aren't you tired of running? From your past? The law? God?"

He was quiet a long time, and she wished she could see his expression. "Don't worry about me. Concentrate on getting home to your family. Once you're home safe and sound, you won't spare me another thought."

Juliana knew that would never happen. Evan Harrison wasn't a man easily forgotten.

"I've heard it said that you can run from God, but you can never *outrun* God," she said quietly. "One of these days you'll grow tired of all this."

"You might be right," he quipped. "For now, why don't we agree to have this conversation another time?"

Far from ready to end the conversation, Juliana quashed her irritation.

Since she couldn't talk to Evan, she talked to the Lord. As the pair rode through the forest, she poured out her concerns to God. The tension gradually eased.

God is in control, she reminded herself. *In the heavens above He hung the moon, the stars, the planets. He created the Earth in six days. Working a miracle in one outlaw's heart was by no means out of reach. With God, all things were possible.*

Chapter Ten

Evan's thoughts were not as upbeat. If he were completely honest, he'd acknowledge his growing attachment to Juliana O'Malley. She was beautiful, yes, but it was her sweet spirit and compassion that touched his soul.

The knowledge that she cared about him while thinking he was an outlaw both thrilled and frightened him.

Of course, he told himself, her only concern was for his spiritual welfare. She couldn't possibly be interested in him as a man. And even if she were, his hands were tied. Evan had a job to do—self-appointed, as it were—to bring to justice the men responsible for James's death.

Vengeance is mine, saith the Lord.

The still, quiet words crept into his mind, catching him by surprise. There it was again. The Lord's voice, so long silent. *But, Father,* he argued, *those murderers took an innocent life—my only brother. They must pay.*

Then Evan remembered another verse he'd learned at his mother's knee.

Let all bitterness, and wrath, and anger, and evil speaking be put away from you. Be kind and compassionate to one another, forgiving each other, just as in Christ God forgave you.

Forgive those monsters? Impossible!

And yet, deep down, he knew if he would but ask, God would help him do just that. Question was, did he really want to? He held on to his anger so the grief wouldn't bury him.

With each passing day Evan missed James a little more. Instead of lessening, his grief only deepened with time. More than brothers, they'd been best friends.

From his earliest memories, their mother had encouraged teamwork. Margaret Harrison had instilled in her sons a sense of responsibility for one another. If Evan needed help milking the cows, James was expected to pitch in. If James was having trouble learning his letters, Evan tutored him.

Left alone after their parents' death, he and James had relied on each other even more. Four years of pouring all their sweat, energy and resources into the farm had paid off—it was now a profitable, well-kept spread.

But because of a senseless act of violence, James was no longer around to enjoy the rewards of their labor. Dead at twenty-one. Evan's saddest moments were when he allowed himself to think about all the wonderful experiences James would miss. Falling in love. Getting married. Babies.

No, he couldn't dwell on that now. Juliana's safety took top priority.

Straightening in the saddle, he focused once more on their surroundings. Juliana was so quiet she must have dozed off. He allowed himself to enjoy her closeness, knowing it would soon be over. He dreaded leaving her. He'd miss her and worry about her every minute they were apart.

She might be able to forget him, but he knew without a shadow of a doubt that he'd never forget her. Evan sucked in a swift breath, amazed suddenly at how quickly she'd turned his life upside down.

Four days ago, he'd been consumed with thoughts of revenge and strategy. All his energy went into maintaining his masquerade as a low-down thief. He'd ignored the Holy Spirit's subtle nudges.

Then Juliana walked into his life.

Not only had his quest for revenge been pushed aside, his mind was consumed with thoughts of her. And he'd actually talked to God. A little.

A flash of white darted across the dirt path, spooking Lucky. The horse sidestepped. Tightening the reins, Evan spoke in low, soothing tones in an attempt to calm him. Juliana gripped the saddle horn.

"What was that?"

"Probably a rabbit. Whatever it was, it's gone."

She kneaded the back of her neck. "Can we stop at the next stream? I don't care how deep it is. I need to get clean somehow. I feel as though I haven't bathed in a month." She twisted her face so that he was presented with her profile. "I suppose it isn't proper to speak about such things in front of you. You'll have to excuse my frank speech—I'm used to being in the company of women."

"I'm not so easily offended. Besides, it's only you, me and the animals out here. I figure the rules of proper society don't apply."

"That's a relief." She laughed. "Because I believe I've broken almost all of them."

Juliana thought she might melt. The humid air pressed against her, and her clothes clung to her damp, sticky skin. A cloud of gnats hummed about her head.

They'd been hiking for miles, it seemed. Her calves

and thighs were burning with exertion, and of course her toes ached from rubbing against the inside of her boots. Her way of coping was to clamp her mouth shut and focus on placing one foot in front of the other.

Evan wasn't speaking, either. His lips pressed in a harsh line, he didn't appear to be any happier than she was with the situation. When they crested the largest of the hills and Juliana spotted a patch of sparkling blue in the valley below, she wanted to jump for joy.

"Is that a lake?" she huffed.

He paused beside her, his gaze following the direction of her outstretched finger. "Sure looks like it." He tipped his black hat up. "Let's go check it out."

Two hours later, they stood on the grassy banks of Lake Restawhile. Someone had erected a rough, hand-made sign proclaiming the name. The name fit.

Weeping willows spilled their trailing pale green branches onto the water's crystalline surface, and larger, more massive oaks rose majestically to the sky. Clusters of bright red poppies dotted the fields. Cheerful blue and yellow forget-me-knots brightened the water's edge. Swans glided in serene splendor across the water.

Juliana glanced at Evan. "I'm going in."

He grinned boyishly. "Me, too."

Her heart leapt at the eagerness in his eyes. Gone were the shadows and weariness.

"I'll unload our stuff over there." He pointed to a nearby oak. "While I'm doing that, you can go on in. I'll keep my eyes averted while you ready yourself."

Juliana felt her face heat. Her sisters would be scandalized…it wasn't proper for her and Evan to swim together unaccompanied. Nor spend the night in each other's company without a chaperone, but it wasn't as if they'd had a choice. Under normal circumstances, they would be expected to marry. However, she wasn't there of her own volition. And he was a criminal. Not exactly normal circumstances at all.

The reminder darkened her mood a bit. If she wasn't careful, she was going to start thinking of this as an adventure with Evan as the dashing hero.

Marching over to the nearest weeping willow, she swept aside the thick veil of branches and stepped inside the natural enclosure. The branches fell back into place with a soft swoosh, effectively cutting off her view of the pond and the surrounding trees.

She undid the buttons on her bodice, stepped out of the dress and folded it in a neat square. Underneath she wore a white cotton camisole, nipped in at the waist with a drawstring, and white knickers trimmed with lace ruffles. They were dingy from dust and sweat. A dip in the pond would take care of that.

Untying her boots, she set them beside her folded dress and hurriedly peeled off her knee-high stockings. The moist, cool dirt felt good against her bare feet, and she wiggled her toes. A sigh escaped her. Finally, release from those stiff boots! Peering through the leaves, she monitored Evan's movements.

His back was to her, his attention on his horse. Praying that he wouldn't turn around and see her unmentionables, she sprinted to the shallow end and waded in. The cool water enveloped her body in a soothing embrace. She dove underwater, darting down deep and back up again for air. After about five minutes of this, she came up for a rest and stifled a scream when she bumped into something solid.

Warm fingers closed over her shoulders.

"I didn't mean to startle you," Evan's husky voice sounded above her. "Are you all right?"

She shoved her hair out of her eyes and stared at him. He was too close for comfort, water droplets clinging to his golden skin. His jet-black hair was slicked back away from his forehead. All that was visible above the water were the tops of his powerful shoulders.

Juliana's mouth went dry. Evan's dark blue eyes roamed her face before zeroing in on her lips. Water gently lapped their bodies. The air hummed with electricity. In a desperate act of self-preservation, Juliana splashed water into his face and slipped free of his hold. As she darted in the opposite direction, a spray of water rained down on her head.

His deep-throated laughter broke the tension. They splashed each other until, tired and lazy, they agreed to a cease-fire. Floating in the water, Juliana couldn't recall the last time she'd had so much fun. Evan had enjoyed himself, too. His laughter made her heart soar.

"Can we camp here for the night?" Juliana asked hopefully.

Evan scanned the area. "We can stay until after supper, but we'll bed down a ways out. I don't want to be here after dark. That's when animals will come looking for a drink."

"You're suited to this life, aren't you?" she said. When he looked at her askance, she amended, "I meant you're at home in the outdoors. You were a farmer, right?"

"I *am* a farmer," he insisted, "always will be. I'm just…sidetracked at the moment."

She really wanted to ask him about that wanted poster. And the mysterious object in his boot. Instead, she said, "Do you like being a farmer?"

He thought for a moment, bobbing up and down in the water. "It never occurred to me to do anything else. I like caring for the animals. I like workin' with my hands. I have an area in my barn where I tinker with tools. I'm always trying to figure out new ways to do things."

"So you're an inventor of sorts."

"I guess you could say that." He nodded. "I've come up with a few handy gadgets over the years—even sold a few to the neighbors."

"That's impressive. Have you thought about selling your gadgets in the mercantile? You could pay the owner a small percentage in exchange for shelf space." And it's legal, she added silently.

He shrugged. "I don't have time to make many extra. It was hard enough to keep up with all the chores when James was alive. After his death, I decided to hire someone to help. Before I could do that, I went to see the sheriff—" He stopped and clamped his lips together.

"And?" she prompted.

"Forget it." He pushed his fingers through his damp hair, and Juliana tried not to stare at his carved biceps.

"Have I given you any reason not to trust me?"

One black eyebrow quirked up. "Hmm, wasn't it just yesterday that you stole my horse and left me stranded in the middle of nowhere?"

"*Stole* is such a strong word." She adopted an innocent expression. "I prefer the word *borrowed* and only for a short time."

He tilted his head to study her. "You're something else, Irish."

"Don't try to distract me, Evan. It won't work."

"I'm trying to protect you."

"From what?" She threw her hands up. What was he hiding?

"From information that could get you into trouble. Let's face it—the less you know about me, the better."

"I don't agree."

"You don't have to." He straightened to his full height and stared down at her. "Doesn't change anything, though."

Juliana averted her eyes from the sight of all that male skin. She was beyond frustrated—why did he have to be so stubborn?

"Juliana." Evan's hard, low voice snagged her attention. "Go and get dressed this instant."

Her head snapped up, alarmed at the urgency in his voice. "Why? What—"

"We're about to have company." He was already striding to the shore. "Do it now," he barked over his shoulder.

Juliana hesitated for an instant, her eyes scanning the fields. There, in the distance, she spotted the approaching riders. There were at least three horses. Evan and she were outnumbered. Her heart leapt into her throat.

In her haste, her legs seemed sluggish in the water. At last she reached the shore, and she dashed to her hiding place behind the curtain of branches. Loosening the drawstring, she ripped her wet camisole up and over her head and pulled off the knickers, not taking the time to dry herself before hurriedly pulling on her navy calico. The sound of horses' hooves grew louder. Her trembling fingers fumbled with the buttons. Stuffing her feet into her boots, she burst out of her hiding place in time to see Evan withdraw his weapon.

Evan assumed an air of calm. Not an easy task considering that he was sopping wet and half dressed. He had no idea what to expect from the approaching trio. Could be normal folks. Or they could be outlaws like Cliff Roberts and his gang. If that was the case, he was at a disadvantage.

Gripping the revolver, he kept his gaze on the riders.

When they got close enough, he was able to see that the lead horse carried a clean-shaven male, the second, a female, and the third a young boy. A family. Evan relaxed his stance, but his gaze remained sharp.

Thank You, God. The thanks were heartfelt and spontaneous. He admitted to himself that he couldn't protect Juliana without help from God.

"Howdy," the man greeted cautiously. He appeared to be older than Evan, possibly in his mid-thirties. All three horses halted. "Mind if we stop and rest awhile?"

Evan smirked, thinking of the handmade sign Juliana and he had seen on the other side of the lake. "Fine with me."

The man's attention volleyed between Evan and Juliana, who stood waiting by the trees. He was assessing the situation, of course, just as Evan had done. With instructions to the woman and boy to stay put, he dismounted and approached with an outstretched hand.

"The name's Henry Talbot."

Evan shook the man's hand. He'd learned to distinguish honest men from the corrupt over the course of the last few months. This one appeared to be on the up and up. "Pleased to meet you. I'm Evan Harrison."

Mr. Talbot's gaze slid to Juliana once more, then to Evan's haphazard attire. "I hope we aren't disturbing you."

Knowing what he must be thinking, Evan felt heat creep up his neck. "No, no...we were swimming, is all."

The man hooked a thumb over his shoulder. "My family and I've been traveling since this morning. We need a break, especially the little ones."

"Yeah, well, this looks like a fine place to camp. Don't mind us."

"Great. I'll go tell my wife."

While Mr. Talbot went to assist his family, Evan holstered his weapon, made quick work of his shirt buttons and tucked the ends into his waistband. He strode over to Juliana. Her face was pale.

He gave her shoulder a reassuring squeeze. "There's nothing to worry about."

Her gaze was on the newcomers. "Who are they?"

"Henry Talbot and family." He threaded his fingers through hers, pleased with how well her hand fit into his larger one. "Come on, let's go meet everybody."

"Wait." She held back. "What are we going to tell them about us?"

Evan met her questioning gaze. "Nothing. Most likely they'll assume we're husband and wife." Her green eyes lit with emotion he couldn't identify. "Does that bother you?"

"I hate the thought of deception."

In the not-so-distant past, Evan would've felt exactly the same way. After months of living a lie, however, he'd pushed aside his conscience enough times to weaken its effect. He felt ashamed.

"I'm sorry I've put you in this position, but that doesn't change reality. A single man and woman traveling alone together—well, it simply isn't done. We don't want them asking questions we can't answer."

"I know."

The look in her eyes made it clear that she trusted him. Juliana humbled him in so many ways. She thought he was a wanted man and yet, she trusted him. Juliana O'Malley was a rare woman.

He leaned in close, so that their foreheads nearly touched. "Why aren't you married, Juliana?"

He heard her swift intake of breath. Her cinnamon-colored eyebrows drew together. "Why are you asking me this?"

"I'm curious, that's why."

"I haven't met anyone I wanted to marry, I guess."

"Have you ever been asked?"

Her chin came up. "You're getting awfully personal, Mr. Harrison."

"Is that a yes?"

"I'm not answering any more of your questions." Her green eyes blazed in bold defiance.

When he spoke, his voice was as smooth as velvet. "Remember, Irish, you're my wife for the next twenty-four hours. As hard as it may be, try to act like you're crazy about me."

On a whim, Evan pressed his mouth against hers. A jolt of lightning-swift heat surged through him clear down to his toes. In that instant, he knew he was lost. Soft and sweet with a hint of honey, her lips were like a cool drop of water to a man dying of thirst.

Of their own volition, his hands crept up to cradle her face, his thumbs stroking her satin cheeks. A tide of unfamiliar emotion welled up within him and threatened to carry him away. He fought the urge to crush her to him and never let go.

He tore his mouth from hers, his breathing ragged. She stood stock-still, her eyes a maelstrom of emotion. Accusation. Longing. Confusion.

"Juliana, I—" he began, his voice gravelly.

"Mr. Harrison?"

Evan dropped his hands and pivoted to find Henry Talbot and his family standing a few feet away. The boy's eyes were wide as saucers, which meant they'd probably witnessed the kiss. His ears burned with embarrassment.

He eased Juliana forward. "Excuse me, Mr. Talbot. I didn't hear your approach. This is Juliana."

Juliana didn't spare a glance his way as she bestowed a welcoming smile on the couple.

"This is Rose." He indicated the small, dark-haired woman by his side, "and this is our son, Matt."

"It's nice to meet you," Juliana offered in a friendly manner. "What's the little girl's name?"

Confused, Evan glanced around to see whom she was referring to. Then Rose Talbot turned sideways, and he glimpsed the sleeping toddler snug in her wrap. He hadn't noticed the material harness strapping her to her mother's back.

"Her name is Joy." Mr. Talbot smoothed her dark hair with a gentle hand and shared a smile with his wife. "We waited a long time for this little treasure."

"She's adorable," Juliana said in a soft voice, clearly enchanted with the curly-headed tot. "How old is she?"

Rose spoke up. "She'll be two next month."

Evan turned his attention to the boy. "You must be about twelve."

Matt's face relaxed into a gap-toothed smile. "Naw, mister, I just turned nine in March."

He feigned disbelief, rocking back on his heels. "I can't believe it. By the way you handled your mount, I thought for sure you were older."

Matt shrugged, his eyes downcast as he toed the dirt with his boot.

"Your pa must be really proud," he added.

Mr. Talbot nodded. "I am at that. Matt's a quick learner."

Evan clapped his hands together. "How about I start a fire and put on some coffee?"

"We'd be much obliged, Mr. Harrison," Mr. Talbot agreed. "Matt, come and help me with the horses."

"Yes, sir." Matt straightened to attention.

"Please, call me Evan."

"And you can call me Henry." He wrapped his arm around his son's small shoulders and led him away.

Juliana stepped forward. "Can I help you, Mrs. Talbot?"

"That's sweet of you, thanks."

While Juliana helped the other woman, Evan went in search of firewood. His mind was not on the task—it was on the kiss. The experience had rocked him to the core. The touch had been so intimate, so sweet… he couldn't imagine kissing anyone else besides Juliana. Just the thought of another man touching her made his stomach clench in anguish.

Face the facts, Harrison. You have no claim on her.

It was true. Besides, he couldn't afford to get side-tracked now. He was on a mission to find James's killers and bring them to justice. Too much was at stake.

He'd have to watch his step from here on out. A couple of days—three at the most—and he'd drop her off in Cades Cove. Leave her in his cousin's capable hands. Time away would help him get perspective on things. He and Juliana had simply spent too much time alone together. What normal, red-blooded man could hold himself aloof from her for very long?

Juliana was beautiful and graceful and sweet, with a little spice thrown in for good measure. He liked her spirit. She kept him on his toes.

Stop it. Listing her attributes won't help matters.

Evan pushed thoughts of her out of his mind and focused instead on the mundane task of finding firewood.

Chapter Eleven

Juliana sat cross-legged in the grass, her arms cradling the petite toddler. The girl's mother was taking a few moments to stretch and refresh herself. Joy's body was a warm weight in her lap, her chubby hands clasped together as if in prayer. Brown curls framed a heart-shaped face. Impossibly long, sooty eyelashes rested against pink cheeks. Her rosebud mouth was parted to form a small *O*.

Unfamiliar feelings stirred in Juliana's chest. Would a daughter of hers look like this precious treasure? Or would she have red hair and pale skin like her? She wondered what Evan's offspring would look like. Glossy black hair, deep indigo eyes and golden skin?

Rose approached carrying a bulging leather satchel and sat across from Juliana. "Is she getting too heavy?"

"Not at all."

"Joy doesn't normally sleep this long, but she's been ill. I didn't want to travel until she'd fully recovered, but we need to get home."

The poor baby. "What was the illness?"

Rose pushed wayward strands out of her eyes, her weariness evident in the way she arched her back and kneaded the back of her neck. "I'm not sure. We've been visiting my sister the last few weeks, and her husband and sons came down with a high fever and chills. Joy was the only one of us to get it." She reached out and smoothed her daughter's hair. "I was worried sick about her. I lost a child to sickness a few years back, and it nearly buried me. Just the thought of losing Joy or Matt..." Her voice trailed off and her brown eyes grew wet with moisture.

The grief in the other woman's voice spurred Juliana to reach over and squeeze her hand. "Are you a believer, Rose?"

She gave her a quivering smile. "I am."

"Would you mind if I said a prayer for Joy?"

"I'd appreciate that, Juliana."

Still holding the other woman's hand, Juliana closed her eyes and uttered a simple prayer. "Dear Lord Jesus, thank You for loving us. Your Word says that You have a plan for each of us, a plan for a future and a hope. Please restore little Joy's health and give the Talbots a safe trip home. We know that You are in control, and You will never abandon us. In Jesus's name I pray, Amen."

Her intent had been to encourage the other woman, but remembering God's promises aloud boosted her own flagging spirits. God had allowed Evan to kidnap her, and He'd been with her every moment since. He hadn't lost sight of her. She didn't understand His reasons, but she recalled reading somewhere in His Word that His thoughts were above her thoughts and His ways above her ways. That made sense, considering that He created the entire universe, and He created her.

"Thank you." Rose sighed and smiled. "Not everyone would take the time to pray for a stranger."

The other woman's face grew serious once more. Her eyes were sharp as she scanned their surroundings in a deceptively casual manner. Seeing no one about, she spoke in urgent tones. "I can help you, too. I know it's none of my business, and my Henry would say I'm putting my nose where it doesn't belong, but I simply have to ask where you got that shiner."

Juliana's hand went to her mouth in surprise. She'd forgotten all about the bruises. What could she possibly say? Certainly not the truth! She couldn't bring herself to outright lie to this kind woman, however. Think, Juliana, think!

"I know it looks bad—" she held Rose's concerned gaze. "You must believe me, however, when I say that Evan would never hurt me. He's a good man."

And she realized that she meant it. Deep down, Evan *was* a good man. He was guilty of making bad choices, of course. But he had admitted to being a Christian and was even familiar with the Holy Scriptures. At some point he'd lived a normal life. How she wished she'd met him back then. Maybe they would've had a chance.

Rose was waiting for her to continue, uncertainty etched in her features.

"There was another man." Joy stirred in her lap and rubbed her eyes with her fists. "Evan rescued me from him."

"Oh." Rose looked at a loss for words, but she appeared to accept Juliana's assertion. "Well, then, I'm glad he was there to protect you."

"Yes," Juliana murmured, dropping her gaze, "me, too."

She hadn't thought about it in quite that way. In an ironic twist, Evan was now her protector.

"Momma."

Juliana looked down into eyes the color of melted chocolate and smiled. The little girl popped her thumb into her mouth and started sucking, content to stay in Juliana's lap. Her wide, curious eyes stared unblinking up at her. Juliana must have passed the inspection, for Joy's lips curled up in an impish grin. Her heart melted at the sight. What a treasure!

A movement at the edge of her vision snagged her attention. It was Evan, returning with an armful of kindling. His intense gaze was centered on her, but he was too far away for her to catch his expression. He was probably wondering what they were discussing so intently.

Juliana watched him drop the sticks and broken branches in a heap before heading their way. Dusting the dirt from his shirt and pants, he walked with long, purposeful strides. There wasn't an ounce of fat on his muscular frame.

"Ladies." He tugged on the brim of his hat, his larkspur blue eyes unreadable as his gaze scanned Juliana's face and dropped to the child in her lap. "Juliana, may I speak with you for a moment?"

"Up!"

All three adults turned their gazes to the little girl, who'd extended her arms in Evan's direction.

Lifting her head, Juliana bit her lip to ward off a grin. Evan looked stricken.

Before he could respond, Joy scrambled off Juliana's lap and tugged on his pants leg. "Up! Pwease!"

"Joy, Mr. Harrison is busy—" Rose began.

"It's all right," he said. Reaching down, he scooped her up and held her against his chest. The toddler and outlaw stared at each other, taking each other's measure. Then, to everyone's shock, Joy slapped a noisy kiss on his cheek and giggled. His low rumble of laughter mingled with hers, a delightful sound to Juliana's ears. She and Rose shared a smile. They watched as Joy laid her head on his shoulder, her tiny arm curling around his neck.

Serious once more, Evan's gaze found Juliana's. The look was full of questions she couldn't answer.

She closed her eyes and relived the moments leading up to his kiss. He'd been talking in that honeyed voice he reserved for those times he wanted to charm her. His breath had fanned out across her mouth, teasing her. His lazy caress had driven all rational thought from her mind. Unable to move, she'd stood mesmerized by his touch and the promise in his eyes.

Evan Harrison might not pose a threat to her physical well-being, but he was downright dangerous to her heart. He had pledged to protect her, yes, but he didn't care about her. Getting her home safe was all that mattered to him. He considered it his duty and his responsibility. He regretted having played a part in her kidnapping and was trying to make things right.

The fact that he'd taken such liberties with her when he had no intention of furthering their relationship angered her. How could he be so casual with his affection... so careless with her heart? Juliana decided then and there to keep him at arm's length. If she allowed him continued access to her body, her heart would no doubt succumb and she'd find herself in love with an outlaw.

She opened her eyes to find him still watching her. Her lungs suddenly seemed devoid of air. He held her captive without laying a hand on her! No. She was through being toyed with.

Jumping to her feet, Juliana murmured an excuse to Rose and strode away, her head held high. How dare he toy with her?

"Juliana, wait!"

Ignoring him, she continued walking away from camp.

"I'll take her," she heard Rose say.

Gritting her teeth, she fought to keep the tears at bay.

Why did she allow him to affect her? Her inexperience with men, perhaps? Or was it him in particular?

"Juliana, please stop and talk to me." Evan was right behind her, following closely but making no move to stop her. "I'll follow you back to Gatlinburg if I have to. You know I'm stubborn enough to do it."

Stopping abruptly, she whirled to confront him. "Can't I have a few moments alone?"

He stood a foot away, hands on his hips, boots planted wide as if braced for a fight. "Not out here, you can't. It isn't safe."

"Being with you isn't safe," she retorted, instantly wishing she could call the words back.

"What's that supposed to mean?" He dropped his hands to his sides, confusion written all over his face.

At the appeal in his eyes, the fight went out of her. Juliana chose to be upfront with him. "I'm not experienced in matters of the heart, Evan. I have a handful of male friends and acquaintances, but I haven't experienced a serious courtship. When you kissed me, I—" She closed her eyes and blew out a breath. "I thought that my first kiss would be with a man I love. A man I intended to marry."

"And instead it was with me," he stated flatly, an odd glint of hurt in his eyes. "I think I understand now why you're angry. I apologize, Juliana. I overstepped my bounds. It won't happen again."

Instead of bringing satisfaction, his words tore at her. *It's for the best,* a quiet voice reminded her. If they kept their distance from each other, she would be able to get through the next few days with her heart intact. Then she could return to her old life with no regrets.

Squaring her shoulders, she pushed the words through her lips. "Thank you, Evan. I knew you'd understand."

He tugged the brim of his hat down low, his manner all cool formality. "We'd better start back. Mr. Talbot will be wondering what happened to that coffee I promised him."

He motioned for her to go in front of him, which she did with reluctance. Conscious of his eyes upon her as they walked through the ankle-high grass, she kept her back stiff and shoulders straight. The exposed skin at her nape prickled as if his gaze was a physical touch. When the pond came into view, Juliana sprinted to reach the edge, leaving Evan behind.

She scanned the rocks and sandy soil for a long, smooth stick. When she'd found one, she crossed the field to where Rose and Joy sat on a blanket sharing a canteen of water.

"Do you know how to fry frogs' legs?" Juliana asked.

Shading her eyes, Rose grinned up at Juliana. "I do. Do you think you can catch enough for all of us?"

"I could if Matt helped me. Would Mr. Talbot mind my borrowing him for an hour?"

The dark-haired woman's head bobbed. "Henry's fond of anything battered and fried. I can fry up some hush puppies, along with some taters and onions my sister insisted on giving us."

"If I have time, I'll hunt for berries to serve as dessert."

"Sounds good to me." Rose tickled the little girl's tummy. "What do you say, Pumpkin?"

Joy nodded. "Yum!"

Juliana smiled down at them. "I'd better get started if we want to eat before dark."

She found Matt in the shade of poplar trees, brushing down the horses. His father was nearby, sorting their supplies. Once she explained her plan, Henry gladly gave his permission. While Matt didn't jump up and down for joy, she sensed his eagerness. He offered to use the knife his pa had given him to sharpen their sticks. Juliana could tell he was proud of that knife. He was a sweet boy, caught in the awkward transition from a child to a young man.

While she and Matt gigged for frogs, Evan started a fire and made coffee. Determined not to glance his way, she kept her head down and eyes on the water. But her ears strained for the sound of his low-timbered voice. To the casual observer, she no doubt appeared to be relaxed and happy. Nothing could be further from the truth.

Juliana was tense, her stomach as jumpy as the frogs leaping about trying to avoid their spears. Her head ached from holding back the tide of tears. Her emotions were a raw, jumbled mess.

"Dear Lord," she whispered, "I need wisdom."

"Did you say something, Miss Juliana?" Matt balanced on a rock nearly submerged in the water. His pants legs were rolled up to his knees, and he was barefoot. His hair was dark and wavy like his sister's, but instead of brown eyes, his were green. Henry and Rose Talbot had been blessed with adorable kids.

"I was praying out loud."

He held his spear aloft. "My ma does that a lot."

"What about you?"

"Nah. I do it mostly in my head." His brows shot up, and he pointed to a spot near her foot. "Look—there's a five-pounder!"

Juliana looked down and spotted the fat frog. While five pounds might be a stretch, three wouldn't be exaggerating. Moving slowly so as not to frighten it off, she lifted her weapon and, with a swift, sure stroke, plunged it down.

"You got him! You got him!" Matt whirled his arms and nearly fell into the water.

Depositing her latest catch into the pail, she said, "I think we have enough, Matt. I'm going to get these ready for your momma."

Awe filled his eyes. "You mean you're gonna skin them yourself?"

"I'd planned on it. Would you rather do it?"

"But you're a girl!" he blurted out.

She paused in the midst of pulling on her stockings and flashed him an indulgent smile. "And?"

He hesitated. "I thought girls didn't like that sort of thing."

"I don't particularly like the task, but I've done it often enough to get used to it. If I want to eat it, I have to know how to prepare it, right?"

"Right."

She could see that he was mulling this information over. Rising to her feet, she asked, "Would you like to help me?"

"Yes, ma'am." He scrambled onto the bank and started tugging on his socks and boots.

"Carry the pail for me?"

"Yes, ma'am!"

As they searched for a place to work, Juliana couldn't resist a glance at the fire. Evan was nowhere to be seen. Frowning, she wondered where he had gone.

Rose was peeling a mound of potatoes. Joy was amusing herself by tossing the peelings in all directions. Henry sat on the other side of his daughter, drinking a cup of coffee and listening to her chatter.

An hour passed. Then another. Evan was nowhere to be seen. Juliana was worried. Just because it was daylight didn't mean there weren't wild animals roaming the woods. Their encounter with the black bear flashed through her mind. What if he'd stumbled across another one?

Or worse, what if Lenny Fitzgerald had caught up to them? The thought of Evan in danger made her heart race. By the time she and Matt were finished, she was trembling with apprehension.

"Are you all right, Miss Juliana?"

Washing her hands in the shallow water, she looked over her shoulder at the concerned boy. "Why do you ask?"

"You're awful pale," he said in a serious tone. "And you got quiet all of a sudden."

Juliana felt bad about causing him alarm. She mustered up a fleeting smile. "I'm sorry, Matt. I guess I was thinking too hard about something." She walked over to where he was crouched down and placed a hand on his shoulder. "Thank you for your help this afternoon."

He beamed up at her. "You're welcome."

With a squeeze and a pat, she picked up the pail containing the frogs' legs and took it over to Rose. Her legs were unsteady, and she felt as if she might lose her lunch.

"Juliana!" Rose scrambled to her feet and took the pail from her. "Sit down right here in the shade while I pour you a drink of water. You look parched."

Juliana sank to her knees, accepting the tin cup pressed into her hand and sipping the cool liquid. She untied her bonnet with her free hand, slipped it off and placed it in her lap.

"I hope you didn't get too hot," Rose commented as she resumed her task. "Would you like a cool compress for your forehead?"

"No, thank you. The water is helping." She met Henry's gaze. "Do you know where Evan went?"

"He went looking for berries," Henry's eyes twinkled. "Heard you had a hankerin' for dessert."

Juliana didn't know what to think. Evan was out there searching for berries in order to please her? That meant that, in a roundabout way, it was her own fault she was sick with worry.

"He's been gone a long time, don't you think?" She brushed a black ant off the corner of the blanket.

"Your husband should be along shortly," he assured her. "Don't worry, he's got protection."

She didn't respond, merely sipped more water. A weapon wouldn't do him any good if he didn't have time to draw it.

Father God, my thoughts are spiraling out of control. You know exactly where he is and what he's doing. Keep him safe. I ask this in Jesus's name, Amen. Oh, and please help me not to worry.

Evan stared down at the smoldering fire pit with dismay. Next to it lay an empty whiskey bottle and the remains of someone's supper. Whoever had been there hadn't taken the time to clean up after themselves.

He picked up the bottle and examined it more closely. The label was partly worn off, but he could make out enough of it to know that it was the cheap brand Fitzgerald preferred. Tossing it to the ground, he searched for more clues, but came up empty.

If Fitzgerald was nearby, he'd have to warn Henry Talbot.

The Talbots' arrival had proved to be a blessing. Before now, he hadn't been able to backtrack and check for signs that Fitzgerald was indeed following them. He hadn't wanted to leave Juliana alone and unprotected.

With Henry to watch over her, however, he'd felt that he could leave her for a while.

He figured he'd been gone about two hours, enough time to relive their last conversation about a hundred times. Her words had seared him clean through to his soul. He'd never been shot, but he figured the pain of a bullet hole couldn't compare to the wound she'd inflicted.

Juliana hadn't wanted him to kiss her. She said she didn't feel *safe* with him.

Burying his face in Lucky's coarse neck, he groaned. What a mess he'd made of things! Her mistrust dealt a harsh blow to his honor. Evan would die before forcing himself on a woman.

Slamming his hat on his head, he swung into the saddle and turned Lucky in the direction of camp.

Memories of the kiss resurfaced. Juliana had been irritated with him beforehand, but she'd responded to his touch. Hadn't she? Had he imagined the longing in her eyes?

His grip tightened on the reins. One thing was for certain—he would not kiss her again unless she asked him to. And, knowing Juliana, that day would likely never come.

Juliana paced before the fire, stopping every few moments to search the darkness and listen for the sound of a rider approaching. Her nerves were stretched to the limit. If Evan didn't show up soon, she would borrow one of Henry's horses and go search for him herself.

Her imagination was running wild, dreaming up all sorts of reasons why he hadn't returned. Fear taunted her, robbing her of peace.

Supper had turned out to be a huge disappointment. The food Rose worked so hard to prepare hadn't tempted her a bit. For Rose's sake, she'd managed to eat a portion of her meal. Even with that small amount, her stomach had cramped up and she'd resorted to sipping coffee.

The other couple had done their best to keep her mind off Evan. They entertained her with stories of the children's antics. They were kind people who shared her love for the Lord. She was thankful for their companionship.

Throughout the evening, Henry hadn't appeared at all concerned over Evan's absence, but Rose hadn't been able to hide her unease.

"Juliana?"

Stopping short, she shot the other woman a hopeful look. "Anything?"

With a sympathetic smile, Rose shook her head. Black curls framed her face and spilled over her shoulders, making her appear ten years younger. Juliana thought she was a handsome woman.

"Would you like for me to pray with you?" Rose asked.

"That would be nice."

Rose approached and, clasping Juliana's hands, she began to pray for Evan's safety and swift return. For Juliana, she prayed for peace and faith in God's goodness.

"Thank you, Rose. I've only known you a day but I already consider you a friend."

Rose's face lit up, warming Juliana. "Not only are we friends, but sisters in Christ."

The weight of her and Evan's deception weighed heavily on her conscience, but she couldn't tell Rose the truth. Not yet. Perhaps someday, when the time was right, she would confide in her new friend and ask for forgiveness.

"The children are already asleep, but Henry and I will be up awhile longer. Just so you know, Henry plans on staying awake until Evan shows up."

"I'll be awake, too. I doubt I'll sleep this night."

"Try not to worry, Juliana." She spoke with conviction. "From what I've seen, it's obvious that Evan loves you dearly. He'll fight to get back to you with everything in him."

Juliana bit her lip. If only he truly did love her. If only he wasn't an outlaw. If only…

"I hope you're right," she sighed, her heart heavy.

"According to Henry, I'm always right," Rose grinned and patted her arm. "Wake me if you need to. I won't mind."

"I'll do that," she agreed. "Good night."

"Good night."

Juliana watched her walk back to where they'd bedded down on the far side of the fire. She spoke to Henry, who turned and waved. Juliana lifted her hand in a limp wave and resumed her pacing.

Chapter Twelve

Exhaustion threatened to overtake Evan. His lower back ached from sitting in the saddle for hours on end, and his head pounded from lack of food. At this late hour, hunger was the only thing keeping him awake. He tried to remember what he'd eaten for lunch and realized he and Juliana had skipped it. He wondered if she'd thought to save him a plate from supper, or if she'd thought about it and decided to let him fend for himself.

The light from the fire was a welcome sight. Sensing water and rest were within reach, his horse cantered into the campsite, arriving winded and nearly tossing Evan to the ground with his abrupt stop.

"Whoa there, big boy." He spoke in low tones so as not to wake the others. He balanced his hat on the saddle horn and ran his fingers through his hair.

Sliding out of the saddle, he jerked at the unexpected sound of Juliana's voice directly behind him.

"Where have you been?"

He turned to face her, taken aback by her undisguised anger. Her eyes were enormous in her colorless face. Tendrils had escaped the once-tidy bun, and there was a smudge of dirt on her chin. She looked fit to be tied.

"Do you realize how worried I—*we* have been?"

Evan stared down at her. The desire to hug away her worries was strong, but he knew she wouldn't welcome it. As hard as it was, he turned his back on her and began to see to his horse, speaking over his shoulder as he worked.

"I'm sorry about that, but I had my reasons."

Silence greeted his remark. Then, "And what might those be, may I ask?"

"Fitzgerald," he grunted, lifting the saddle and dropping it on the ground nearby. His glance flicked to her face, then away. "He's on our trail." He removed the saddle blanket from Lucky's back.

"Did you see him?"

"Nope."

"Then how—"

"Whiskey bottle." He brushed the black's coarse hair until it shined in the low light. "I know the brand he drinks. That, and the place was a mess. Typical of him."

When she didn't respond, Evan paused. Heaving a sigh, he slowly turned around. Fear was written all over her. When he noticed her trembling, his willpower took a nosedive. Still, he managed to hold back.

"Please try not to worry, Juliana." He gazed deep into her eyes, trying to impart comfort without actually touching her. "He'll have to go through me to get to you."

"That's what I'm afraid of," she whispered.

Evan's fists clenched. He swallowed hard. How much was a man supposed to take? He wasn't made of steel.

"I don't plan on losing, darlin'," he drawled, his voice a soft caress.

"Evan, I—"

"Glad to see you made it back." Henry strode up and clapped him on the shoulder. "Everything all right?"

"Actually, I need to speak with you." He glanced at

Juliana. "Do you happen to have any leftovers? I'm starving."

She stared at him. "I'll get a plate ready for you. How about coffee as well?"

He flashed her a grateful smile. "I'd like that, if you're not too tired."

"I'm too wound up to be tired."

"You can keep me company while I eat then."

With an arched brow, she whirled away and went to ready the food. He stared after her, content simply to watch her move about. Henry cleared his throat, and, pulling his gaze away, Evan began to lay out the facts.

After stoking the fire, Juliana set the coffee on to heat. The night air was fresh and sweet and pleasant. Crickets chirped. The fat, luminescent moon cast a glow over the land as mist rolled in across the pond.

Her eyes drank in the sight of Evan, safe and sound in her presence. In the pale moonlight, she could make out his profile as he spoke with Henry. Wide forehead, straight nose, angled jaw, determined chin. His short black hair lay smoothly against his head.

His bearing spoke of self-assurance and resolve. Did he fear nothing?

Her own battle with fear had left her limp and worn out. It had taken her on a wild ride that day—from the heights of worry to the depths of despair. She knew that God had not given her a spirit of fear, but of power and of a sound mind. Instead of trusting in Him, however, she'd allowed herself to become consumed with the emotion.

Now there was new reason to fear—Lenny Fitzgerald was hot on their trail.

God, I'm so confused. I'm falling in love with one

outlaw and being hunted by another. Where are You in all of this? How will I find my way?

Juliana missed her family, especially her sister, Megan, and her cousin, Josh. Megan was a good listener, and her faith was solid. As roommates, it was their habit to confide in each other while everyone else slept. In the comfort of their beds, they often talked long into the night. Megan would surely have something constructive to say concerning Juliana's growing attachment to Evan. Josh was a good listener, too. He gave sound advice from the male perspective.

She wondered what they were doing at that moment. No doubt her entire family was in turmoil over her disappearance. She wondered if there were men still searching for her. She knew Josh would never give up. Her cousin would search until he found her.

Josh and Evan were alike in that they were both determined men. Once their purpose was set, they would do anything to accomplish it. If the circumstances had been different, she had no doubt the two would've been great friends. As things stood, she would have a hard time convincing her cousin not to shoot the man who'd kidnapped her.

Evan was saying good-night to Henry, who looked tense. Evan would've warned him of the danger without telling him the whole truth about their situation. She prayed that no harm would come to the Talbot family. She wouldn't be able to live with the guilt if Fitzgerald harmed her new friends.

Lowering his tall frame to the ground, Evan propped his arms on his bent knees and stared intently at her. "Are you all right?"

"I'm fine." She focused on pouring them each a cup of coffee, all the while avoiding his direct gaze.

"Are you still angry at me?"

As she handed a cup to him, his fingers closed over hers. A jolt of awareness shot through her. Her gaze flew to his face. Carefully releasing her fingers while still holding onto the cup, his expression became guarded and his eyes watchful.

"Well?" he prompted. "Are you?"

"I'm not angry. I reacted out of fear, I suppose."

His dark gaze roamed her face. "Does that mean you care what happens to me, Juliana?"

She stiffened, her mind scrambling for a proper response. Had she been that obvious? "Of course I care for your safety," she stammered. "If something happened to you, who would take me home?"

He winced as if she'd inflicted physical pain. "That's right. I'm your ticket home."

For the second time that day, Juliana wished her words had been left unspoken. She'd hurt him. "I didn't mean that how it sounded, Evan. Really—"

He held up a hand. "You don't have to explain. I understand."

"Evan, please—"

With a feather-light touch of his finger, he lifted her chin. "I wasn't expecting a declaration of love, Juliana."

Dropping his hand, he turned his head to stare into the fire.

Juliana squeezed her eyes shut. She'd led him to believe he was merely a means to an end. Her ticket home, as he put it. That was a lie. Against her better judgment, she had begun to care deeply for him. Worrying and fretting about his whereabouts all evening had brought that fact to light.

"Why do you associate with men like Fitzgerald?" she said suddenly. "You're nothing like them."

He sipped his coffee. "As I said earlier, it's a temporary thing."

"Is it the money?"

He shot her a look of dismissal. "I don't need money."

"What is it you need, Evan?"

He didn't speak for the span of a few seconds. The smile he summoned up bordered on a grimace. "I need to eat, Irish. That's it."

Frustration bubbled up deep inside, and she bit back a retort. Why couldn't he trust her? If he didn't do it for the money—and she'd seen the evidence of that back at the cabin where he'd left the money from the mercantile heist—then what was his motivation? Was he a thrill seeker? Or was it something else entirely? What had driven Evan Harrison to leave his farm for a life of crime?

Juliana wanted desperately to press the issue, but the circles of exhaustion under his eyes and the weariness in his posture aroused her compassion. He was spent. And hungry. This conversation could wait until later.

Grabbing a square cloth, she lifted his trencher from the coals and handed it to him. "I hope you like frogs' legs. Matt and I caught them."

"Sure do." He accepted the trencher with eagerness. "I'll bet Matt had a great time." He bit into one and heaved a contented sigh. "This is the best meal I've had in a long time. Thank you."

"Rose prepared it—not me."

"Yes, but you helped catch the critters. Something else Josh taught you?"

"Yes." She smothered a yawn, and he looked up.

"You're tired," he stated. "Go to bed."

"I can wait until you're finished."

"I'm gonna be up awhile, so you go on ahead. It's been a long day."

She brushed the escaped tendrils away from her face. "Aren't you tired?"

His mouth full of food, he swallowed and wiped his mouth with his handkerchief. "I am, but considering Fitzgerald is out there, I think it's wise if someone stands guard."

"But you've been in the saddle all day!"

"It's just for a couple of hours. Henry's gonna take the second shift."

"I suppose you'll want to sleep in tomorrow morning."

"I was planning on it, yes," he said wryly. "Is that okay with you? Or do you have plans for me that can't wait until after breakfast?"

"No, no plans." She yawned for the second time in five minutes.

"Good night, Juliana." His tone left no room for argument.

"Good night, Evan."

Juliana hadn't been able to sleep for thoughts of Evan. The long night of tossing and turning had left her feeling out of sorts. What was driving him? What was he hiding? Frustration with him, his refusal to trust her and her own wayward heart bubbled up within her.

With jerky movements she scrubbed the pots clean, but her attention was not on the task at hand. Like a magnet, her gaze was drawn repeatedly to his sleeping form and the black boots propped a few feet away. Her thoughts turned to the paring knife she'd slipped in her pocket at breakfast. Could she really do this?

After all she'd been through, Juliana felt as if she deserved some answers. And if Evan refused to give her the information she sought, then she'd just have to take it upon herself to find it. Her mind made up, she wiped her hands dry and checked to see whether or not the others were watching. They seemed to be sufficiently occupied.

She didn't give herself time to change her mind. She approached Evan with cautious steps, her gaze on his relaxed features. He didn't stir. He was so handsome, perhaps even more so now that he was unguarded and peaceful. Her heart gave a painful twinge. She felt horrible doing this, as if she herself were a criminal. The last thing she wanted to do was hurt him. If only Evan would confide in her...

Fat chance. Ignoring the warning voice inside her head, she scooped up the boots and hurried to an area of tall grass near the water's edge and sank down, her back to camp. The knife poised in midair, she hesitated. Was this really the right thing to do? After all, she was about to destroy his property. There would be no repairing the lining, so he would know it had been tampered with. And who else but her would do such a thing?

Juliana worried her bottom lip, debating. No matter the consequences, she *had* to know. Perhaps this *thing,* whatever it was, would give her some insight into what he was hiding.

Her mind made up, she sliced through the stitches. Her hands were unsteady as she explored the lining with her fingers. It took a few tries, but she eventually managed to retrieve the object.

A sheriff's badge. She faltered, her stomach tightening. No. It couldn't be.

"What do you think you're doing?"

Her heart slammed against her chest at the sound of Evan's deep voice directly behind her. She clutched the star in her fist and bolted to her feet.

He looked grim. Dark brows winged low, his mouth was turned down in intense displeasure.

"I—I—" she stammered, her mind a complete blank.

His hands on his hips, he waited for her answer. There was no avoiding the issue. He could plainly see what she was doing. She stuck her hand out, palm open, the gold star shining in the light.

"How did you get this, Evan?" she demanded, suddenly angry. Had he lied to her? "Please tell me you didn't kill a lawman and then hid the evidence."

She held her breath as she waited for his response, half-afraid to hear it. She couldn't tell by his expression what he was thinking. That frustrated her.

"I've never killed a man," he said slowly, his eyes narrowing, "I thought I made that clear."

"So why are you carrying a badge around in your boot? Whose is it?"

"I'd like to know how you found it. Do you make a habit of examining men's footwear?"

Her cheeks heated. "Absolutely not. I was trying to move your boots out of the rain yesterday when I discovered it. You were asleep at the time."

With a backward glance over his shoulder, he advanced toward her. He held his hand out. "May I have that back now?"

Reluctantly, she relinquished it. He brushed past her and, scooping up the knife, shot her a look of exasperation before dropping it in his pocket. Then he bent to tug on his boots. When he straightened, his jaw was set.

He came to stand directly in front of her. "I understand your need to know the truth. I'd do the same thing if I were in your position. But let me make myself very clear—" his blue eyes skewered her "—don't put your nose where it doesn't belong. My business is just that—mine."

His words hurt. "Are you threatening me?" she asked incredulously.

His mouth firmed. "Call it whatever you want, Juliana."

Spinning on his heel, he strode away without another word.

Juliana watched him leave, her mouth hanging open. What in the world? She'd expected his anger, but threats? It didn't make sense. He hadn't been that abrupt with her since the first day.

She was no closer to the truth. In fact, the badge had only sparked more questions.

She stamped her foot in frustration. Why did he have to be so stubborn?

Evan tried to smother the annoyance roiling in his gut. She had some nerve! Why couldn't she leave well enough alone?

The badge was safe in his pants pocket. For now. He shook his head in disgust. He'd thought he'd found the perfect hiding place. Either he was that bad or she was that good.

He strode back to camp and quickly rolled his bedroll into a tidy bundle. What he really wanted to do was go back to sleep. He'd gone to bed with a raging headache. The long rest hadn't helped this time. It felt like an axe was being driven into the base of his skull.

Retrieving his shaving kit, he walked to the opposite side of the lake to shave. As soon as he was finished, he would get a cup of coffee and a plate of food. Maybe that was the reason he felt out of sorts this morning.

His thoughts strayed again to Juliana. He could tell her everything, he supposed.

Yet something inside him resisted. If she knew the truth, there would be no more barriers. No reasons to keep her distance. No more defenses.

The walls protecting his heart were not rock-solid. Against his better judgment, he already cared more than was wise. If he told her the truth now, he wasn't so sure he could remain detached. And falling in love was *not* an option.

By the time he finished shaving, Evan realized that breakfast would have to wait. He needed to lie down again or risk collapsing in a heap. He just barely made it back. As it was, he didn't have the strength to fix his blankets, so he stretched out in the grass and promptly fell into a dark oblivion.

A feather brushed over his nose. Lifting a limp hand, Evan batted it away and turned onto his side, his arm cushioning his head. Sleep sucked him back down.

A feather tickled his ear. Grumbling at the disturbance, he swatted again. All he wanted was to sleep in peace. He felt as if he'd been flattened by a runaway wagon.

"Baba!"

A child's voice interrupted his dreams and a warm weight plumped down onto his rib cage. Jerked awake, he opened his eyes in time to see a curly haired moppet tumble sideways into the grass. Unfazed, she scrambled on top of him once more, her chubby hands clutching his blue cotton shirt for balance. Leaning in close, her brown eyes were large with curiosity as she gazed at him.

"Fafa!"

Careful not to dislodge her, he maneuvered himself

onto his back. She picked up a broken willow branch and waved it in the air.

Studying the little girl, he was struck by her sweet face and wide-eyed curiosity. Her sunny yellow frock combined with her large, heavily lashed brown eyes and coffee-colored curls put him in mind of the tall sunflowers growing along the far edge of his property.

Ah, to be a child again, innocent and free of the worries of this world.

She slid off his chest and toddled in the direction of the water. Evan sat up and pushed a hand through his rumpled hair. He had no idea how long he'd been out.

He tracked the little girl with his gaze. She was headed for the wildflower patch, no doubt drawn by the rainbow of bright colors—blue, red, yellow, pink and purple blossoms swaying in the wind.

The girl's mother was hunched over the fire, stirring the contents of the iron kettle. Henry sat nearby sharpening his knives. Matt wasn't in sight, nor was Juliana.

He stood and ambled after the child. She wasn't near the water, but snakes liked to hide in tall grass and he didn't want to take any chances.

On her knees in the midst of the wildflowers, she buried her nose in the fragrant blossoms. Occasionally, her tiny pink tongue jetted out to lick a petal. He shook his head in amusement. When she reached for a pale pink, bell-shaped flower, he hurried to warn her.

Squatting to her level, he said, "Hey, princess, don't mess with that one," pointing to the cluster of foxgloves. "These flowers will make your tummy hurt real bad. Don't touch them and don't put them in your mouth."

"Fafa?" She quirked her head, her tiny brow wrinkled in dismay.

Flower? He pointed again. "Fafa no good."

A shadow fell across his body.

"When did you learn baby talk?"

Despite his irritation with her, pleasure curled through him at the sound of her lyrical voice. "How long have I been asleep?"

"A long while."

When he rose to greet her, black spots danced before his eyes and he swayed. He squeezed his eyes shut in hoping that the light-headed sensation would pass.

"What's wrong?" Juliana moved closer. Her slender hand closed over his wrist, thrilling him despite his discomfort.

"Probably stood up too fast," he muttered, pinching the bridge of his nose between his thumb and finger. His head throbbed.

He opened his eyes and was relieved to find his vision clear. Juliana's face was within touching distance, her forehead puckered in concern. Pale eyelashes framed dark green irises, tiny flecks of gold reflected by the shafts of sunlight peaking through the puffy clouds overhead. A breeze picked up, teasing strands of hair from the neat bun at her nape.

"Are you okay now?"

"I'm fine."

A tug on his pants leg had him looking down. The little girl held her hands up to him. "Up!"

"I guess that means she wants me to hold her again, huh?" he said, bending to pick her up.

"Wait, Evan," Juliana cautioned, "are you able to carry her? She may look light, but she's not."

With the girl perched in his arms, he turned to Juliana. "I'm fine, really. Let's deliver this bundle to her parents. My morning coffee is long overdue."

Gauging from the expression on her face, Juliana

wasn't convinced. She walked beside him without speaking. The gusts of wind took the edge off the humidity. He eyed the darkening sky. They were likely in for a squall.

"I see you finally decided to roll out of bed, Harrison," Henry called out, his ready smile in place. Evan liked the man and would be sorry when they parted ways.

"I found something that belongs to you." He set the girl down. She hurried to her father's side. Henry set aside his tools to pull her into his lap. Evan nodded to Talbot's wife. "Good morning, Mrs. Talbot."

"I told you to call me Rose," she scolded in a light tone. "Would you like your breakfast now? We saved a plate for you. Bacon, beans and corn bread."

His stomach revolted at the notion of food. "Thank you kindly, ma'am, but I believe I'll just take a cup of coffee if you have any."

Her brows rose in surprise. "Sure, we have plenty."

"I'll get it." Juliana moved to fill a tin cup with the dark brew. When she handed it to him, she lowered her voice. "Are you sure you're okay? It's unusual for you to skip a meal."

He accepted the cup with a nod. "I'm just feelin' a little off today." He sipped the steaming liquid. "Probably a combination of not eating all day yesterday and not enough sleep."

"Maybe we should stick around here another day," she suggested. "We could leave early tomorrow morning."

She had a point. With the way he was feeling, hitting the trail in this heat held little appeal. Still, he didn't like the idea of sitting in one place with Fitzgerald on their trail. And time was an issue—he needed to get her settled in Cades Cove and then report back to Roberts and the gang.

"Your idea is tempting, but we need to get home." He tried to convey with a look what he couldn't say aloud.

"What's your hurry?" Henry joined them, his daughter on his hip. "Stay with us one more night. It'll give us a chance to visit a bit more before we say our goodbyes."

Evan couldn't think straight, what with the sledgehammer pounding away in his skull. The coffee tasted bitter going down, so he threw it out. Juliana gave him an odd look. He shrugged.

"I can't think…" The edges of his vision went black, and he stumbled back.

"Evan!"

Juliana calling his name was the last thing he heard before he lost consciousness and slid to the ground.

Chapter Thirteen

Juliana reached for him, but wasn't fast enough. He hit the ground hard, his head glancing off a fallen log. A thin stream of red trickled from his temple down past his ear and into his hair.

Alarm spiraling through her, Juliana fell to her knees. "Evan!" She cradled his face in her hands. "Speak to me."

Stepping over his prone body, Henry kneeled, held Evan's wrist and checked his pulse. "Does he have any health problems?"

"No." Evan hadn't mentioned a thing. He seemed so strong and healthy. But she'd only known him a few days. "At least, none that I know of."

Rose rushed up and placed a hand on Juliana's shoulder. "What can I do?"

Her thoughts scattered, Juliana's only focus was on Evan himself.

Henry spoke with utter calm and authority. "We need clean water and bandages for his head wound." Letting go of Evan's arm, Henry placed a hand on his forehead. "His pulse is thready. And he's burning up." He looked at her. "Does he have a tent among his gear?"

"I don't think so."

"You can borrow ours." He gave instructions to his wife. "Have Matt empty the tent of our things and ready a pallet for Evan."

"All right," Rose said before Juliana could protest. "I'll be right back."

With a squeeze of Juliana's shoulder, she left, taking Joy with her.

"You really don't have to do that," she said.

"Evan's ill. He'll need cover if it starts to rain."

"Thank you." She paused. "What do you think is wrong with him?" She tore her gaze away to look at Henry.

Henry's dark eyes were somber. "Could be any number of things. Did he get bit by anything recently?"

"Like a spider?"

He nodded. Her eyes drifted back to Evan's still form. "He didn't say. But he was really tired last night. We didn't talk long before I went to bed."

Rose brought the bandages and a bowl of clean water. She offered to clean the wound, but Juliana declined, preferring to perform the task herself. With great care, Juliana cleansed the gash and wrapped long strips of cloth around his head, tying it off tight enough to stem the flow of blood. She was thankful the wound wasn't deep and wouldn't require a sewing kit. She was in no mood to sew his skin back together. She was worried by the fact that not once during her ministrations did he flinch or flutter an eyelid.

"I have an idea." Henry's voice broke into her reverie. "Once we get him inside the tent, why don't you undress him and look for marks or spots that look suspicious."

Dread filled her as his words registered. Setting the bowl aside, she looked over at him. "I can't do that."

"Why not? You're his wife."

"Well, I—" She scrambled for a solid reason for her refusal and came up blank. As much as she wanted to help, she couldn't bring herself to do as he suggested. "Could you do it, Henry? You probably have a much better idea of what to look for than I do."

He studied her a moment, and Juliana felt a flush creep up her neck.

"Yes, of course." He moved to rise. "Will you stay here with him while I help Matt?"

"I won't leave him."

"Holler if there's any change."

"Okay."

She scooted closer and gently took his head in her lap, smoothing his hair with trembling fingers. Against the dark material of her dress, his face was deathly pale. His skin was dry and hot. His chest rose and fell in shallow, rapid breaths.

"What's wrong with him, Lord?" she whispered, brushing aside the wetness on her cheeks. "I'm scared."

She checked the bandage. So far, there was no sign of blood soaking through the thick cotton. A small blessing.

Juliana racked her brain, trying to think if Evan had eaten anything odd in the last day or so. As far as she knew, he'd eaten the exact same food as she. Unless he'd eaten something on the trail he'd failed to mention.

The wind picked up, tugging at her skirt and whipping strands of hair across her face. Slate-gray clouds swirled in the sky overhead, blocking out the sunshine. Henry and Matt worked with quick, efficient movements to ready the tent. She prayed the rain would hold off.

Rose brought Juliana a bowl of clean, cool water and strips of cloth with which to bathe Evan's face and neck. With a light touch, she swabbed his forehead, cheeks, chin and neck. She unbuttoned the top buttons of his sky-blue shirt and spread the material wide so that she could access more skin. Curiosity overriding common sense, she slipped her hand beneath his shirt and flattened her palm against the hard muscles, the light covering of hair teasing her fingers. His heart thumped an angry rhythm, his skin fiery to the touch. Yanking her hand back, she ignored the flare of heat in her middle.

"Miss Juliana?"

She jerked at the sound of Matt's voice behind her, the sudden movement jarring Evan's head. He groaned but didn't open his eyes. "Yes, Matt?"

"The tent's ready."

Henry rushed over. Between the three of them, they were able to lift his body off the ground and carry him to the tent beneath a magnolia tree. With the thick, inter-woven branches, it was a good choice. Rainwater would sluice off the outer leaves and flowers onto the ground, leaving the inner circle of ground beneath the branches relatively dry. They settled him inside the cozy interior on a soft pallet.

Juliana stopped Matt's departure with a hand on his arm. "The water is already tepid. Would you mind refilling it?"

His dark eyes were wide with uncertainty. "Yes, ma'am."

"Thanks."

The sound of Evan's labored breathing stirred fear in Juliana's soul. Whatever was ailing him was serious.

Miles from the closest town and doctor, they would have to depend on herbs or plants to provide a remedy.

"Mrs. Harrison." Henry spoke as he untied Evan's bootlaces. "I'm going to check him now. Do you plan to stay or would you rather wait outside?"

"I'll go speak with Rose." With a last caress of Evan's cheek, she scooted outside and looked up at the dark sky. She thanked God for holding off the weather until Evan was settled. She headed toward the fire where Rose sat with Joy, who was apparently unhappy with the choice of beans for lunch.

"No!" Crossing her arms, the little girl averted her face.

Rose held the spoon aloft, encouraging Joy to eat. She looked up at Juliana's approach. Her black hair was damp with sweat from cooking over the fire. Lowering the spoon to the bowl, she waited for Juliana to speak.

"He's not doing well," she said, discouraged. "I'm worried, Rose. We're out in the middle of nowhere, and we haven't a clue what's wrong with him. He's so hot. If the fever gets out of control—"

"Let's hold off on the what ifs, okay?" Rose held up a hand. "Someone very wise once told me that what ifs open the door to fear. We don't need that. We need clear-headed thinking."

"Of course you're right."

"What's the first thing we need to do?" Rose asked, thinking aloud. She tugged on Joy's shoe. "Come sit next to me, Joy baby." The child obeyed. Intent on watching them, she ate the beans her mother again offered her.

"We have to get that fever down," Juliana uttered on a shaky breath.

"Right. My grandmother used coneflowers for pain and fevers. Have you noticed any growing around here?"

"No, but I haven't been on the lookout for them."

"Why don't you search in this area while I finish feeding Joy? If you don't find any, Henry can look farther out."

Careful to keep the camp in sight, Juliana combed the area for the large purple flower. Her gaze swept across the prairie. With its thigh-high grasses and sparse tree cover, she didn't hold out much hope that she would find what she was looking for. The coneflower was a woodland plant, preferring the shady forest floor to direct sunlight.

In the distance, she spotted Henry leaving the tent. She sprinted toward him and arrived winded.

He was the first to speak, his eyes kind as he looked at her. "I didn't see a thing. Nothing at all that would call for suspicion. He must have some sort of sickness."

"How is he?" Her gaze darted to the opening.

"The same. Fever, shallow breathing." He touched her elbow briefly. "I need to speak with Rose. While I do that, why don't you try to get some water into him?"

"Tell her I didn't find the coneflower."

His mouth drooped. "I will."

Stooping over, she entered the tent and waited for her eyes to adjust to the faint light. He was dressed in his white undershirt. A cheerful red, blue and yellow patchwork quilt covered him to his chest, adding a dash of color to the dim space.

She settled on the pallet and brought his hand to her lap. With her fingertip, she traced the blue veins beneath his tan skin. Testing the weight of it, she took comfort in the strength and capability she knew he possessed. These hands had caught her when she stumbled, comforted her when she cried, held her close when she was afraid. She lifted his hand and pressed her cheek into his palm.

His eyes remained closed, shutting out the rest of the world.

When had his face become so dear? Five days ago, she would've passed Evan Harrison on the street without a second thought. How had he come to mean so much to her in such a short time? A better question would be how had she allowed herself to fall in love with an outlaw? A man who courted danger?

Alice O'Malley had raised her daughters to fear God and live upright, godly lives. She expected her daughters to choose men of moral character and good standing in the community. Her mother would be horrified if she knew that her eldest daughter had fallen in love with the very man who'd kidnapped her.

What was the secret he guarded so closely?

"What are you hiding?" she whispered softly.

The flap lifted, and a stiff wind circled through the space. Henry ducked his head in and beckoned her outside. With reluctance she left Evan's side. Henry and Rose stood side by side waiting to talk to her, while Matt played with his baby sister. Their grave expressions gave her pause.

"Mrs. Harrison," Henry began, "I'm inclined to believe that Evan has contracted the same sickness that swept through my sister-in-law's house. Joy had similar symptoms, but as you can see she's almost recovered."

"Remember I mentioned it yesterday?" Rose prompted.

"Yes, I remember." She kneaded her stiff neck muscles. Dread flooded her entire being. "But she and the others were given medicine to control their fevers, right?"

Husband and wife exchanged a look. "Yes. And the adults fared slightly worse than the children. Took longer to recuperate."

Her heart hammered against her rib cage. "Tell me directly, Henry. Without the medicine, what do you think Evan's chances are of surviving?"

He didn't flinch at her words. "He's young and healthy. If we can bring the fever down and get him to drink plenty of fluids, I believe he has a fighting chance."

A tiny bud of hope burst forth in her heart.

"How are you with a gun?" he asked.

"Me? I know my way around a firearm."

"Good." He lifted a weapon from his left holster and gave it to her. "Don't be afraid to use it."

"What about Matt?"

"Matt has his own rifle."

Her gaze strayed to the boy playing peekaboo with his sister. She prayed he wouldn't be forced to use it. "Evan told you about Fitzgerald, didn't he?"

His lips flattened. "Yes." He shifted, his arm going around his wife's shoulders. "I wouldn't be leaving if it wasn't absolutely necessary. As it is, I'm not going far. I figure it's about an hour's ride to the forest edge. Once there, I'll travel on foot until I find the coneflower. Pray I find it soon, for everyone's sake."

Rose lifted her face to his. "I'll be praying every minute you're gone."

His expression softened, and he dropped a kiss on her cheek. "Thank you, my dear."

"Me, too," Juliana added. "I appreciate all you're doing for Evan."

Settling his hat on his head, he returned, "I know he'd do the same for me."

Juliana recognized the truth of his words. Evan would be quick to help a man in need. She watched the pair walk arm in arm toward the horses, turning away when they embraced. The clouds overhead rushed past without releasing a single drop of water. While the wind was still brisk, it had lessened in the last ten minutes or so. It seemed as if the storm would pass them by. Praise the Lord!

"Oh, Father God, please protect Henry. Again, stay the weather as he searches. Bring him back swiftly, and protect us while we wait. In Jesus's name, Amen."

Juliana headed for the fire, determined to get some broth into Evan. She would do everything in her power to help him get well. The alternative didn't bear thinking about.

Juliana spoke in soothing tones as she coaxed Evan to sip the lukewarm broth. He'd drifted in and out of consciousness as the afternoon wore on, at times mumbling random words she couldn't make sense of. It was suppertime now, around five o'clock or so, she guessed, and the fever still raged through his body.

Holding the cup to his parched lips, she managed to get a bit of the broth into him. She set the cup aside and gently lowered his head back down to the pillow. Then, as she'd done countless times, she dipped the cloth into the water bowl and, wringing out the excess, began to wipe his face. Not that it appeared to be helping.

Outside the tent, the constant wind had given way to occasional gusts. While the sun still hid behind a thick layer of clouds, it hadn't rained. Every now and then, she lifted the flap and peeked out to see if Henry had returned yet. She hoped he hadn't run into bad weather.

Evan couldn't seem to lie still. Restless, he moved his head from side to side. His low moans tugged at her heartstrings. Watching him suffer while she sat helplessly by made her want to weep with frustration.

She leaned in close. One bright spot in this whole ordeal was that she was free to look at him and touch him and speak without reservation. "Evan, darling," she murmured, smoothing his damp hair, "hold on a little while longer. Henry will be back before you know it with that coneflower and you'll soon be on the mend."

She prayed that her words would prove to be true.

The nightmare was back.

James was driving the wagon, minding his own business, when six masked men on horseback emerged from the woods with guns drawn. A mix of anger and disbelief marked his expression. With no choice, he halted the team and faced his enemies with courage. True to his character, he didn't give in. He didn't go down without a fight.

The scene distorted into chaos, and James was lying facedown in the dirt. Evan was there, tugging on his shoulder to turn him over. James flopped over and his hat slipped back. Instead of his brother's dear face, an eyeless skull with a gaping mouth stared up at him.

"James!" His brother's name was ripped from his lips. "Where?"

"Shh," a familiar voice close to his ear soothed, "You're all right. I'm here."

Juliana. At the sound of her sweet voice, the horror of the dream slipped away. Evan tried to say her name, but he couldn't. Blackness overtook him once again.

* * *

Henry rode into camp about an hour after supper.

She ducked outside as soon as she heard the sound of an approaching rider. Rose walked swiftly over with Joy in her arms. Matt followed close behind.

He dismounted near the tent. One glimpse of his expression was all it took for Juliana's hopes to fly away on the wind.

"You couldn't find it, could you?" Hands clasped at her waist, she braced herself for his answer.

His eyes held a wealth of regret in their dark depths. "I'm sorry, Mrs. Harrison." His gaze flicked to his wife at her gasp of dismay. "I stayed away as long as I dared. I think it may be too late in the season for that particular wildflower, because I didn't see a single one."

"I don't understand," she heard herself saying. "We all asked God to lead you to it. Why didn't He answer our prayers?"

"God always answers our prayers," Henry said kindly, "it's just that sometimes His answer is no."

"Then what are we supposed to do?" she demanded, a single tear sliding down her cheek. "If his fever doesn't break soon, he could—" She clamped her lips shut, her eyes darting to Matt. She couldn't say it in front of the boy.

"One thing we're going to do is continue to pray and ask God to spare Evan's life."

Juliana buried her face in her hands. *Dear Father, I don't understand why You didn't allow Henry to find that flower. Based on Your word, I know in my mind that You love Evan and have a plan and a future for him. But my heart is rebelling, Lord. Help me to trust You, God. Please spare Evan. I love him.*

And now she might not have a chance to tell him. She'd led him to believe that he meant nothing to her. In trying to protect herself, she'd hurt him.

Henry and Rose stepped closer and took turns praying out loud. Her heart heavy, Juliana couldn't stop the tears from coursing down her cheeks. Their heartfelt words of petition humbled her. These relative strangers were pouring their hearts out to God, requesting healing for a man they didn't know. A man they thought was her husband.

Juliana hated that they'd deceived this dear couple. She was tempted to tell them the truth, but felt like she'd be betraying Evan's trust if she did. After all, how would they react when they found out he'd kidnapped her?

Of course, she could tell them the truth without giving them all the details. She made up her mind that if—no, *when*—Evan got well, she would discuss the matter with him.

"Mind if I take a look?" Henry splayed a hand toward the tent.

"Please do."

"Juliana." Rose placed her arm around her shoulders and steered her toward the fire. "You've been in there with him all day. Come and sit in the fresh air awhile. Eat something. It will do you good."

"I don't like to be away from him," she protested.

"Henry will sit with him until you return. He won't be alone."

"Momma." Matt's quiet voice halted their progress. "Can I take Joy to the water's edge and show her the frogs?"

"Yes, you may." She bent to put the girl down. "But don't take your eyes off her."

"I won't, I promise." He held out his hand. "Come on."

Grinning, Joy placed her tiny hand in his.

"Mind your brother, Joy," Rose called after them. "And try not to get wet."

At the fire pit, she pressed a cup of coffee into Juliana's hands. "Have a seat."

"No, thanks. I'd rather stand awhile." Her legs and back were stiff from sitting in that cramped space most of the day. The coffee tasted fresh and strong. She was finally learning to appreciate black coffee.

"So what now?" She faced the other woman. "Do you have any suggestions?"

Rose chewed on her lip. "I know this sounds crazy, but we could try putting him in the shallow end of the pond. Having most of his body submerged in the water might bring his temperature down."

Juliana looked over at the placid water drenched in muted hues of orange-gold. In the distance, the sun was an orange ball hovering above the horizon. Above their heads, the clouds had finally dispersed. The sky was a pale, whitish-blue color. "At this point, I'm willing to try just about anything."

"We'll ask Henry, but not until you've eaten." She passed Juliana a bowl and spoon. "It's not much, but it will fill your stomach."

The aroma of rabbit stew teased her nose and her stomach growled in response. She was hungrier than she'd realized. Eating standing up, she savored every bite of the tender meat, wild mushrooms and ramps.

"Thank you." She licked her lips. "Very tasty. You're a great cook."

"Would you like more? There's plenty to go around."

"I'm tempted, but I think I'll pass for now. Have you eaten yet?"

"Not yet." She tucked a curl behind her ear and blew out a breath. She looked tuckered out. "I was waiting for Henry."

"Why don't you take a couple bowls over there." She hooked a thumb over her shoulder. "Discuss your idea with him while you both eat. You'll be near enough to hear Evan if he calls out." Juliana began gathering the dirty dishes and utensils. "Meanwhile, I'm going to wash the dishes. I feel horrible about leaving all the work for you to do."

"Don't. You've been exactly where you should be—at your husband's side."

Ignoring the twinge of guilt, she paused in the midst of stacking the dishes. "I'm so glad you both are here. I don't know what I would've done if Evan had taken ill when we were alone on the trail. I wouldn't have been able to tend to his needs while trying to hunt for food and cook and wash dishes. I have that much to be thankful for, at least."

Rose sent her a tired smile. "I'm happy God worked it out so that we could be here. I've been in your position before. I know what it's like to be on the receiving end, and it's nice to be able to give back for a change."

"Well, I appreciate all you've done. Now go eat," Juliana insisted. "I'll watch out for the kids."

After a moment's hesitation, Rose dipped a portion for herself and her husband into two bowls. "I'm sure he'll want coffee, too, but it can wait until after we eat."

"I'll leave it, then. Don't rush. Enjoy some time alone with your husband."

"Thank you."

Juliana watched her walk away before turning to her task.

Crouched at the water's edge, Juliana inhaled the fresh

air. Although she wanted to be near Evan, it was nice to be outside doing something useful with her hands. The tent was a small, confined space, made smaller by Evan's wide shoulders and long legs.

The children's laughter reached her, followed by sounds of splashing water. Resting her hands on her knees, she watched the brother and sister toss pebbles into the pond. Joy's high-pitched squeals mingled with Matt's carefree laughter. Watching them interact, her thoughts drifted to her own siblings.

In her mind's eye, she summoned a picture of each of her sisters. Jessica and Jane in the kitchen preparing supper, their faces smudged with flour. Megan curled up on the couch with a book, oblivious to everything around her. Nicole sewing in her favorite chair by the window, the picture of a prim and proper young lady.

She missed them—plain and simple. Longed to see them face-to-face. Her heart ached at the fear and worry and pain they must be enduring on account of her disappearance. Her family had no idea whether she was alive or dead. And now that Evan was ill, delaying their arrival in his hometown, they would have to wait and wonder even longer.

The fact that she would see them again in the near future brought her immense comfort.

Evan, on the other hand, wouldn't see his brother again this side of heaven. From the depth of the grief she'd glimpsed in his eyes whenever the subject came up, the two had been extremely close. Considering they'd lost their parents as young men, she could imagine how they'd leaned on each other during that time of loss.

He'd obviously been dreaming about his brother. Could his death be the reason behind Evan's current situation? Juliana realized that she didn't know the details surrounding his passing. She'd neglected to ask.

Clearing her thoughts, she checked on the children and, spotting them chasing a butterfly, continued with her task. By the time she was finished, dusk had settled around her. She called for Matt and Joy to join her, which they promptly did. Upon reaching the fire pit, she noticed the flames had died down so she added a couple of logs to the heap.

"Juliana." Henry and Rose approached. "He's asking for you."

"He's awake?"

"He's groggy. His communication is fuzzy, but he's very clear about his wish to see you."

Her heart skipped a beat. "And the fever? Has it broken?"

"I'm afraid not."

"Rose, I hate to ask…" She indicated the clean dishes.

"I'll put everything away." She gave Juliana a gentle shove. "Go. Be with him."

Gathering her skirts, Juliana jogged across the narrow field. His eyes were open and searching for her when she reached him.

"Juliana?" he rasped, his head turning toward her. His ebony hair was slicked back, his forehead wet with sweat. The strips of cloth holding the bandage in place were twisted from so much movement. She would need to re-dress the wound soon.

"I'm here." She hurriedly kneeled at his side, her water-splotched skirt a cloud about her knees. She sand-wiched his hand between hers.

In his larkspur-blue eyes she saw regret and pain. "I'm sorry."

"Evan," she whispered, her vision blurring with tears, "don't do this."

He licked his dry lips before continuing. "I never should've—" He broke off, too weak to continue, his frustration evident. "Taken you."

Juliana leaned closer, smiling tenderly through her tears. "I'm not sorry."

His lids fluttered closed, and she thought that perhaps he'd drifted back to sleep. Disappointment skittered through her. She wanted, no *needed,* to talk to him.

"You're not?" he grunted after a moment, leveling a look at her.

"You asked me if I care about what happens to you." She dipped her head, focusing on the rapid rise and fall of his chest. "And I led you to believe something other than the truth." Taking a deep breath, she gazed down into his eyes. "I don't regret going to the mercantile that morning. I don't regret our kiss. And, yes, I do care about you."

I love you. But she couldn't say the words aloud. Not yet.

A tiny spark of hope lit in his eyes. "You…forgive…me?"

"Yes, of course," she rushed to say, the corners of her eyes crinkling as she smiled.

His gaze roamed slowly across her face, as if memorizing her features. "You're…beautiful…Irish."

The nickname brought a fresh wave of emotion, and she blinked to dry her eyes. She'd shed more tears in the last several days than she had her entire life!

Scooting closer, she reached for the tin cup. "Try to drink some water, okay?"

His eyes never left her as she cradled his head and helped him drink. "Good nurse," he murmured.

With trembling fingers, she touched his stubbly jaw. "You should rest now."

His fingers gripped hers, his expression turning urgent. "Something I need...tell you." His voice faded and his eyelids drooped. "I'm not..."

Juliana moved closer. "You're not what?" she prompted softly.

When he didn't respond, she realized that he'd fallen asleep. She sat there, watching and waiting for him to stir again. What had he been about to say? Whatever it was would have to wait until he regained consciousness. And by that time he would've probably already forgotten.

Fatigue weighed her down, and she couldn't resist stretching out on the blanket next to him. Just for a few minutes, she told herself, and then she would go and talk to Henry.

Chapter Fourteen

Juliana awoke some time later to the sound of Evan's moans. Through the slim openings in the tent, she could see that it was night. Though exactly how long she'd slept she had no idea.

"C-cold." His teeth chattered, and, because of her close proximity, she felt the tremors that racked his body.

Pushing her unkempt hair out of her eyes, she scrambled to her knees. The kerosene lamp in the corner cast a faint glow across the small interior. She thought his face appeared paler than normal, but it was hard to tell.

His body trembled beneath the single blanket covering him. "P-please…"

"I'll go for more blankets," she reassured him. "I'll be right back."

Outside, she waited for her eyes to adjust before starting across the field to where the Talbots slept near the fire. When she had just about reached them, a tall figure stepped out from behind a tree.

She stopped short, her loud gasp splitting the silence.

"It's me, Henry." He whipped off his hat, but with no moon in the cloudless sky, his features remained indistinguishable. She recognized his voice, however.

"Henry!" Her hands went to her throat. "You scared the life out of me!"

"I'm sorry," he said, "I didn't mean to startle you. I thought it best to keep watch, considering. Are you all right?"

"I'll be fine," she said, though her heart continued to race. "Evan has the chills. I've come for extra blankets, if there are any to be had."

"Good thing for us, Rose likes to be prepared. She insisted we bring every last one."

"I imagine that when traveling with children, one must expect the unexpected."

He chuckled in the darkness. "Yes, ma'am."

He quickly gathered up the extras while trying not to disturb his slumbering family. He carried the bundle back to the tent for her and helped her cover Evan.

"I don't understand," she said, tucking the material beneath him, creating a cocoon. "How can he be so cold and yet so hot at the same time?"

Resting on her haunches, she looked over at Henry.

"It's his body's way of trying to cool itself. Same thing happened with the others."

"Did Rose talk to you about her idea?"

"She did. I don't think it's wise at this point, what with the chills and all."

Frustration at the whole situation sharpened her tone. "I hate seeing him suffer like this."

"I understand," Henry commiserated. "If it were my Rose lying here sick, well, I don't know if I would've handled it as well as you."

"I don't like feeling helpless." She sighed.

"You're taking care of his needs as best you can, and even though he's unconscious much of the time, I'm certain he senses your presence. That must be a huge comfort to him."

Her gaze slid to Evan's shivering form. "I hope so."

"I'm going to make some sassafras tea." He turned to go. "Maybe that will help."

"It certainly can't hurt. Thank you."

"I'll be back in a jiff."

Juliana scooted next to Evan and tugged the layer of blankets up so that they nearly reached his chin. Placing her palm against his forehead, she found it damp and clammy.

"God in heaven above," she prayed with her eyes shut tight, "I ask You to please spare Evan's life. Give him another chance. Give *us* a chance, if it is Your will. Drive the fever from his body and restore his health. In Jesus's name I pray, Amen."

Time passed slowly. The tremors began to come quicker and harder than before. She hugged him tighter, trying to ease the violence of them. His lips quivered with cold. His moans became low pleadings for the pain to stop.

Juliana cried in earnest, her heart ripping in two. He was getting worse. She feared that she was losing him.

Voices penetrated the fog surrounding his brain. Hushed, worried voices. He tried to concentrate on what they were saying, but his mind wouldn't cooperate.

He couldn't seem to stop shaking. So cold. And weak. He doubted that he could lift his little finger, he was that exhausted.

Where was Juliana? He needed to talk to her. There was so much to say…

The voices were louder now. He focused on the words, stunned to discover that they were praying for him. Begging God for his life. His heart hitched within his breast, unease skittering through his limbs. Was he hovering near death?

He didn't want to die. He wanted to live! Not the way he had before, bent on revenge and consumed with hatred. More than anything, he craved peace. He understood now that God could handle his anger and his grief, but He would not tolerate his rebellion.

It was hard to put his thoughts together, but he prayed as best he could.

Forgive me, Lord, for blaming You for James's death. Forgive me for holding on to the hate in my heart. Help me. I want to be near You as I was before.

At the completion of his prayer, he felt at peace for the first time in almost a year. How he'd missed that sense of calm and comfort only the Lord could bestow. He was forgiven, and that's all that mattered.

Feeling his deep sigh, Juliana lifted her head. His tremors eased.

"What's happening?" Rose asked, in part fearful, in part hopeful.

Juliana felt his forehead again. "Hotter than ever." Disappointment weighed her down.

"We could try willow leaves," Henry said quietly. "I don't know why I didn't think of this before, but my sister used them to make a concoction once when my mother became ill and there wasn't a doctor available. There were weeping willows on our property just like the ones here."

Juliana had never heard of that particular remedy. "You know as well as I do that a homemade remedy can be tricky. Too little and it has no effect. Too much can be deadly. Do you remember if she used the leaves and bark together? And what about the quantity?"

"I was just a boy. I don't remember much about it."

"Are you certain it was a willow tree?" Rose said.

"Absolutely."

"I don't know. It's risky." She looked at Rose. "What do you think?"

"It appears to me he's getting worse, not better. We can either wait and hope he can fight this on his own or try the willow leaves. Henry is positive that's what was given his mother, so we could try a small amount at first."

Juliana studied Evan's still form. The decision was ultimately hers, she knew. She was torn between the need to act and the fear of things going horribly wrong. What if they gave him too much? Or if he had some sort of adverse reaction? She would never be able to forgive herself. On the other hand, if they did nothing and he got worse...

"Let's do it," she blurted before she could change her mind.

Henry moved to get up. "I'll go."

"I'll brew the tea," Rose added.

Needing reassurance, Juliana stopped Rose with a hand on her arm. "Am I doing the right thing?"

"I believe so, yes." She placed her hand over Juliana's. "Remember, God is watching over him."

"I know," she breathed, her attention already on Evan. She hoped she wouldn't regret this decision.

That night was one of the longest in Juliana's life. Despite Henry's urging to get some rest, she refused. Since she'd slept much of the day, she wasn't at all sleepy. And even if she was, she couldn't leave him. Not until she knew whether or not the willow leaves were going to work.

They managed to get a few cups of the brew into him. While he didn't appear to have a reaction, neither did his condition change. Juliana was growing more frustrated by the minute.

Rose ducked her head in. "Juliana, I made coffee. Why don't you come outside for a little while? You need a break. Fresh air will do you good."

Henry nodded. "Go on. I'll be here."

Evan was sleeping peacefully, so she decided it wouldn't hurt to leave him in Henry's care for a bit.

"It's nearing daybreak." Rose moved back to give her room to exit. "We could start breakfast."

"Hey," Henry spoke up, "both of you stay alert."

Juliana didn't want to think about Fitzgerald, not with Evan lying here so ill. But Henry was right. There was a very real possibility that Fitzgerald would find them. They couldn't let their guard down simply because they were worried about Evan.

"I'll take the gun you loaned me, Henry."

Outside the tent, Rose handed her a cup of steaming hot coffee. "Let's go sit by the pond."

"We'll get eaten up by mosquitoes," she objected. "How about here on this old log?" She indicated a spot not far from the tent. "We'll be close by but still able to see the children."

"That's fine."

They sat and sipped their coffee in companionable silence. Around them the animals began to stir as the darkness slowly lifted.

"How are you holding up?"

Cupping the warm mug in her hands, Juliana turned her head to look at the other woman. "I've been better."

"You're very devoted. You two seem to share a special bond."

The corners of her mouth lifted a fraction at the irony of that statement. "Yes, I guess you could say that. How did you and Henry meet?"

Rose spoke at length about how they'd been neighbors and she'd fancied Henry, but he'd hardly seemed to notice her. Absorbed in Rose's story, Juliana lost track of the time.

"Do you mind my asking how you met?" Rose asked.

At Juliana's uneasy expression, Rose continued, "You seem so well suited is all—that's why I asked. Don't feel as if you have to answer—"

Henry poked his head out, his expression urgent. "Juliana! He's awake!"

In her haste, she toppled her mug, spilling most of the contents on the ground. Her heart in her throat, she rushed to Evan's side. Her sole focus was on Evan, so she didn't notice when Henry left to speak with his wife.

"Juliana?" His deep voice was rough from disuse.

"Oh, Evan, you're awake!" Her first thought was to check his temperature, and she pressed her palm against his forehead. Cool and dry. Thank God! All the stress and worry of the last few days drained from her body.

"Your fever's gone," she whispered.

His clear gaze clung to hers. "What's wrong with me?"

Suddenly self-conscious, she removed her hand and let it fall to her lap. "You've been ill. Do you remember anything at all?"

A wrinkle formed between his brows. "The last thing I remember is holding Joy. What happened? Did I pass out?"

"Yes, Evan. You've been in and out of consciousness for the last two days."

"Two days?" His eyes widened. When he tried to sit up, Juliana put restraining hands on his shoulders.

"Don't try to sit up. You don't have the strength—"

"We've lost a lot of time." He struggled a moment then fell back with a grunt. "Why am I so weak?" As was to be expected, he was irritated and confused.

She smoothed the blankets across his chest out of habit. He watched her every move. "Your body has been fighting this sickness. On top of that you haven't eaten anything."

"You're wearing a gun," he stated, his eyes going dark with concern. "Has Fitzgerald been here?"

"No, it's just a precaution."

"Have there been signs of anyone around the camp?"

Juliana covered his hand with hers in an effort to re-assure him. "No. Stop worrying. Henry and I both carry weapons. We're being careful."

His fingers gripped hers. "How experienced are you, though? Fitz is a professional."

She couldn't help but smile. "You're forgetting my cousins."

"Oh." His expression eased. "Right."

"Your only concern right now should be regaining your strength."

His gaze roamed her face. "I heard your prayers. That meant a lot. I said one of my own as well."

"Oh?" Her heartbeat quickened.

"There's so much I'd like to tell you." His lids grew heavy. "But I'm tired. Can't seem to keep my eyes open."

"There'll be plenty of time to talk later," she reassured. "Your body needs rest."

His fingers relaxed their hold on her hand. Within minutes, his breathing evened out. Juliana watched him sleep, her heart bursting with gratitude.

"Thank You, Jesus," she whispered.

God had heard their prayers, and in His infinite wisdom and kindness, healed Evan.

Knowing the others were expecting her, she went outside.

"Well?" Rose asked hesitantly.

Juliana's smile rivaled the sun. "He's fine. He's tired, of course. A little confused about what's been happening. But overall he's okay."

Henry put his arm around his wife and hugged her to him. "I do believe we've witnessed God's hand moving upon this man, just as we asked."

"Yes," Juliana agreed. "Words can't express how happy I am right now."

"Now that you know he's going to be okay, you need to rest. Henry and I will fix breakfast and wake you when it's ready, okay?"

"I can help—"

"No."

She *was* tired. No, exhausted. Not knowing whether Evan would live or die had taken a huge emotional toll on her. "You're right. I'm worn out. But be sure and wake me when breakfast is ready. I'll take cleanup duty."

As soon as she got comfortable on her pallet in the shade, she fell into a deep sleep. When she awoke, she had the feeling that she had slept a lot longer than an hour. Immediately she went to check on Evan. He was sleeping still, and she could tell by his breathing that he was resting soundly. She sat there watching him for a few minutes before hunger drove her outside.

Brilliant blue stretched across the wide expanse above her. The sweet-scented air was calm today, the sun heating the fertile earth. A hawk made lazy circles in the air before swooping down into the field to catch his lunch.

Like the graceful bird, her heart soared, free of its

burden. Evan would recover, praise God. She refused to ponder the future with all its unknowns and what ifs. She would focus on his recovery and the blessings of today.

Her friends waved her over. There was a bounce in her step as she made her way to join them. The women spent the day catching up on laundry and entertaining Joy, while Henry and Matt fished for their supper.

Juliana checked on Evan throughout the day, at times hand-feeding him tea and broth. He was drowsy and not inclined to talk. She was a bit disappointed but realized his body needed time to mend.

The next morning, she was so eager to see Evan she tossed aside her blankets and rushed into the tent, heedless of her appearance. She was surprised to find him already awake, propped up into a sitting position and supported by a mountain of blankets. She hesitated just inside the opening.

"Good morning," she said with a tentative smile, "How long have you been up?"

"Long enough to wonder if you were ever coming to check on me," he drawled. The heavy growth of black stubble covering the lower half of his face made him look dangerous, at odds with his usually clean-shaven appearance. His eyes tracked her every movement, as if hungry for the sight of her. "You must've been exhausted to have slept so late."

"I was," she admitted. "I feel rested this morning, though."

He nodded. The silence stretched between them, thick with unvoiced emotions.

Juliana longed to feel his arms around her. She wanted his reassurance that everything would be all right.

"Juliana." He sighed heavily. "Don't look at me like that."

"Like what?" Her lower lip trembled, sudden tears burning her eyes.

"Come here," he said softly, his arms outstretched.

She hesitated a fraction of a second before vaulting into his arms and burying her face in his shoulder. He wrapped his arms around her in a comforting embrace, his fingers stroking her unbound hair, his low voice murmuring reassuring words as salty tears slipped from beneath her eyelashes.

Juliana was independent by nature, accustomed to being the one everyone else leaned on. How wonderful it was to be able to lean on someone else. To not have to be the strong one for once.

Once the tears had abated, she sighed contentedly and snuggled deeper into his embrace. He held her tight. Being close to Evan made her soul sing. Right now, in this moment, she refused to think about how wrong it was to love him.

Evan closed his eyes, buried his face in her hair, and inhaled deeply. Images of lush green meadows dotted with pale lavender blooms flooded his mind. He pictured Juliana in that meadow, dressed in purest white, her golden-red hair spilling over her shoulders, her green eyes brimming with laughter. He was there, too, in a three-piece suit fit for church. Or a wedding.

No, he cautioned, *don't think about forever. It's too dangerous. You'd never survive another loss. Especially not losing Juliana.*

Gradually, her trembling ceased. She sighed a small, contented sigh that told him she was comfortable in his arms. The need to tell her the truth gripped him. She deserved to know everything. He only hoped she could find it in her heart to forgive him. Again.

Chapter Fifteen

Juliana did not want to move from this spot. She felt safe. Protected. Cherished.

"Juliana."

His deep voice rumbled through his chest. She felt his hands come to rest lightly on her shoulders. With reluctance, she eased away from the haven of his embrace to stare up at him.

His gaze was a tender caress, filled with longing, affection and regret. With great care, he wiped away the wetness from her cheeks.

"I haven't been completely honest with you."

It took a moment for his words to register. She sat back, her thoughts bouncing off each other.

"About what?" She heard the tremor in her voice.

Oh, Lord, please don't let him have a wife. I'll die if he tells me he's married.

He hesitated, clearly uneasy, which caused her stomach to tighten with anxiety.

"I've kept certain things from you in order to protect you. At least, I *thought* I was doing it to protect you. Maybe I was protecting myself. I don't know." He paused to draw in a lung full of air. "I'm not who you think I am."

What did that mean? He had an alias? "Your name isn't Evan Harrison?"

"No. I mean, yes. I am." He plowed his fingers through his hair, accidentally dislodging the bandage. "Can I take this thing off?"

"Maybe tomorrow," she said, distracted.

With his thumb and finger, he untwisted the strips and smoothed them against his forehead. "I'm not an outlaw. Despite evidence to the contrary, I am a law-abiding, God-fearing, honest-to-goodness farmer."

Juliana didn't move. She couldn't believe it! He was lying. Lying with a straight face. And oh, he was *good*. If she hadn't found that paper, his air of innocence would've fooled her. The knowledge stung. What else had he lied about? Her thoughts turned to the badge in his boot. No lawman in his right mind would give it up without a fight.

Evan paused, his head cocked to one side. "What is it?"

She forced the words out. "It's no use, Evan. I've seen the sign with your picture on it."

He was momentarily taken aback. "What are you talking about?"

Outrage and despair warred within her. She loved this man...a man who apparently had no qualms about lying to her. She'd never felt so low. How she wished she'd heeded her instincts!

"Your gun, remember?" she muttered. "I found the wanted notice with your name on it. Evan Trey Harrison."

His mouth quirked. "Ah. I see. You found that, did you?" A disbelieving laugh burst from him. "Why am I not surprised? After all, you found the badge I'd so carefully concealed. You are one surprising woman, Juliana O'Malley."

His reaction didn't make sense. Why wasn't he more concerned?

"Sheriff Tate and I had that drawn up just in case Roberts didn't trust me. You see, I had to make him believe I was an outlaw."

He was determined to conceal the truth. "Forget it." She moved to get up. "I'm done believing your lies."

His hand on her shoulder stopped her. "Juliana, please." His husky voice was pleading, bordering on desperate. "Hear me out. I'm telling the truth."

She stared into his molten blue eyes. There was no trace of deceit, only sincerity.

"What about the mercantile? I was there, remember?"

"And I ushered you inside, which landed you in a heap of trouble," he supplied, his gaze probing hers.

"Yes," she murmured, "we mustn't forget that."

His expression turned rueful. "I felt certain no one would come in until later. That's what I'd counted on, anyway. I figured we could get in and get out without being seen. Tell me, why were you there at that hour? You must've gotten an early start."

She recalled complaining to Megan about the early hour. "I needed supplies for my mother's birthday celebration. We had a lot to do to prepare, since we were expecting a lot of guests that night. Mr. Moore's a talker and, like you, I wanted to get in and get out as quickly as possible."

"Talk about bad timing."

"Why were you there in the first place, Evan?"

"Ten months ago, my brother James was gunned down in cold blood." Pain flashed across his face, stark emotion that couldn't be faked. "That day, I pledged to hunt down those responsible and bring them to justice."

Stunned into silence, Juliana couldn't breathe. His brother? *Murdered?*

"It is my mission," he continued. "That's why I was at the mercantile, and why I've been hanging around low-lifes like Fitzgerald and Roberts."

His jaw was set, his blue eyes hard and unyielding. His expression promised retribution.

Juliana's head spun. No wonder he hadn't acted like a criminal—he *wasn't*. She remembered all the things about him that just didn't add up. Her gut instincts had been on the mark. She hadn't lost her heart to an outlaw, but to a farmer-turned-undercover detective!

The implications were too huge for her to grasp at that moment.

"What happened?" she managed.

His hand covering his eyes, he massaged his temples with his fingers. His words were muffled when he spoke. "James was attacked by a band of thieves. He was traveling to Knoxville with a large sum of money. My guess is he resisted, and they killed him." When he lifted his head, Juliana sucked in a breath at the sorrow etched in his features. "James would've stood his ground even if he was outnumbered. He wasn't the type to give in without a fight."

Her heart ached for his loss. She tried to imagine what she would do in his situation and couldn't. The idea was too horrific to even comprehend. Reaching over, Juliana wrapped her hand around his. "I'm so sorry. I can't imagine how much it must've hurt to hear the news."

He flipped his hand over and held on tight. "I was ill." He spoke the words almost as an apology. "Pneumonia. I told him the trip could wait until I was well enough to go with him, but he wouldn't listen. If I had gone, I could've protected him. James would still be alive today." Regret rolled off him in waves.

"You can't know that for sure," she insisted, determined to make him see reason. He blamed himself for something he had no control over. "One extra gun wouldn't have made that much of a difference. If you had gone, in all likelihood you would've been killed, too."

"I could've tried to outrun them. I could've bargained for his life. Something, *anything* to change what happened."

Juliana searched for the right words. "I know this might be difficult for you to hear, but God alone controls our destinies. His Word says each person has a set number of days on this earth. Nothing we can do can change it."

A muscle in his jaw twitched. "Does that bring you comfort when you miss your father?"

"Knowing God is in control brings me comfort and peace," she answered, ignoring the sting of his words. He had responded out of hurt. "Of course I don't understand the reasons or the timing of my father's death, but I trust in God's goodness. When I was consumed with grief, He gave me the strength to go on."

He stared hard at her. "I've heard when tragedy strikes, a person either draws closer to God or falls away. Two guesses which category I'm in."

"It's okay to be angry with God. He already knows what's in your heart. The key is not to shut Him out. Talk to him. He'll help you work through your emotions."

He was quiet, staring straight ahead. "I've been angry with Him for a long time," he confessed, his shoulders slumping. "My parents' deaths didn't affect me the same way, maybe because of the way they died. No one was at fault. One day they got sick and died. I don't know why, but something inside me snapped when I heard what happened to James. Someone was to blame. Someone cut his life short."

He swung his attention back to her. "Before you came along, I was in pretty bad shape. Thoughts of revenge consumed my every waking moment. When I was with the gang, it was all I could do not to strangle each and every one of them while they slept. I was haunted by James's face. I studied each man, wondering which one of them had pulled the trigger. After a while, the only emotion in my heart was hatred. Then, suddenly, I had you to worry about, and everything changed. Avenging James's murder wasn't my sole focus anymore. Keeping you safe was my first priority.

"I believe God used this illness to get my attention. When I heard your prayers, I realized what a mess I'd made of things. I didn't want to die. I told Him I couldn't bear this burden any longer. And because He's a loving, patient God, He forgave me."

Her heart swelled with gratitude. God had worked a miracle in his heart. "I'm proud of you, Evan."

"Please don't say that. I'm not proud of the man I've become these last few months. And I have to be honest— it's gonna take some time for me to come to the place where I can forgive the men responsible. A big part of me still craves vengeance."

"It takes courage to own up to sin, even when we feel we're justified in our feelings. That's why I'm proud of you. Admitting when you're wrong is the first step toward change. Eventually, by God's grace, you will be able to forgive them."

She remembered the gold star. "Is the badge yours?"

"Temporarily. Sheriff Tate, whose office I'm working

with, gave it to me. Just in case I got hauled into jail, I'd have proof to back up my claim."

Juliana was relieved he wouldn't be lumped in with the other outlaws, should they ever be caught. The authorities would only need to contact the Cades Cove Sheriff's Office to verify Evan's story.

"Are you positive you've got the right group of men?"

"Yeah, I'm sure." His mouth thinned. "But I don't have solid evidence. Before you came along, my next plan of action was to go back to the scene of the crime, to Knoxville. Visit the gang's hangouts and try to snuff out a witness. Those men like to brag about their crimes. I'm hoping they talked the night James was killed."

For his sake, she hoped he was able to find the answers he sought. As for his deception, Juliana needed time to sort out her feelings. If she were honest, his decision not to confide in her early on hurt. He hadn't trusted her.

"What are you thinking?" he asked.

"I'm wondering why you didn't tell me this in the beginning."

He closed his eyes. "I figured the less you knew, the better." Opening them, he looked at her with regret. "Now I know it would've made it easier for you, at least in the sense of knowing that I'm not dangerous."

Oh, how wrong he was, she thought. He *was* dangerous. In an ironic twist, he was even more of a threat now than before. There were no obstacles, no reasons for her to deny her feelings. And that was downright scary.

"I realize an apology can't make up for all the mistakes I've made," he continued, "but I am sorry. If I could go back to that morning at the mercantile, I'd do it all differently, anything to have spared you and your family this grief. Do you think you can forgive me?"

* * *

Evan held his breath as he watched the emotions marching across Juliana's face.

"What happened wasn't entirely your fault. And you've worked hard at keeping me safe, even though it put your mission at risk. I wish you would've confided in me, however. You're right—knowing your identity would've saved me a lot of worry."

He could see the hurt reflected in her clear green eyes. His heart dipped. He didn't deserve her forgiveness, but he craved it. How could he live with himself if she couldn't move past this?

"I also understand that you felt you were making the right decision not to tell me."

He blew out the breath he'd been holding. The glow from the kerosene lamp highlighted the copper streaks in her thick tresses, tumbling down around her shoulders. How he longed to take her in his arms and hold her close. That was out of the question, of course.

"I never intended to hurt you, Juliana," he murmured.

Her lashes swept down to hide her eyes. "I know." Her voice lowered to match his.

"There are others my deception has hurt."

She lifted her head. "Henry and Rose?"

"Yes. I think it's best if I tell them the truth about us."

He paused to gauge her reaction. He sensed her apprehension. Would she agree or disagree?

"I definitely think it's the right thing to do."

He should've known she'd want to do the right thing. He exhaled. "They won't be too happy with us," he warned. "Are you prepared for that?"

"They have every right to be upset. We tricked them. And they've been nothing but kind to both of us. They deserve the truth, even if it doesn't affect them directly."

"I agree." It wouldn't be pleasant, admitting his deception to his new friends, but he didn't want to put it off. "When do you want me to talk to them? Now?"

Juliana moved to her knees, lifted the flap and peered out. "Rose is busy. Henry is playing a game of chase with the kids. How about after lunch?" she suggested, peering over her shoulder at him. "We can talk over a cup of coffee."

"Coffee?" His black brows rose hopefully.

"You'll be having tea," she replied firmly, refusing to be swayed by his entreaty.

"Tea is for females," he grumbled. "I want coffee."

"I'm going to ignore that remark." She arched a brow at him. "Maybe tomorrow. For now, let's stick with the tea, okay?"

He scooted down until he was lying flat and stared up at the top of the tent. "Yes, ma'am," he sighed, amazed that a simple conversation could wear him out.

"Evan?"

She was crouched in the opening, looking like a vulnerable young girl with her earnest expression. "I'm glad you're better. There were times when I feared you wouldn't pull through. In fact, I—" Her breathing hitched, and her gaze skittered away. "Never mind. The important thing is that the worst is over, and you're on the mend."

He swallowed hard, with effort reining in his runaway emotions. "Any other woman would've bolted the moment I passed out," he declared. "You're a woman of great mercy and compassion, Juliana. I'll never forget your kindness toward me. I wish I could repay you somehow. Saying *thanks* doesn't seem to be enough."

"Your getting well is reward enough." Her tender

smile warmed him deep inside. "Think you can get some rest?"

He didn't want to rest. He wanted to talk to her. "I'll try," he huffed, doing his best to sound pitiful.

Her eyes narrowed. "I'll be back soon."

She slipped out the opening, and Evan watched her boots, skimmed by the hem of her dress, until they disappeared from sight. His eyes remained on the spot she'd vacated, wishing for what he couldn't have. He closed his eyes and, although he wasn't sleepy, within minutes he drifted off to sleep.

Gnawing pains in his stomach woke him some time later. He was warm, so he tossed off the quilt and reached for his pants. It was a struggle to put them on while he was on his back, but finally he succeeded and had just finished buttoning them up when Juliana entered the tent. When her gaze fell on him, she almost dumped the soup on the ground.

"Oh! I'm sorry! I can come back—"

"It's okay, I'm decent. I hope it tastes as good as it smells." He had his long-sleeved undershirt on, so he didn't bother with finding his button-down.

"Be careful, it's hot."

Evan accepted the stoneware bowl and spoon from her. A quick glance at her face revealed two bright spots of color on her cheeks. He didn't comment. Instead, he focused on the steaming vegetables floating in rich broth.

Juliana had brought a bowl for herself, and she sat down opposite him. He was pleased she had chosen to share her meal with him, even if they weren't inclined to speak. The silence was a comfortable one. At times, they commented on the weather or the Talbot children, but all in all it was a quiet affair.

When they had finished, Evan began tugging on his boots.

"What are you doing?" Juliana demanded, eyes wide.

"Four of us can't fit in here, can we?"

"I suppose not. Still, I'm not sure it's wise for you to be up and about so soon."

He heard the undertone of concern in her smooth-as-velvet voice, and it warmed him. "Juliana, I'm only walking to the nearest shade tree, no farther. I'll be just fine."

She bit her lip. "You might experience some dizziness. I'll walk beside you in case you do."

Evan didn't have any objections to that, of course. She went out first and waited for him. After being in the tent's dim interior for so long, it took a minute for his eyes to adjust to the bright sunshine. He would've liked to have his hat, but he hadn't seen it since before he got sick.

As Juliana predicted, weakness assailed him, and his knees threatened to buckle. Immediately, he curled his arm around her shoulders and leaned into her, allowing her to steady him as they slowly crossed the grass. Holding her close filled him with contentment.

His heart felt lighter than it had in a long time. As soon as he'd prayed to God and asked for forgiveness, peace had flooded his soul. Instead of being burdened by guilt, he now felt free to pray anytime he wished. The grief that had been his companion for nearly a year was still there, but now he didn't carry it alone. His Lord was there to help share the burden and make it bearable.

He was glad to be out in the fresh air. The sweet perfume of wildflowers teased his nose, and the whack of a woodpecker's beak filled his ears. Bees buzzed between blossoms, hovering for a time before darting off to the next one. As they passed beneath a leafy bower, he spotted a fuzzy-tailed squirrel above their heads. The little animal scurried away as soon as he saw them.

They settled in a shady area not far from the tent, but the short walk had left him feeling weak and out of sorts. That worried him. They needed to get on the trail as soon as possible.

Seeing Henry striding their way, Evan pushed his worries aside. First things first. He had some explaining to do. He didn't peg Henry Talbot as the type to hold a grudge, but he'd been wrong before.

Henry had two cups in his hand, one of which he passed to Evan. Seeing Henry's wink, Juliana protested.

"You know he's not supposed to have that." She eyed Henry sternly.

"He needs the energy." Henry smiled, not looking the least bit repentant.

Evan inhaled the aromatic steam rising from the dark liquid and sighed. The coffee smelled strong and bracing, just the way he liked it. Taking a long drink, he eyed Juliana over the rim of his cup. Then he held it aloft.

"I'm willing to share."

Her eyes widened and her lips parted. He didn't get to hear her response because Rose appeared at that moment with a cup for Juliana. Too bad. He rather liked sparring with her.

Evan didn't immediately bring up the issue of his and Juliana's true relationship. He listened as the other couple spoke of their departure and their plans for the near future. Beside him, Juliana grew increasingly fidgety. Without looking at her, he snatched her hand up and, placing it on his knee, gave it a reassuring squeeze. She squeezed his hand in return.

He cleared his throat and threw a glance her way before addressing Henry and Rose.

"I, uh, have a confession to make," he began, feeling heat rush into his face. "There are some things I haven't told you about Juliana and myself, about how we met and the true nature of our relationship."

Henry looked bewildered. His wife's gaze searched Evan's face as if trying to guess the meaning behind his words.

Drawing in a deep breath, he said, "Juliana and I are not really husband and wife."

Henry stared hard at Evan, his dark gaze dropping to their clasped hands. With a light squeeze, Evan released her hand, which she quickly withdrew. He knew what the other man was thinking. Henry had witnessed that kiss and other displays of affection normally reserved for married couples. No doubt he thought they were living in sin.

"I want to assure you both that nothing improper has happened between the two of us. We met five days ago when our paths crossed unexpectedly, and we've been traveling together out of necessity. When you and your family showed up, I figured it was best to pretend to be married. Juliana didn't want to do it but I insisted, knowing how it would look if we didn't." He looked from husband to wife. "I'm sorry I lied to you both."

"I'm sorry, too," Juliana rushed to add, her expression full of remorse. "I think of you as a dear friend, Rose, and I hope you can forgive me."

"Of course I forgive you," Rose said, her eyes full of questions. "I would just like to know what's going on. The man who's following you—the one who hurt you— is he the reason you are traveling together?"

"We know it isn't any of our business—" Henry began.

Evan interrupted. "No. You deserve an explanation. I'll have to start from the beginning, though."

Starting with the death of his parents, Evan told them everything leading up to that day in the mercantile. They listened with rapt attention, scarcely believing he'd actually kidnapped Juliana. When he'd finished, they sat in stunned silence.

Henry was the first to speak. "Juliana, you obviously have been through quite a lot this week. Are you sure you're all right? Would you like to add anything to Evan's account?"

"I'm fine—honest. God has carried me through these last few days. He's protected me, and I'm sure He's comforted my family as well. Evan has been a perfect gentleman. He's done nothing to make me feel afraid or uncomfortable."

Evan didn't know about the perfect part. He regretted the pain he'd caused her family, and realized he'd have to face them one day soon. That was one confrontation he wasn't eager to have.

"I see." Henry appeared thoughtful.

Rose Talbot's curiosity was not so easily satisfied. "I'm curious about something. Henry will likely say I'm being nosy, but I have to say what's on my mind. It seems to me the two of you have come to care for each other a great deal. The affection between you isn't pretend, is it?"

Evan feared they could hear his heart banging against his rib cage. How could he possibly answer this question? He wasn't ready to face the truth himself, much less admit to it in front of Juliana. She'd already said she didn't love him—the day he kissed her. And really, how could she? After everything he'd put her through...

His mouth dry, he took another swig of coffee. "Juliana is a remarkable woman, Mrs. Talbot. She's put up with a lot, and yet, she has found it in her heart to forgive me. I count myself lucky just to know her."

He hoped his answer would satisfy the other woman. He felt the weight of Juliana's stare, but he couldn't bring himself to meet it.

"I think I know the reason for my wife's questions." Henry leaned forward to address Evan. "You see, the two of you have spent days in each other's company without a chaperone. When Juliana's family finds out, they'll expect you to marry her. Have you thought about that?"

Evan bowed his head. It was true. A single man and woman traveling for days and nights on their own—no one would believe they were innocent of wrongdoing. Juliana's reputation was at stake.

"No," he heard Juliana say. When he lifted his head to look at her, he recognized the defiant tilt of her chin. She met his gaze, her eyes full of fire. "I won't be forced into marriage. It's not fair to Evan or myself."

Evan's gut twisted. He wanted to do what was best for her, but marriage wasn't in his plans. Marriage meant commitment and, eventually, attachment. He didn't want that. It hurt too much to lose someone you loved.

"Think what the townspeople will say, Juliana," Rose insisted, her face a mask of concern. "You'll be shunned by many."

"I don't care," she declared. "Those who know me know I'd never do anything to bring shame upon myself or my family."

Evan noticed her fisted hands in her lap and longed to soothe her, but he didn't think she'd welcome his touch right about now. He'd put her in this position. She had every right to be angry.

Rose's voice was gentle. "It's not fair, I agree, but it's the way of things. And it won't just affect you, my dear. Your mother and sisters will be treated the same as you."

Juliana shook her head. "I can't believe it of my friends. The people of Gatlinburg will understand. They have to."

Rose looked on her with kindness. "Perhaps you're right."

"What do you think, Evan?" Henry spoke up.

He caught Juliana's gaze and held it. Her inner turmoil was plain to see in her beautiful green eyes. It hurt to know he was the cause. "I want what's best for Juliana. If that means marriage, then so be it."

The second the words left his mouth, he knew he meant every one. He was willing to give her his name if it meant sparing her pain and humiliation. Somehow he'd find a way to protect his heart.

Her hand flew to her throat. "You can't mean that, Evan. It's not what you want, and you know it."

"What do *you* want, Juliana?" He searched her face for a clue. A myriad of emotions crossed her face—anger, fear, longing.

"I know what I *don't* want," she huffed, "and that's a sham marriage!"

Scrambling to her feet, she strode away.

"Wait—" He moved to rise, but Henry held up a staying hand.

"Maybe you should give her a few minutes alone. It's a lot to sort through."

Evan settled back down, his gaze following her to the lake. He doubted he could make it that far on his own strength, and it frustrated him. He didn't like feeling helpless.

He felt a hand on his arm. Rose said, "Don't worry, she'll come around. She just needs some time."

He summoned a small smile of thanks before excusing himself. Refusing Henry's offer of assistance, he made his way back to the tent and lay down to rest and think.

Chapter Sixteen

Juliana watched the swans glide gracefully across the sun-dappled water. How she envied their peace and tranquility! Her own soul was in turmoil. Like a tumbling house of cards, her thoughts heaped one upon another in quick succession until she couldn't make sense of a single one.

When she'd imagined how the conversation would go with the Talbots, talk of propriety and social expectations hadn't been on the list of topics for discussion. And certainly not marriage!

Remembering the expression on Evan's face when Henry brought it up, she dropped her head in her hands and groaned. The idea *terrified* him. Whether it was the prospect of marriage in general or marriage to her in particular she didn't know.

She had to admit—his reaction cut deep.

He didn't want a life with her.

Oh, she believed he liked her—perhaps even admired her—but he didn't love her.

Of course in the end he'd agreed to marry her—*if* she wanted him to. What girl wanted a husband on those terms? What kind of marriage could they have? Besides, she had a feeling he said it out of a sense of obligation.

Face it, you're just a liability to him, a little voice said, *an unwanted responsibility.*

As the truth sank in, the place around her heart ached with a dull pain. Tears traced uneven tracks down her cheeks. If she'd known how much it would hurt to love someone, she would've guarded her heart more closely.

But from the start, she'd been overwhelmed by her reaction to him. Evan was the first man to make her feel alive and very aware of her femininity. With a single touch of his hand, he could set her pulse racing and make her feel as if she'd just run a mile. Simply being near him thrilled her.

With each new glimpse of his soul, her compassion had taken root and developed into something more, something deeper. Their shared experiences had forged a unique bond between them. He'd seen her at her worst, and she him. They understood each other.

It had taken almost losing him to force her to face the fact that she loved him. And she hadn't cared that he was an outlaw. She was still adjusting to the fact that he wasn't a criminal at all, but a respectable man.

A life without Evan would be bleak. Miserable. Unbearable.

And yet that's the future she faced. In the coming days, she would be reunited with her family, and he would continue his quest for justice. She would go back to her mundane life while he spent his days and nights with criminals.

She wondered if he'd even miss her.

The sound of children playing reached her ears and, lifting her head, she swiped at the wetness on her cheeks. The swelling was gone, and it hurt only if she touched it.

She hoped the bruises disappeared before she returned home. She didn't want to go into the details of how and where she'd gotten them.

Tugging her snug bodice down, she went to find an empty pail. She wanted to be alone, and the best excuse was to go berry picking. Juliana found Rose tending to Joy. To her relief, the other woman didn't mention Evan or their earlier conversation, nor did she question Juliana's intention to go searching for berries. She did, however, insist that Juliana stay close by. With her bonnet and holster in place, she set off.

Juliana spent much of the afternoon meandering through the fields surrounding the lake, venturing as far as the tree line in the distance. She used the time to think and pray. While she didn't find a single berry bush, she did locate a cherry tree. With her pail swinging from her arm and brimming with plump, crimson fruit, she strolled back into camp.

She spotted Evan right away sitting in the shade, peeling potatoes. Matt was hunkered down next to him, chatting happily. The boy was clearly relieved to see Evan up and about. She'd seen how worried he'd been during Evan's illness.

As soon as Evan caught a glimpse of her, his hand stilled in midair and his back stiffened. Her steps slowed at his reaction. He didn't look at all pleased.

But she couldn't change course now. So she approached the twosome, unable to tear her gaze away from his. When she drew near, he rose to his feet and with a parting word to Matt, met her halfway.

He stopped a foot away and slipped his hands in his pockets. She was still trying to come to grips with the fact that he wasn't an outlaw. He was a law-abiding citizen and a believer.

Juliana swallowed hard, resisting the urge to throw herself in his arms. He was gorgeous, his pale blue shirt a complement to his tanned skin and dark hair, and so very dear. The only reminder of his illness was the pallor of his skin. She longed to caress his cheek as she'd done while he lay unconscious. Instead, she clasped her hands behind her back, the pail dangling from her fingers.

"You were gone a long time. I was worried."

His gaze roved over her from head to toe as if assuring himself she was unharmed.

"As you can see, I'm fine. I have protection." Her palm settled over the gun handle at her waist.

One black eyebrow quirked up. "I already know you're an adept hunter. But how much experience do you really have with a weapon?"

"Enough."

"Care to elaborate on that?"

His eyes held a hint of challenge, and she seized on it. "It'd be easier to show you than tell you. How about a demonstration after supper? We can even make it into a contest, if you want."

His expression turned disbelieving. "You against me? Are you sure you're up for the challenge?"

She flashed him a confident grin. "I'll do my best." Was he in for a big surprise!

"I'd expect nothing less." He grinned then, white teeth flashing. "I've got work to do." He hooked a thumb over his shoulder, indicating the pile of potatoes. "I'd better get back to it."

"It's nice of you to help Rose."

He lifted a shoulder. "I've been idle long enough. I needed something to occupy my hands."

"How are you feeling?"

"Normal, except for the fact I tire easily."

"That's to be expected. Are you sure you'll be ready to travel tomorrow? We could always wait an extra day."

With a look of determination, he said, "No, we can't. We need to get a message to your family as soon as possible. Besides, we'll be in the saddle most of the way. Lucky will be doing the exercising, not me."

Juliana had her doubts, but she could see that he wouldn't be swayed. She hoped he wouldn't overdo it and end up having a relapse.

She lifted the fruit for him to see. "Do you like cherries?"

"I do. Got anything special in mind for those?"

"Not exactly. I'm going to see if Rose has any suggestions."

"Ask her if she knows how to make a cherry crumble. If so, I've got plenty of cornmeal to spare. She's welcome to it."

"Is that a favorite of yours?"

"Not mine. My father's. I can still remember his excitement each time my mother made it. He was like a little kid in a candy store."

Hearing him laugh lightened her heart. After all the pain and suffering he'd endured, he deserved to be happy.

She realized that she didn't know much about his likes and dislikes. "If cherry crumble isn't your favorite, then what is?"

He thought for a moment. "I'm partial to apple pie. With lots of cinnamon."

For the first time in her life, Juliana wished she'd learned how to cook. She would've liked to make something special for him.

"I guess it's been a while since you've had a homemade meal."

"Too long," he muttered. "Restaurant food is the closest I've had to Mom's cooking, and it still can't compare. I've enjoyed Rose's, though. She's done wonders, considering her limited supplies."

"Yes," she agreed, "maybe when I get home I'll ask Jessica or Jane to teach me a few things."

"That's a wise idea." His expression turned serious. "You'll have a husband and children to cook for someday."

"Yes, perhaps."

He took a step forward. "Juliana, we need to talk."

She stepped back, sensing he wanted to continue the marriage discussion. "Not now, Evan. Later. I—I have to go."

She made to move past him, but he caught her wrist. "You can't avoid the subject forever."

Juliana gazed at her boots. "We both have things to do."

He dropped his hand. "You're right. But we *will* talk about it. Soon."

She walked away without a word.

Arms folded across her chest, Juliana watched as Evan took aim at the target and fired off a shot. The ping of the bullet against tin reached her ears, and she knew he'd hit it dead on. As she'd suspected, he was a good aim. Now it was her turn.

They'd chosen this cool, quiet meadow because it was a good distance from camp and the noise wouldn't bother the children or the horses. A tranquil place, Juliana would've liked to stretch out in the grass and relax amid the lilacs and daisies. Instead, she stepped to the spot he'd vacated and waited as he strung up a new target.

Juliana had managed to keep her distance from him during supper and cleanup, but she knew better than to expect him to drop the subject. He wasn't a man to let an issue fester. Once a matter came to his attention, he wanted it settled.

She checked her weapon. Everything was in order.

Evan came striding back, his long legs quickly eating up the distance. He stopped in front of her. "Are you ready?"

"I am."

He moved to the side, putting enough space between them so as not to crowd her. She felt his gaze on her, and with difficulty she tamped down her sudden nervousness. She was used to people watching, just not this particular person. She realized his opinion mattered a great deal.

Raising the gun to eye level, she focused on the target with one eye open and one closed. Then she squeezed the trigger. Again the loud ping reached her ears, and she let out a breath she hadn't realized she was holding.

Evan whistled as he approached, admiration in his gaze. "I'm impressed, Irish."

The tension left her body and, confidence in its place, she tossed out another challenge. "How about we do it again from farther away?"

His eyebrows darted up. "Are you sure you wanna do that? I've had lots of practice the last couple of months."

"Very funny," she retorted with a toss of her head. "I wouldn't have suggested it if I didn't think I could pull it off."

His hands braced on his hips, he leaned in close. His familiar clean scent wafted toward her. "Tell me something. If this is a competition, then what's the prize? What are you willing to give me if I win?"

Evan's nearness stirred her senses. She stood her ground, however. "Assuming you win, what is it that you want?"

His brilliant blue eyes dropped to her mouth, lingering there before ever so slowly lifting to meet her gaze once more. "One kiss."

Juliana felt as if she would melt into a puddle at his feet. Swallowing hard, she unconsciously licked her lips. "And if I win?" she croaked.

"Name your prize."

She couldn't think with him so close. "I don't know."

He flicked a gaze at her hair, still in a haphazard ponytail. "I could always braid your hair for you as I did the night of the rainstorm."

Juliana thought back to that night, recalling all too well the intimacy created by such an act. No matter who won, the outcome would be the same. Too much closeness for her peace of mind. It would be foolish to agree and, yet, she was tempted. She wanted nothing more than to be in his arms.

"If I win, you teach me to cook."

"You're on." A lazy grin curled his lips. "I'll be right back."

Her heart rate sped up as anticipation set in. He changed the target again and returned. "Are you sure you don't want to go first?"

"No, thanks. You go ahead."

Evan walked about fifteen paces past the first spot, turned on his heel and sought her approval. "Far enough?"

"Looks good to me."

He took his time, judging the distance with his eyes before lifting his arm to aim his weapon. Again, his aim was true. Juliana moved into position, wiping her damp palms down her skirt. When all was ready, she lifted her gun. At the same instant that her finger put pressure on the trigger, a bumblebee buzzed past her ear and she jerked. The bullet strayed a few inches to the left, missing the tin can altogether.

Disbelieving, she stood there, the gun still in her hand at her side. Evan rushed over. "What happened?"

"It was a bee." Feeling the heat rushing to her face, she couldn't meet his eyes. He probably thought she had lost on purpose. She sheathed the gun in its holster.

He chuckled. "A bee, huh?"

A thought struck her. She lifted her face to his. "How about giving me another chance? If it hadn't been for that bee, I could've made the shot."

He stroked his chin, as if considering her request. "Uh-uh. I don't think so."

"Why not?" she demanded.

Evan stared at her, all amusement fading. His voice dipped. "Because. Bee or no bee, I won, and I want the kiss you owe me."

Juliana's pulse accelerated and she struggled to breathe. She felt light-headed, and her knees threatened to buckle. "You're not playing fair," she accused in a whisper.

"*I* didn't send that bee."

He closed the distance between them and tugged her against his muscular body. His hands gripping her waist, he swooped down to cover her mouth with his own. He gave her no time to resist. Her hands splayed against his chest. Beneath her palm, his heart pounded fast and hard.

His soft lips moved over hers with insistence, coaxing and tasting until she couldn't think, only feel. Emotion left her weak, and she leaned against him for support. She slid her hands up and locked them around his neck.

He emitted a low, guttural moan. His hands moved up her back, and he pressed her even closer. He deepened the kiss, and trembling, she clung to him.

Evan became her anchor. In the haven of his embrace, she felt safe, cherished and more alive than she'd ever felt before. Pushing aside her reservations, Juliana kissed him with abandon, willing him to feel the depth of her love.

When he abruptly broke off the kiss and set her away from him, she nearly cried out in protest. His chest heaved as if he'd run a mile, and she could clearly see that he was fighting an inner battle. With a searing glance, he strode to where he'd left his hat. Retrieving it from the ground, he settled it smoothly on his head and walked back, stopping several feet away.

It was plain to see that he was upset and trying to conceal it. "When we get back to Gatlinburg, there are going to be a lot of questions. Your family will expect me to marry you and rightly so."

Juliana opened her mouth to speak, but he held up his hand to forestall her. "I don't want your reputation to suffer, Juliana. I don't want you to be treated like a social outcast just because you unwillingly spent a couple of days and nights in my company. You don't deserve that kind of treatment. You've done nothing wrong.

"I can shield you from all that by marrying you. I know it's not the best situation. I'm certain you pictured your life turning out a different way, but I'm willing if you are. The truth is I wouldn't mind being married to you."

Juliana couldn't speak. The man who had captured her heart was offering to marry her. That meant living together as husband and wife, day in and day out, sharing life's ups and downs, trials and blessings. Perhaps they'd even have children some day.

Oh, she was tempted. In time, she reasoned, he could grow to love her.

Or he could end up resenting her.

Did she dare take that risk?

Tears threatened, and she blinked them back. Squaring her shoulders, she dug down deep for the courage to say what was in her heart. "Thank you, Evan, for your kind offer. But you see, I don't want a man who simply doesn't *mind* marrying me. I want a man who *yearns* to be with me, whose utmost desire is to make me his bride. A man who believes life isn't worth living if he can't share it with me. Call me romantic or even foolish, but I'd rather face the disapproving stares and whispers of the townspeople than a loveless marriage."

Evan closed his eyes, as if her words caused him pain. "Love opens you up to a whole world of pain, my dear. I should know. I've lost every single person I've ever loved. Let me tell you, I wouldn't wish that kind of grief on anyone."

"It was good while it lasted, though, wasn't it?" she countered, desperate to make her point. "Isn't it better to experience love and joy for a little while than not at all? Yes, it hurt when I lost my father, but do I wish I'd never known him? Of course not." Juliana approached him and slipped her hand into his. "Evan. Do you honestly want to spend the rest of your life all alone? With no one to care for you?"

His eyes roamed her face, questions lurking in the dark depths. "I don't think I could endure another loss, Juliana." Lifting his hand, he gently cupped her cheek, his thumb stroking her skin. "A lot of marriages are built on friendship alone and are very successful. I may not be able to offer you my heart, but I can give you my friendship. Isn't that enough?"

His words stabbed at her. Pulling his hand away, she stepped back. "I'm afraid not."

His shoulders slumped in defeat, and she almost

changed her mind. Instead, with a look at the setting sun, she muttered, "I think we'd best be getting back. There's a lot to do before we leave tomorrow."

Evan turned away, oddly defeated. He cared more for her than he knew was wise. Why else would he be pushing her to marry him? Of course he understood what she was up against if she didn't, and he didn't want to see her hurt. Especially because of something he'd done.

He fell into step beside her, his gaze on everything *but* her. He was afraid that if he chanced a glance at her now, he would kiss her again. And that would be a huge mistake.

Kissing Juliana was dangerous. It had taken every ounce of his willpower to stop. He'd wanted to go on holding her forever. If they were husband and wife, he reminded himself, he wouldn't have to stop. He could kiss her whenever he liked.

The thought kicked his heart into a wild gallop, and his stomach did a flip-flop.

Juliana was a beautiful, desirable young woman. He couldn't deny that he was attracted to her. When she was near, he was lucky if he could put two words together. With those innocent green eyes and sweet mouth, she had the power to drive all rational thought from his mind.

He didn't necessarily enjoy not having control over his emotions like that.

Camp came into view then, and they parted ways without a word. It was just as well. He hadn't a clue what to say.

Chapter Seventeen

Breakfast was a solemn affair. After prolonged good-byes, they finally hit the trail. Juliana didn't seem inclined to talk, which suited him just fine.

He glanced upward, pleased to see not a single cloud in the vast blue sky. Anticipation bloomed in his chest. Soon he would be home. *Home.* It seemed like a lifetime had passed since he'd seen the place. He was eager to see for himself how the animals and crops were faring under his cousin's supervision.

In hindsight, Evan realized that he hadn't really handled the whole situation as well as he could have. His letters home had been few and far between. And he hadn't told Luke how much he appreciated everything he'd done since James's passing.

Well, he would have a chance to correct his wrongs that night. By suppertime, he fully intended to be sitting at his cousin's table.

"You weren't exaggerating, Evan. It's absolutely breathtaking."

Standing on the ridge overlooking his beloved valley, Juliana surveyed the scene.

Far below, encircled by majestic blue-green mountains, lay his home. Fields and fences, cabins and barns crisscrossed the verdant valley basin. Even the white clapboard church, with its white cross reaching toward the sky, was visible from the mountaintop. Shimmering ribbons of blue cut large swaths across the valley.

Evan appeared pleased by her declaration. He grinned at her, and she could see the excitement in his eyes. "Shall we go?"

Their descent took just under two hours. Evan halted Lucky near the first homestead.

At the mix of emotions crossing his face, Juliana asked, "Is that your cabin?"

"No, this is Luke's place. My land starts on the other side of that tree grove." He pointed to a spot about a mile distant. "We'll have supper with him first."

Apprehension warred with curiosity. She could only imagine the man's reaction when Evan showed up on his doorstep with a strange woman.

Juliana spotted a large dog on the front porch. He noticed them at the same time and let out a warning. The animal's noisy barking alerted Lucas Harrison, because almost immediately the front door swung open and a man appeared in the doorway.

Evan tipped his hat back and waved. "Hello, cuz," he called. "I sure do hope you've got supper on the table 'cause I've been dreaming of a home-cooked meal for days!"

A wide smile broke out on the stranger's face. With a word to the dog to stay put, he leapt off the porch and strode quickly across the grass to meet them. "My eyes must be deceiving me! I was beginning to wonder if you were ever coming home."

Evan held out his hand, which Lucas accepted only to

tug Evan close for a quick but enthusiastic hug. Releasing him, Lucas turned his attention to Juliana.

Her cheeks burned beneath his scrutiny. He was obviously curious as to her identity but too polite to question her.

"Hello," he offered with a kind smile. "I'm Lucas Harrison. But my friends call me Luke."

Evan stepped closer to her, and she caught the warning glance he shot his cousin. "Luke, this is Juliana O'Malley."

He tipped his head. "It's nice to meet you, Miss O'Malley."

"It's a pleasure to meet you as well, Mr. Harrison." Evan's cousin was handsome and charming, although not quite as striking as Evan.

"Please, call me Luke. Whenever someone calls me *Mr. Harrison,* I automatically look around to see if my father's nearby. Can't seem to get used to it." His gaze volleyed between the two of them. "You both look parched. How does a glass of lemonade sound?"

"Wonderful," Evan huffed. "Juliana?"

"I'd love some."

"Evan, why don't you show Miss O'Malley to the house? I'll see that Lucky gets a drink, and then I'll be right in. We've got a lot of catching up to do." He clapped Evan on the shoulder. "Think you can remember where everything is?"

"I'll do my best." At Evan's dry response, Juliana hid a smile. She sensed the two cousins teased each other often.

Inside, the smell of meat roasting in the stove tantalized her nose. They'd had a light lunch of beef jerky and hard biscuits hours ago, and she was hungry.

A glance around revealed a home that was neat and

tidy, if sparsely furnished. The windows were bare and the only touch of color in the room came from the blue settee sitting in front of the fireplace. Gauging from his home, Luke Harrison struck her as a man of simple tastes.

"Here you go." Evan appeared at her side with a tall glass of lemonade.

She sipped the cool, tart liquid and sighed. "That's delicious."

"We've been walking for hours. Why don't you have a seat? If you don't mind being on your own for a few minutes, I'd like to have a word with Luke before supper."

"I'll be fine." Placing her glass on the oval coffee table, she sank down onto the settee and untied the strings of her bonnet. "He must have a lot of questions."

He drained the remainder of his drink and set it on the table next to hers. "Juliana," he began, his eyes searching, "I plan on telling him the truth about our situation. Do you mind?"

"As I see it, we have no other choice."

He cocked his head to one side. "I could tell him it's none of his business."

Juliana could tell by his serious demeanor that the decision was indeed hers to make. Clearly, Evan wanted to tell his cousin everything, which meant he trusted him to keep it quiet.

"If you trust him, then so do I."

"I do."

"Who is she?"

Leaning against the stall door, Evan stroked the mare's nose and tried to formulate an answer. No matter how he said it, his cousin wasn't going to be pleased.

"I'm not going to like what you have to say, am I?" Luke said finally.

Evan decided to be blunt. "I kidnapped her."

"*What* did you say?"

"She walked in on a robbery. I tried to get her out of there, but my *colleague* had other plans."

Feet planted wide and arms folded across his chest, Luke leveled a steady glare in Evan's direction. "Do you realize how outrageous that sounds coming from *your* mouth? Those words don't even begin to match up with the man I know you to be. Explain yourself."

"I realize this is hard for you to swallow. Believe me." He thrust his fingers through his hair. "I'm having a hard time understanding it myself."

"Juliana didn't appear to be here against her will, however. In fact, the two of you seem to be on friendly terms."

"Yeah." Evan's mind drifted to the kiss he'd won and how it felt to hold her in his arms. Many times today he'd been tempted to do it again, but had resisted.

"Evan," Luke prompted sternly, "you look like a man in love. Tell me, how could that be?"

In love? With Juliana? He cared about her, of course. Surely he wouldn't have been foolish enough to let himself fall in love with her.

"I didn't come out here to talk about my feelings."

"So you admit to having feelings." He cocked an eyebrow. His lips tugged upward in a teasing grin.

Evan shot him a warning glance, but said nothing.

"Fine, I'll drop it. For now." Luke turned serious once more. "So why didn't you let her go? Why bring her here?"

He told him everything that had happened, including his belief that Fitzgerald had been trailing them.

"Oh, this is getting better by the minute," Luke groaned.

"I know I'm out of favors, but I need you to promise me that you'll keep an eye on her while I'm gone."

"You have my word," he agreed. "You look peaked. Have you been taking care of yourself?"

He really didn't want to go into his illness at that moment. He was bone-tired. Maybe he'd pushed himself too hard. He'd be hitting the hay early that night. Literally. "You know how life on the trail can be. Not the best of conditions."

"Let's go eat then, so you can go home and get some rest." He started for the barn door.

"Luke?"

He paused and looked back at Evan. "Yeah?"

"Thanks." Gratitude overwhelmed him, making it hard to speak. He'd missed him. "I owe you."

Understanding dawned, and Luke smiled. "Who knows? One day I may need a favor from you."

"All you need to do is ask."

As they waved goodbye to Luke Harrison, Juliana felt content. The meal, while nothing fancy, had been delicious—the tender beef roast dripping in rich gravy had melted in her mouth and the biscuits slathered with freshly churned butter and a touch of honey made her moan in delight. She grinned, remembering how surprised both men had been at the number of biscuits she'd consumed.

She'd enjoyed the lively conversation as well. Evan and Luke had entertained her with stories of their childhoods and teenage years. It was obvious the two men shared a close friendship, and she could tell both were pleased to be in each other's company once again.

As they left the front yard, Evan urged Lucky into a canter. His arm held her fast, securing her against his muscled body. She reveled in their closeness, knowing it would soon come to an end. He would take the next day to do errands in town and check on his animals and garden, then leave the following morning. How long it would be before he returned she hadn't a clue.

He slowed the big black when they emerged from the trees. They were on his land now. Crossing a shallow stream, they intersected a field with knee-high grass and entered another small cove before emerging beside long, even rows of plants. In the distance, a one-story cabin stood in the midst of several apple trees, the profusion of pink blossoms shining in the sun. Chestnut trees with spotted trunks lined the drive. A tall barn rimmed with animal pens stood just beyond the cabin.

Lush and green, with rounded blue mountain peaks in the near distance, his home took her breath away. With its tranquil scenery, she thought it even more beautiful than her beloved childhood home.

His cabin faced the mountains, with a wide porch on which to relax and enjoy the view. As they neared, she noted a glass-plated window on each side of the front door, as well as two rocking chairs. Stacked stone, likely from the nearby river, formed the foundation.

Halting Lucky directly in front, Evan jumped down and helped her out of the saddle. For the briefest of moments, he gazed down at her, his hands a warm weight on her waist. When he stepped back, she tried to hide her disappointment.

"Well, what do you think?" He swept his arm in a wide arc, his excitement showing in his sparkling eyes and bright smile.

She quashed her sense of loss. "It's beautiful, Evan.

You must be so proud. Did you and James help your father build it?"

"Yes, we did." He nodded slowly, his gaze moving along the roofline of the cabin, lost in memories. "Took us a month, only because we had a few locals helping. Otherwise, it would've taken longer."

"Where did you live during that time?"

"Live?" His black brows winged up. "Here. Under the stars."

"Your mother must've liked that," she responded in a dry tone. A few days sleeping outside was tolerable, but an entire month? Mrs. Harrison would've been itching for a stove to cook on and a nice soft bed.

"She didn't complain, but I'd catch her watching us at odd times during the day while we worked, as if she could somehow will the house to go up faster."

Juliana smiled at that but said nothing.

"Once the cabin was finished, we had a barn raising. That took three days because the entire community came out to help. Despite the hard work, it was fun. Everyone brought food and we ate under those trees yonder." He pointed to the sugar maples and oaks beside the barn. "When the sun went down, we had bonfires and music and dancing. Momma was thrilled to meet the other women."

"How long did your parents live here?" she asked gently.

He turned to her, a bittersweet expression stealing across his face. "Not nearly long enough. Four years."

"They were happy here? They didn't regret leaving North Carolina?"

"Very happy." Again, his gaze roamed the landscape. "We all fell in love with this place. About a year after we moved here, the tract next to ours came up for sale and, at my father's urging, my Uncle Clarence and Aunt Willa—Luke's parents—bought it sight unseen. The three of us grew up together."

In her mind's eye, she imagined the three boys racing across this land. "So when James died, in a way Luke lost a brother, too."

It was clear the notion hadn't occurred to Evan. He was quiet a long moment. "Yeah, I suppose you're right. I've never thought about it, but Luke was like a brother to us. I left immediately after the funeral. We never talked about our loss."

"It's never too late, you know."

"You're right. I might stop by his place before I head out in the morning."

Juliana gave him an encouraging smile. "I think that will help the both of you."

He held out his hand. "Come, let me show you inside."

Juliana took his hand and allowed him to lead her inside the cabin. Standing inside the front door, she scanned the spacious living area and kitchen. Considering the sparseness of Luke's cabin, she hadn't expected Evan's to be any different. But here there were cheerful yellow curtains adorning the windows, crocheted pillows piled on the sofa, and hand-stitched samplers hanging on the walls. Then she remembered that this had been his parents' home, and his mother had likely added the feminine touches.

"There are two bedrooms down here." He pointed to a ladder lying against the wall. "And as you can see a loft up there. That used to be my room when my parents were alive."

"I see."

Still holding her hand, he urged her toward the largest bedroom. A pretty blue-and-white wedding-ring quilt covered the wide bed. She wondered if his mother made it. "This is mine now." He ran a finger along the dresser and scrunched up his nose. "Sorry about the dust. No one's been in here to clean while I've been away." He turned to face her. "You'll sleep in here tonight and the remainder of the time I'm gone."

She opened her mouth to protest, but he raised a hand. "No arguments. I'm sleeping in the barn tonight and tomorrow tonight, so you don't have to feel uncomfortable."

"The barn?" Her brows lifted. "There's plenty of space in here. Why not the loft? I don't mind."

Standing very close, he tilted her chin up with his finger. "I do."

Swallowing hard, she managed, "You've been ill. I'm not sure it's wise for you to sleep out there. If it's anything like our barn, there's no telling the measure of filth in the hay. And the varmints…"

"Juliana," his voice dipped to a husky rasp, "you don't realize the temptation you are to me, do you?"

At first the meaning behind his words didn't sink in. When she didn't speak, he gave a curt laugh and dropped her hand. "I didn't think so. I'm sleeping in the barn."

Evan awoke to the sounds of the cows shuffling down below and the hens clucking in their pen outside the barn. A glance outside the door told him it was after dawn, time to feed and water the animals before going inside to cook breakfast for himself and Juliana.

As he climbed down the ladder, he was met with the sound of an approaching rider. He strode outside, his hand on his gun. The tension left his body when he recognized Thomas Latham, the young man Luke had hired in Evan's absence to do chores around the farm. The two spreads were too much for one man to tend to, of course. The Latham family had moved to the cove a few years after Evan's, and he remembered Thomas as a shy sort.

He greeted the young man with enthusiasm and invited him to breakfast. Thomas refused with the excuse he'd already eaten. Evan explained he'd be leaving again the next day, and that Miss O'Malley was not to be bothered. Blushing, Thomas assured him profusely that he would not go near the lady. Satisfied with his response, Evan helped Thomas with the care of the animals before heading inside with a basket full of eggs.

The smell of coffee met him, but Juliana was nowhere to be seen. Then he noticed the closed bedroom door. He carried the eggs into the kitchen, and after washing his hands at the washstand, he prepared the cornmeal batter. He was in the midst of pouring it into the hot skillet when Juliana appeared with a soft greeting.

At the sight of her, Evan swallowed hard and willed himself not to drop the bowl on his toe. The white blouse she wore, with its fitted bodice, billowing sleeves and cuffed wrists, accompanied by a full skirt, lent her an air of elegance. Her hair, a deep, rich red with golden highlights, hung in a straight, silky curtain around her shoulders. She'd inserted a tiny silver clip just above her ear for decoration. Her porcelain skin was dewy fresh, her green eyes luminous in her oval-shaped face.

She fidgeted beneath his stare. "Are you regretting letting me borrow your mother's things?"

"What?" He shook his head to clear it. "Uh, no. Actually, I don't remember her wearing that at all. Probably reserved it for special outings, which back then were few and far between. You look beautiful."

Long, sooty lashes swept down to hide her eyes. A soft flush infused her skin. "Thank you." She touched her fingers to her hair. "I found this clip in the bottom of the trunk. I hope it's okay for me to use it."

"I told you, Juliana, help yourself to anything you need. Or want."

A line formed between her brows. "I waited for you last night."

He turned his attention back to the hoecakes, lest they burn. "I was worn out. After breakfast I have to head into town."

"I suppose I'll need to stay here," she said quietly, unable to mask her disappointment.

He held the spatula aloft. "I wish I could take you with me, but your showing up on my arm now would stir up a hornet's nest of questions. I don't have time for that."

"I understand. I'll use the time to explore your land, if you don't mind."

"I don't, but I want you to promise me that you won't wander too far." He told her about Thomas Latham and assured her that she wouldn't be bothered by him.

"I'll stay within sight of the house. Now, what can I do to help?"

Evan glanced around the kitchen. "You can pour the coffee and set the table. I keep a jar of molasses in the upper cupboard there."

Within twenty minutes, they had everything ready. At the last minute, he remembered to pull out her chair for her and wait until she was seated to seat himself. He sat at the head of the table, with Juliana on his left. They simply stared at each other, silly smiles on their faces.

He could hardly believe that she was here—in *his* home—sitting at his table and sharing a meal with him.

With his palm outstretched, he waited for her to slip her slender hand in his and then bowed his head to say grace. It was with reluctance that he released it when the prayer was finished. As they ate, he answered her questions about the farm and the community, more than happy to talk about the home he loved. By the end of the meal, she was looking suitably impressed.

"I wish I could give you a tour of the place myself," he said over his shoulder as he carried empty plates to the kitchen. "I'll probably be gone a couple of hours, so I'll stop by Addie's eating establishment and bring us home some lunch. She makes the best fried chicken I've ever eaten."

"I'll clean this up while you haul in the bath water," she said, moving past him to grab a washcloth to clean the dishes. "Thank you for breakfast. I do feel bad that you have to cook every meal."

"Don't. I'd much rather cook than wash dishes."

"Ah, well, I'm a master dish cleaner because that's all I ever do in the kitchen." She smiled, a sparkle in her eye. "Jessica, Jane and sometimes Megan are in charge of the cooking and Nicole and I handle the clean up."

Evan moved to the door, his hand on the handle. "Speaking of that, the first thing I'm going to do when I get to town is send that telegram to Gatlinburg. Your family will finally get the news they've been waiting for."

Her smile widened and her expression was one of true happiness. "They will be so relieved."

Eager to get ready and be on his way, he hooked a thumb over his shoulder. "Well, I'd better get a move on if I'm going to get everything done before lunch."

"Go." She shooed him out. "Do whatever you have to do."

"Remember what I said," he reminded her an hour later from his perch on the wagon seat.

"Yes, of course." She stood on the front porch, one hand shading her eyes from the bright sun. "Be careful."

Evan stared down at her, wondering if it had been a mistake to bring her here. Forever stored in his memory would be Juliana in his home—standing on his porch, sitting on his sofa, eating at his table. He wouldn't have to imagine her presence here, which meant her absence would be all the more noticeable.

Not for the first time, his thoughts returned to their conversation of the evening before when she'd rejected his offer of a marriage based on friendship. He knew that he was fast approaching the point of offering her his heart merely to keep her near. When he was with Juliana, the grief and loneliness faded away and he felt content to simply be in her presence.

The truth was that Evan didn't want to be alone anymore. Why not share his life with her? Everyone would expect them to marry anyway for propriety's sake. If they married, he would have a companion and her reputation would be protected. Problem solved.

Now all he had to do was convince Juliana.

He tipped his hat. "I'll be back as soon as I can."

Chapter Eighteen

Juliana watched his wagon disappear around the curve before going back inside. As she walked past the fireplace, her glance fell on a small daguerreotype lying flat on the mantel. Picking it up with the tips of her fingers, she stared at the image of a handsome couple and two teenage boys. She recognized the taller boy right away. If her guess was correct, Evan looked to be around the age of fourteen or fifteen. Although thinner, his features less defined, he was handsome even then.

Next to him stood his younger brother, James.

After studying the image, Juliana decided that both boys took after their father in height and coloring, but their noses and mouths resembled their mother's. She placed it back upon the mantel, propping it up against the wall.

Juliana wondered what it would feel like to be the last one left of her entire family. To have nothing left but bittersweet memories. The mere idea made her unbearably sad.

Moving past the mantel, she retrieved her bonnet from the bedroom and walked back outside into the golden sunshine. The air was heavy with moisture, the sun's rays already uncomfortably hot.

Turning in the direction of the barn, she passed beneath the branches of several apple trees, inhaling the pleasant scent of apple blossoms. The shade was pleasant. Beyond the trees, she encountered a chicken coop and a small shed that she didn't explore.

Inside the darkened interior of the barn, she made friends with a calico cat and a sweet gray mare who appeared to be the sole occupants. Everything was neat and tidy—not unlike Evan himself—until she stumbled upon the tool area he'd mentioned before, the place where he liked to invent things. In the far corner of the barn stood a rough wooden table piled high with tools and gadgets of all shapes and sizes. She didn't dare touch a thing lest the whole pile tumble to the dirt floor. If there was enough time, perhaps he would agree to give her a demonstration of one of his devices.

The moment she stepped outside, a warning bell went off inside her head. Something was different. Wrong. The cheerful day had taken on a menacing edge.

Her wide eyes cast about for a clue as to what had sparked her alarm and came up empty. Nothing was out of place. No wild animals. No revenge-seeking outlaws.

Then, a flash of color in the woods. Adrenaline surged through her veins, and she automatically reached for her gun. When her fingers found the empty holster, her heart sank. A lot of good it would do her back in the cabin!

Crouching down, she used the barn door as a shield. Her stomach clenched into a hard knot. She scanned the woods again. Nothing.

She stayed in that position until her legs ached with fatigue. Maybe she'd imagined the whole thing.

Another fifteen minutes dragged by. Finally, she

bolted for the cabin. Slamming the door closed and sliding the lock in place, she rested against it trying to catch her breath.

Her gun. She needed her gun. Now.

She found it where she'd left it, checked the chamber and placed it in her holster.

Filled with unease, she peered out the window for what seemed like an hour. When Evan's hired help strode into view, she gasped. Unaware that he was being watched, he strolled casually toward the animal pens.

Irritated with herself, she dropped the curtain. *Silly, Juliana. That's what you are.*

She decided then and there *not* to tell Evan. She wouldn't bother him with what was probably a result of her overactive imagination. He had enough worries. No need adding to them.

He would be leaving in the morning, and she would stay here. Alone.

The more she thought about it, the less she wanted to be left behind. Although she knew he wasn't likely to agree, she would at least try to change his mind.

"I need to talk—"

"There's something I want—"

Speaking at the same time, they both stopped and smiled.

"You first." Evan gestured from his spot on the blanket. They had polished off a delicious lunch of crispy fried chicken, boiled new potatoes, coleslaw and yeast rolls. There were two slices of peach pie, but dessert would have to wait. They were stuffed.

Juliana sat with her legs curled to the side, her pale skirt billowing around her. She watched the river water meander past, the grayish-brown stones glistening in the sun.

"I want to go with you tomorrow." There, she'd said it.

His brow wrinkled in confusion. "We agreed this was the safest place for you. I know you're eager to see your family, but you won't have to wait long. Alone, I can ride hard and fast and be there in two days. I'll be back for you in no time."

"Don't leave me behind. If I rode one of your other horses, I wouldn't have any trouble keeping up with you. You won't have to worry about me slowing you down, I promise."

"What is it, Juliana?" He gave her a measuring look. "Does the thought of being here alone make you uneasy? If you want, I can arrange for you to stay in town with one of the families there. There will be questions, of course, but we can handle it, if we must."

She thought back to her scare earlier in the day, but brushed it aside. "No, it's not that. I feel safe enough, especially knowing your cousin is nearby. To be honest, I'm worried about your traveling alone." A grasshopper landed on the sole of her boot, and she flicked it off with her finger. "What if you get sick again? Who would take care of you? Or what if something happened to Lucky? What then?" The idea of him stranded in the mountains, perhaps sick or hurt, worried her to no end.

His voice firm but kind, he said, "I appreciate your concern, but you're borrowing trouble. I feel fine. My strength has returned, and I haven't had a weak spell in two days. We'll just have to trust the good Lord to keep me safe. Wasn't it you who reminded me the other day that God is in control?"

His admonition shamed her. She knew better than to

give in to worry. Rose's words came back to her—what ifs opened the door to fear. Juliana needed to place Evan's safety in God's hands and trust in His protection.

Her head dipped. "You're right, of course."

With his finger beneath her chin, Evan lifted her face. "I'll be fine, you know."

A sigh escaped her lips. "With God's help, I'll try not to worry while you're gone."

"Good girl."

His affectionate smile eased her tension, making her want to reach over and hug him close. She wanted to feel his strong arms around her, sheltering her.

"Your turn," she announced, shifting position to ease the stiffness in her legs. "What were you about to say before?"

Hooking a hand behind his neck, he hung his head. Whatever it was, he didn't appear eager to discuss it. When she'd decided she couldn't handle the suspense any longer, he lifted his head and looked her square in the eye.

"Look—I like you, Irish. I like being around you. I'm comfortable with you, and I think you feel the same way. This is hard to admit, but I-I'll miss you when you're not around. I think we make a good team, don't you?"

He stared at her, waiting for her to answer. She couldn't. It was as if her brain had suddenly stopped working. When she didn't respond, he plunged on ahead, his words jumbling together in his haste. "You made it plain what you want in a marriage. What if I said I'm open to more than a friendship marriage? Maybe you thought I meant that I didn't want children, but I do. You and I…well, there's something between us. Call it what you want, but I've no doubt we'd be good together."

Juliana sat there, dumbfounded. Was he talking about

the marriage bed? A dozen butterflies danced in her stomach as her skin heated beneath his gaze. Evan apparently felt no embarrassment discussing such an intimate subject.

"Exactly what is your point, Evan?" she managed to get out.

"While I can't offer you my heart, I can offer you a normal husband-and-wife relationship. With God's blessing, of course, you'd be able to bear children and be a wife and mother and perhaps even someday a grandmother. What do you say?"

Juliana felt her cheeks burn with humiliation. With hurried movements, she began to stuff the food back into the basket. "I don't think this is a subject I'd like to discuss."

"I didn't intend to offend you, Juliana. I apologize."

She couldn't look at him. "It's too hot out here. I'm going in."

He placed a staying hand on her forearm. "Please, stay. I promise not to bring it up again."

"I can't," she murmured, pulling her arm from his grasp. Forgetting all about the food, she hurried back to the cabin. Mortified both by his words and by her reaction, Juliana fled to the bedroom and bolted the door.

Juliana dashed away the tears leaking from her eyes. So Evan *liked* her. He thought they made a great *team*.

With a soft moan, she sank down on the bed and buried her face in her hands.

So this is what misery feels like.

That day in the mercantile had turned her life topsy-turvy. It was as if that one event bisected her existence— pre-Evan, a time of stability and simple pleasures, and post-Evan, a time of unpredictability and upheaval. Her emotions were not in the least reliable anymore. Her heart had been ensnared by a man who didn't return her love, and she feared that she was destined to mourn for him for the rest of her days.

A fresh wave of tears threatened and, sinking back down on the mattress, she curled into a ball on her side and fell into a troubled sleep.

Juliana awoke to the sounds of Evan knocking around in the kitchen. A glance at the window told her that she'd slept through the evening hours and all night. No doubt her mental anguish had played a part in that. She lay there staring up at the wooden beams, praying for enough strength to make it through the next hour or so until he left.

After yesterday's conversation, she had mixed feelings about his leaving. A part of her was relieved he was going so she wouldn't have to be constantly reminded of what she couldn't have. The other part wanted to fall down at his knees and beg him to take her with him.

A knock on the door startled her out of her reflections.

"Juliana." Evan's voice was muffled. "Are you awake? Breakfast is ready." A pause. "I'd like to see you before I leave."

Exhaling, she sat up. "I'll be out in a few minutes."

"All right." Was it her imagination, or was there relief in his voice?

From among his mother's things, she chose to wear a buttercup-yellow dress with simple lines—a scooped neck, flowing sleeves, a fitted waist and a fluttering skirt. Using the same silver clip, she gathered the hair above her ears and clipped the mass in the back, allowing the rest of her hair to flow around her shoulders.

Stiffening her spine, she sailed with determination toward the dining area.

You can do this, she assured herself. There was no need for tears. Throughout the entire meal, she would remain calm. She could collapse into a worthless heap after he'd gone.

"Is there anything I can do?" There, her voice sounded almost normal.

When his bright blue eyes collided with hers, her lungs struggled to draw in air. The force of his gaze threatened to turn her knees to jelly, and she reached out for something to hold on to. Fortunately, she was standing behind the table and her hands encountered the chair back.

"Have a seat." He indicated with a dip of his head. "Coffee's hot, but I can make tea if you prefer."

She slid out the chair and sank into it gratefully. "Coffee's fine."

He placed a steaming mug in front of her, along with a small jug of cream and a bowl of sugar. That he'd remembered touched her. As if reading her mind, he smiled knowingly. He placed a plate heaping with bacon, eggs, grits swimming in butter and two biscuits in front of her. She waited with her hands in her lap as he readied food for himself. When he sat down beside her, his clean scent wafted in her direction. She breathed it in without being too obvious about it.

"Juliana?"

Her eyes flew open, heat rushing to her cheeks. She hadn't even realized her lids had drifted closed! "Yes?"

"I'm going to pray now," he said, his open palm sliding toward hers.

She placed her hand on top of his and bowed her head. As he prayed, his thumb lazily grazed her skin, making the nerve endings along her arm tingle with awareness. At his *amen,* she snatched back her hand and, ignoring his questioning expression, began to eat without really tasting anything.

Neither one spoke. The silence was almost unbearable for her, not because she knew what to say but because she felt as if they should be taking advantage of this last time together instead of being awkward. When at last he set down his fork and leaned back in his chair, she followed suit even though there was still quite a bit of food left on her plate.

"You're not hungry this morning?" he asked, concerned.

"Not really."

"There's food in the larder for sandwiches and soup. Do you know how to make soup?"

"I won't starve, if that's what you're worried about." She flipped her hair behind her shoulder, irritated at herself. He was worried about her having enough to eat because he knew she had no culinary skills.

"I didn't mean to make you mad," he began, his mouth pensive. "That applies to yesterday, too."

No, she would not rehash *that* conversation, not in her present state. Standing abruptly, she began cleaning the table. He joined in the cleanup without a word, and in minutes the table was wiped clean.

Evan stood near the door. He cleared his throat. "Lucky's outside. My bags are packed and loaded." Lifting the curtain, he glanced out the window. "Dawn's approaching. Guess it's time to hit the trail."

Juliana was so nervous her palms were sweating. Her emotions were in a jumble. She didn't know what to say or do. So she said nothing.

Their gazes locked, they stared at each other from opposite sides of the room.

"Juliana," he bit out, his voice strained, "aren't you going to say anything?"

Swallowing past a lump, she managed, "Take care of yourself."

"That's it?"

"What else do you want me to say?" She splayed her hands wide.

A muscle jumped in his jaw. He shifted from one foot to the other, an expression of indecision on his handsome face. How she wished she could read his thoughts at that moment.

Especially when he flung his gloves on the table and strode across the room. Juliana was too shocked to move or speak. What was he doing?

He stopped directly before her, his body crowding her back against the cupboard. Not daring to meet his gaze, she allowed hers to roam over his neck and shoulders. The top two buttons of his shirt gaped open, revealing the smooth hollows of his throat and the rapid beat of his pulse.

With deliberate movements, he cupped her neck and eased her face up with slight pressure from his thumbs. As if in slow motion, he lowered his mouth inch by excruciating inch. Perhaps he was giving her a chance to protest. She couldn't. She craved his kiss.

When at last his lips brushed against hers, a sigh of contentment escaped her. He eased back and his blue eyes, hazy with need, sought permission to continue. In answer, Juliana lifted her mouth, and he met hers once again in an unbearably tender kiss.

Overwhelmed by his need for her, Evan forced himself to go slow. Her lips clung to his in sweet innocence as he explored her generous mouth.

Holding her in his arms, Evan entertained thoughts of forever. The thought of leaving her weighed heavy on his heart. If he were completely honest with himself, he'd own up to the fact he didn't want to ever let her go.

When he abandoned her lips to rain kisses along her jawline and the sensitive spot beneath her ear, her swift intake of breath stopped him in his tracks. Lifting his head, he gazed into her green eyes. That one look was all it took. With an abruptness that startled her, he set her away from him and strode across the room. If he didn't put some space between them, he wasn't sure what he might say or do.

"Goodbye, Juliana."

Slamming the front door, he bounded off the porch and hurled himself into the saddle, burying his heel in Lucky's flank.

Chapter Nineteen

Juliana stared at the door. He was gone. Without a single word. How could he kiss her as if she were the most precious thing in the world and then turn around and leave like that?

She rushed to the window and pulled the curtain aside. There was a cloud of dust in the distance, but she couldn't make out his form or that of his horse. She lingered there until the dust settled and the spark of hope that he'd turn around and come back flickered out. He wasn't coming back. Not today, anyway.

Emotions running high, she turned back to the kitchen and attacked the pile of dirty dishes. She was shaky and weak, her lips still tingling from his kiss. His scent lingered in the air, which only intensified her misery. She tried to pray, but the words simply wouldn't come. So she said the only thing she could manage. *Jesus, I need You.*

When she finished cleaning the kitchen, she went to the bedroom to retrieve Evan's Bible. She needed to read those reassuring words and hear her Savior's quiet voice. Nearing the bed, she spotted a small brown package tied up with white twine. There was a note attached with her name printed neatly across it.

Juliana stared at it for the longest time. What had Evan left for her?

With trembling fingers, she picked up the white paper. It fluttered open in her hands. She stared at the tidy black script and imagined him seated at his desk composing the letter.

> *Dear Irish,*
> *I noticed that day in the mercantile your dress appeared quite new. It didn't take long for it to succumb to the rigors of the trail, however. I've taken the liberty of purchasing you a new one, although it isn't an exact copy. If it doesn't fit correctly, there is a seamstress in town we can visit as soon as I get home. Please don't think me forward. I know it isn't the proper thing for a single man to purchase personal garments for a lady, but I owe you. And you did say it was a favorite of yours.*
> *Sincerely,*
> *Evan*

Laying aside the note, Juliana slid the bundle close to the edge of the bed and untied the string. She lifted the brown paper, a tiny sigh escaping her lips at the sight of the luxurious fabric. The dress wasn't blue at all. Instead, it was the same lush, vivid green as the forest. The same hue as her eyes. Which was the reason he'd chosen it, she supposed.

Holding up the dress, she saw that it was very similar in style to her other one, with a fitted bodice, full sleeves and pleated skirt. Eager to see how it fit, she quickly undressed and slipped it over her head. The smooth material felt wonderful against her skin. Twirling in a circle, the skirt billowed around her legs before swishing back into place. Perfect.

If only Evan were here to see her in it. With a sigh, she sank down on the bed and picked up the note, reading his words until she had them memorized. She missed him so much it hurt.

How would she ever get through the days ahead?

Evan was so lost in thought that he nearly rode straight past Luke's place.

Slowing the big black to a walk, he approached the cabin and dismounted.

He didn't bother knocking. Luke looked up from his place at the table, surprise registering on his face.

"Morning." He wiped his mouth with a napkin. "Want something to eat before you head out?"

"No, thanks." He went over to the table and sat down opposite Luke. "I came to remind you to keep an eye on Juliana."

"Do you want me to go over there at lunchtime or wait until the afternoon?"

"Thomas will be around during the day, so why don't you go around suppertime? She doesn't know how to cook. Could you rustle up something simple?"

Luke's brows shot up. "I thought every woman knew how to cook."

For some reason, Luke's reaction set his teeth on edge. He was immediately defensive. "Apparently not. Don't mention it to her, okay? She's touchy about it."

He held up his hands. "My lips are sealed. I'll make it appear as if I'm just being neighborly." A speculative gleam entered his eyes. "We've known each other a long time, Evan. I've never seen you act this way, which tells me this girl is special. Tell me the truth. Are you in love with her?"

Evan's gaze fell away. "Don't be ridiculous."

Luke fingered his chin. "Oh. Then you won't mind if I court her? In case you've forgotten, I've always been partial to redheads."

He *had* forgotten. The thought of any man—family or no—looking at Juliana with romance on his mind set his blood boiling. "Don't even think about it," he said through gritted teeth. "She's off-limits."

Luke drew his head back. "Well, if you don't want to pursue her, why can't I?"

Evan glared at Luke. He got the feeling his cousin wasn't truly interested, but was testing him. Standing abruptly, Evan rocked the chair back; it would've crashed to the floor if he hadn't caught it. He strode to the window and looked out. Streaks of pink and orange brightened the horizon. He didn't need this right now. Time was slipping away. Still, something held him back.

"Or do you really want her for yourself?" Luke moved up beside him. "That's it, isn't it? You love her, but you don't want to admit it. To yourself or anyone else."

He shook his head, irritated with himself, his cousin and the conversation. "You wouldn't understand." He ignored the little voice inside that said it was too late.

Luke's hand settled on his shoulder. "Don't let fear ruin your chance at happiness."

Unwilling to listen to reason, Evan pushed past him. "I have to go."

"Still running, I see."

Evan stopped in his tracks. He slowly turned around. "I've got a job to do."

"Why don't you let the law handle it?"

"This is personal, and you know it."

Sorrow etched his features. "I lost James, too. I grieve for him just as you do. Every day. You two were the brothers I never had. And I've been mighty worried about you, Evan. I've spent many nights by my bedside asking God to keep you safe and bring you home where you belong."

"You're right." Shame and guilt coursed through him. "I was so caught up in my own grief that I didn't stop to think how James's death had affected you. I'm sorry. Will you forgive me?"

"There's nothing to forgive. I know you didn't do it intentionally."

"Thanks, Luke." Evan made to leave. "Would you mind continuing those prayers? I have a feeling I'm gonna need them."

Evan had been on the trail about an hour when he suddenly changed direction. As much as he hated to prolong his absence, he couldn't shake the feeling something or someone awaited him in Knoxville. It wasn't that far out of his way, and he would stay just one night.

James's murder had happened in the outskirts of the sprawling city, and if there were any witnesses to be found, they'd most likely be there. Shortly after his brother's death, Evan had spent two weeks frequenting saloons and gentlemen's clubs, searching for information. It was in one of these saloons that he'd overheard Cliff Roberts and his men boasting about a large amount of cash they'd lifted from an unsuspecting traveler.

But in the eleven months he'd spent with them, he hadn't been able to get his hands on a single piece of evidence. Nor had he gotten any of them to talk. Sometimes he had the scary thought he had the wrong group of outlaws. That another gang was responsible for James's murder, and he'd wasted nearly a year of his life.

No, his mind rebelled. He had the right gang. He could feel it in his gut. But how long could he live like this? How could he ever leave Juliana and go back to living a lie?

He prayed for guidance. He also asked God to lead him to the right place, to help him find evidence so that he could finally bring those responsible to justice.

The sun was setting when he entered the city, down near the waterfront. Mostly men loitered on the street, some searching for entertainment, some for trouble. Normally, Evan wouldn't frequent this part of town, but he wasn't going to find what he was looking for among the upstanding citizens of society.

He dismounted near Lucy's Café, unhappy about the prospect of eating in the greasy establishment. But he didn't want to waste time searching for a reputable eatery. He just needed something to fill his stomach so he could get on with his search.

A half hour later, he exited the place with a bad case of heartburn. With a sigh, he headed down the street toward his first stop for the night—the Red Rose Saloon. The moment he stepped inside the dark, smoky room reeking of unwashed bodies and stale liquor, he knew it was going to be a long night.

Juliana stood with Lucas Harrison on the front porch of Evan's cabin. He was eyeing the darkening clouds with some concern.

"Looks like we're in for a storm. I'd better head home before it lets loose."

"Thank you for the lovely meal." She smiled over at him. "You're a wonderful cook."

Evan's cousin had arrived a few hours earlier with a whole chicken for them to share. He'd also brought green beans with bacon, corn on the cob, and those light-and-fluffy biscuits she liked so much. There were enough leftovers to feed her for a week.

At first she'd been self-conscious in his company, but he'd quickly lightened her mood with silly jokes and more stories of his and Evan's childhood pranks. Luke was a kind man with a good sense of humor. He was also handsome. She'd found herself wondering which of her sisters would be a good match for him.

"Glad you enjoyed it," he interrupted her musings, his eyes twinkling. "My mom taught me everything I know about cookin'. I'm real glad she did, too, since I don't have a wife to cook for me. I'd hate to eat beans and corn bread every night like some bachelors I know."

Juliana merely smiled and dipped her head. She wouldn't pry.

He dropped his hat on his head. "You know where to find me if you need anything. You can trust Thomas, too. He's a good kid."

As he descended the stairs, she walked to the edge of the porch. "I'm glad you stopped by, Luke. You helped get my mind off things."

He stood next to his horse, his expression serious for the first time that night. "Don't worry. Evan will be back as soon as he can manage it."

She hoped he was right. Thunder sounded in the distance, and she felt a spatter of rain. "You'd better hurry."

He climbed into the saddle. "Remember, keep your eyes and ears open. And don't go anywhere without your weapon."

Juliana nodded, thinking he sounded a lot like Evan at that moment. "I'll be careful. Good night."

He lifted his hand in farewell. She waited until he disappeared from sight to go inside.

She slid the lock in place and walked to each of the windows, pulling the curtains closed. Lightning flashed in the distance. Suddenly, the rain pounded on the rooftop and battered the windows. The dirt turned to mud within seconds.

She doubted Luke made it home in time to stay dry.

Once she had lit the kerosene lamps, she retrieved her coffee and got comfortable on the sofa, her thoughts consumed by Evan. Where was he? Was he safe? Well or ill? Was he thinking of her and, if so, what were his thoughts?

A loud crash near the back of the house brought her to her feet. Heart hammering, she hastily set down her coffee mug and reached for her weapon on the side table. Nerves on high alert, she gripped the gun handle and forced her feet to move toward the bedroom door.

Her mind raced with possibilities. A fallen tree limb? A lightning strike? Or something more sinister… She couldn't be sure if the sound had come from outside the house or inside.

When she reached the doorway to Evan's bedroom, she regretted not grabbing a lamp. Shadows lurked in the corners. Squinting, she was barely able to make out the outlines of the heavy furniture.

Her blood roaring in her ears, she stood stock-still, half expecting someone to jump out at her. Nothing happened. Exhaling, she crept toward the windows she'd forgotten to cover.

When she reached the first window, she peered out into the inky darkness. Flashes of light illuminated the yard. She couldn't see any fallen limbs or overturned barrels. She slid the curtain in place.

As she rounded the bed and neared the second window, she noticed a hairline crack in the glass, so tiny it was barely visible. Bending over to get a closer look, she touched the tip of her finger to the cold pane. Strange. She hadn't noticed that before.

In that moment, lightning split the sky just as thunder cracked directly above her head. She screamed and jumped back, her hand pressing against her heart.

The sky went dark again. She blew out a breath. *You're being silly, Juliana. There's nothing out there. You're letting your imagination run wild.*

Setting the gun on the side table, she reached for the curtain. As her fingers closed over the material, the sky brightened once more. There, near the barn door, stood a man.

Juliana froze. No. Couldn't be. Was she seeing things? She closed her eyes. When she opened them, darkness once again shrouded the outbuildings.

Feeling ill, she wrenched the curtain closed, grabbed her gun and ran back into the living room. She extinguished all the lamps except one.

Adrenaline pumping through her body, she hurried up the ladder to the loft. She crouched with her back against the wall. Up here, she would have a clear view of the front door. She extinguished the light, plunging the cabin into utter darkness.

If and when Lenny Fitzgerald walked through that door, she would be ready. Waiting.

At two in the morning, Evan left the saloon on Collier Street, his eyes gritty from cigar smoke and a bad taste in his mouth. Sharp disappointment settled on his shoulders. He'd struck out. A dozen saloons. Countless questions. No answers.

Lord, I know You want justice for James as much or more than I do. I don't know where to turn. I could use some help here.

He was beyond tired. Weariness seeped into his bones. And he missed Juliana. He was lonely without her.

Despite the late hour, men—most of them drunk—still milled about the street. Evan mounted Lucky and pointed him toward the hotel where he would sleep a few hours before making his way to Gatlinburg.

He had almost reached his destination when he noticed a pair of men engaged in a heated argument. He urged Lucky to the opposite side of the street. This late at night, the men were likely to be drunk. And whenever alcohol was involved, an argument could quickly turn deadly. The last thing Evan needed was to get caught in the crossfire.

Wary, he watched them carefully. Light from the lamp-post illuminated their faces. There was something oddly familiar about the shorter man. Evan racked his brain. Who was he and where had he seen him before?

He was young, possibly early twenties. Light hair. Angular jaw. Ears that stuck out a bit too far...

Evan straightened in the saddle. Randy Roberts. Cliff Roberts's son.

Something told him he needed to stop and talk to Randy. With a silent petition for wisdom, Evan halted Lucky and dismounted. The other men paid him no mind, so intent were they on each other. He approached them with caution.

"Randy Roberts? Is that you?" he called out in a friendly voice.

The blond man turned startled eyes on Evan, while the other man scowled. Evan's gaze noted that the man's hand moved to his weapon. To Evan's surprise, neither man appeared to be under the influence.

"I haven't seen you in months!" Evan walked closer. "How've ya been?"

Randy's brow furrowed. "Do I know you, mister?"

"Not exactly." He nodded to the other man before turning his full attention to Randy. "But I know you. I work for your father."

A curtain fell over his features. "My father and I haven't spoken in nearly a year."

"What do ya want, stranger?" the other man growled. "We've got business here."

"Cliff is in a heap of trouble, Randy," Evan tried to appeal to the young man's sense of duty, if he had any. "He needs your help."

A worry line appeared between his brows. "What kind of trouble?"

"Forget it, kid," the man said. "Like you said, you haven't seen your old man in months. Why should you care?"

Evan watched as various emotions danced across Randy Roberts's face. Somehow, he had to get Randy alone.

"Look, I just want to talk to you for a little while about your dad." He shot a glance at the other man. "Alone."

Randy hesitated. Then he looked at his partner. "If my father is in trouble, I need to know about it. We can talk tomorrow."

"This won't wait," the other man bit out.

"Look, if the law comes down on my father, it could affect what we've got going here. And I don't think you want that."

He shot Evan an irate glance. "I'll be around tomorrow afternoon. You'd better be where I can find you."

Randy watched without a word as the other man walked away. Then he turned to Evan. "Silver Creek Café is around the corner. We can talk there."

The café was practically empty, not surprising considering the late hour. Evan led the way to a table in the far corner, ordering two coffees when the waitress stopped for their order.

Across from him, Randy sat on the edge of his seat, his expression a mix of concern and resignation. "So what's the charge against my father?"

For a brief moment, Evan considered lying in order to get his information. But he'd had enough of deceit. He would be honest and hope the young man would cooperate.

Leaning back, his arms crossed, Evan shrugged. "There isn't any. Yet. Truth is, I'm not here to talk about Cliff. I need information, and I figure you might be able to help me get it."

Randy stiffened in anger. "Has the law caught my father or not?"

"Nope. He's still a free man."

"Then I'm out of here."

When he made to rise, Evan spoke. "Don't you want to hear what Fitzgerald's up to these days?"

At that name, Randy froze halfway out of the seat. The waitress appeared then with two steaming cups of coffee, her gaze curious. Evan passed her enough money to pay the bill plus a little extra.

"At least stay and drink the coffee," he suggested after she'd walked back to the kitchen. "I can fill you in on what's been going on since you left."

Randy sat with a huff. He was holding the warm mug between his palms but not moving to take a drink. "I disliked that no-account on sight. Never did understand why my father took up with him. Before that, we stuck to stealin' money. Maybe a horse here and there. The first time I watched Fitzgerald shoot a man, my gut told me it wouldn't be the last." Bitter regret hardened his young features. "Tried to reason with my father, but he wouldn't budge. So I left."

"Why didn't you take Art with you?"

"Art?" His brows drew together. "He's still with you? He told me he was leaving after the next robbery. Needed money to get home."

Evan wondered what had happened to those plans. The next time he saw the young man, he'd be sure to ask. He didn't like to think he'd been intimidated into staying, but that could've happened.

"If you see Art again, tell him to come and find me," Randy said.

Evan agreed that he would, then gave him the short version of the events of the last eleven months. "He's trailing me now. Wants revenge for what my friend Juliana did to him." He told Randy how she threw hot grease in Fitz's face in order to escape.

A glimmer of amusement entered his hard eyes. "I like the way she thinks."

"Yeah, well, she's alone right now. And Fitz is still out there."

"Which begs the question, why are you here and not with her?"

Evan inhaled sharply. "My brother was shot and robbed not far from here. I have reason to believe someone in Cliff's gang is the shooter. I think you might know who that man is."

"No." He shook his head vigorously. "I'm not a squealer."

"Randy." Evan leaned over the table, crowding the

younger man as anger surged. "I don't think you understand the seriousness of this situation. An innocent man was gunned down in cold blood. Someone must pay."

"Look. I'm sorry about your brother, but I won't talk." He clamped his lips shut in defiance.

Trying to rein in his emotions, Evan leaned back against the hard wooden chair and glared at him. "Fine. But when I go to the authorities about Cliff and his gang, I'll conveniently remember you as one of the former members."

He barked a laugh. "Right. *You're* gonna go to the law. And what about the bounty on your head? Think they're gonna overlook your crimes just for information? Information you can't prove?"

Slipping his hand in his pants pocket, he held up the sheriff's badge. The color drained from Randy Roberts's face and he slumped in his chair.

Evan smirked. "Still don't feel like talkin'?"

Juliana ached all over. Weak sunlight filtered through the curtains down below, which meant the storm was long gone. And so was the mysterious intruder, if, in fact, there had ever been one. She struggled to her feet, every muscle in her body protesting the movement.

Down in the kitchen, she started a fire in the stove and put on a pot of water for coffee. While waiting for that to boil, she went to the windows and peeked out. Looked the same as it had the day before. Nothing out of the ordinary.

What she saw had probably been a shadow. A trick of light. Perhaps she needed spectacles.

Sitting at the table with her coffee and a biscuit left over from the night before, her thoughts strayed to Evan. She prayed for his safety and swift return.

The ache in her heart was so great that she was seriously considering marrying him, despite everything. At this point, she couldn't imagine life without him. The mere thought of him dropping her off at her mother's and leaving her behind filled her with sorrow.

The biscuit, which had tasted so delicious the night before, now felt like sawdust in her mouth. Her appetite had fled. Resigned to the long day ahead, she gathered her dirty dishes.

She was elbow deep in dishwater when she heard heavy footfalls on the front porch. She stilled. Had Evan changed his mind and come back for her? Hope surged within her breast.

The door burst open with such force it banged against the inside wall. The man in the doorway was not Evan. Lenny Fitzgerald's evil presence filled the doorway, his soulless eyes boring into her.

Her heart sank. Her gun was six feet away. On the table.

He spotted it and grinned. Then he slammed the door behind him and advanced toward her.

Her last thought before her piercing scream rent the air was that Evan would never know how much she loved him.

Chapter Twenty

Peace. Sweet, glorious peace. The need for justice no longer smoldered like a cantankerous ulcer in his gut.

Evan stood on the boardwalk in front of the sheriff's office and watched Randy Roberts melt into the bustling morning crowd. He took a deep breath.

James, he thought, *you're finally going to get the justice you deserve.*

Thank You, Father, he humbly prayed. If it hadn't been for Randy's testimony, Evan would still be on the hunt for evidence. Still living a lie. He'd be headed for Gatlinburg right now.

Instead, a dozen or so sheriff's deputies, armed and carrying arrest warrants, were on their way to the little cabin outside Juliana's hometown. They would also be hunting Fitzgerald.

He flashed back to Randy's statement. Seemed his instincts had been right all along. Fitzgerald and another man Evan had never met, Harold Greene, were there the night of James's murder. Both men had fired their pistols. Both were guilty of murder.

It had been tough, sitting there in that stale, dusty office and listening to Randy recount the events of that night. He relived every emotion his brother must've experienced. Shock. Anger. Disbelief. The need to fight back.

But he'd sensed God's presence, helping him work through the fresh wave of grief and pain. Again, he reminded himself that God would handle the wicked. Evan's job was done.

Approaching his mount, he swung up in the saddle and pointed Lucky toward home.

Once on the open trail, he lifted his face to the cheerful morning sun and tried to imagine Juliana's surprise when he arrived home unexpectedly. Lord willing he'd get home by late afternoon. He wondered if she'd still be angry or if she'd be pleased to see him.

One thing was for sure—he had to convince her to marry him. He wanted to share his life with her. While he wasn't ready to admit that he loved her, he had his doubts about whether he'd ever be able to ride away from her.

Because he was eager to get home, time dragged. Seemed he was checking the position of the sun every twenty minutes. He stopped only a handful of times, when he felt Lucky needed a rest and a drink.

Finally, at about four o'clock, he rode onto his cousin's land. As he neared Luke's house, he decided he'd forgo a visit. Time enough tomorrow to let Luke know about his return. He was impatient to see Juliana.

But then he spotted Thomas barreling into the yard on his chestnut. Evan was suspicious at once. The young man wouldn't be here unless there was a problem.

Yanking on the reins, he turned his horse around. By the time he'd reached the cabin, Thomas and Luke were waiting for him.

"Evan!" Luke shouted. "What are you doing back here?"

Evan ignored the question, his gaze focused on Thomas, who was red-faced and winded. Evan steeled himself for bad news. "What's wrong?"

"Mr. Harrison," he panted, "I can't find Miss O'Malley anywhere."

"Why were you looking for her in the first place?" he demanded.

The young man's eyes widened. "I wasn't. I walked past the cabin on my way to the barn and noticed the door ajar. I thought that was unusual, so I called for her. I called and called and she didn't answer."

"Did you go inside?" Evan said, trying to keep a firm rein on his emotions. There had to be a logical explanation. "Maybe she was taking a nap."

"I didn't want to, it being your home and all—"

"Just get to the point," Evan interrupted.

"Yes. And she wasn't there."

"What about the loft? Did you check up there?"

"Well, no, I didn't."

Evan had heard enough. While it was entirely possible she could've gone up to the loft to lie down, he didn't think that was likely. And she would've heard Thomas calling her. Something was very wrong.

"Let's hope she decided to go swimming." He strode past Thomas toward Lucky.

"I checked the water. She wasn't there, either."

"I'm coming with you," Luke called out, already on his way to the barn to saddle his horse. "Go on ahead, I'll catch up."

When Evan rode into the yard and saw the door standing wide open, an odd feeling washed over him. This couldn't be good.

"Juliana? Are you in here?"

He stormed into the cabin. The air was still and silent. "Juliana?"

As he turned to go back out the door, his gaze fell on a smattering of dark spots on the floorboards near the base of the washstand. Strange. He rounded the ceiling-high cupboard and stopped, his mouth falling open when he spied the mess.

Dishes lay in a heap on the floor. Everything else in the room was in order except for this one spot. He snapped his mouth shut. Dread flooded his soul. It was as if she'd dropped the pile of them and had left in a hurry.

One question burned in his mind. Had she left of her own free will or had she been forced?

Evan searched the entire cabin with an urgency born of desperation. Nothing was out of place, not a pillow or quilt disturbed. He ran out into the front yard, yelling her name in hopes that she had merely to run to the outhouse. Or perhaps she'd heard an animal in distress and had gone to check it out.

A shiny object on the bottom step caught his eye, and he lunged for it. Holding it in the palm of his hand, his stomach did a nosedive. It was his mother's silver clip, the one Juliana often wore in her hair. Surely it wouldn't have come undone by itself!

Had she dropped it there intentionally for him to find? Or had it fallen out during a struggle?

Panic was quickly setting in. The one suspicion he couldn't ignore was that Fitzgerald had followed them here and bided his time until Juliana was alone and unprotected to make his move.

She wasn't in the barn. Or the shed. Nor was she anywhere near the animal pens.

Dear God, no. Please. I can't lose her. I can't face—

He broke off midprayer, incapable of finishing the thought.

He squeezed his eyes shut. If he lost her now, he would never recover.

Unbidden, a verse he'd learned long ago came to mind. *For God has not given us a spirit of fear, but of power, of love and of a sound mind.*

Help me, Father. Lead me to her. Keep her safe.

Feeling slightly more in control of his emotions, Evan tried to think rationally. If Fitzgerald had indeed taken her, where would he go? What would he do?

He knew Fitzgerald well enough to figure he'd want to see Evan suffer. If Fitz thought he could get to Evan by hurting Juliana, he'd do it in a heartbeat. Which meant he wouldn't go far. He'd wait until an opportune time to show himself. After that, it was anybody's guess what he'd do.

Luke and Thomas rode up in a hurry.

"Anything?" Luke asked, his horse prancing from side to side.

"No." Evan scanned the grounds, on the look out for anything out of the ordinary. "I think I know what happened. And this is what we're gonna do about it…"

Juliana was living her worst nightmare. Slumped against a tree, she strained at the tight ropes binding her wrists. The gag in her mouth smelled of stale sweat and alcohol, making her stomach roil with nausea.

She kept a wary eye on her captor. Crouched down behind a bush, gun drawn, he kept watch on the cabin. So far he hadn't hurt her. But what would he do when he realized Evan wasn't coming back any time soon? Shuddering with the possibilities, she pleaded to God for mercy.

Lenny Fitzgerald hated Evan and wanted to make him suffer. And he wanted revenge for what she'd done to him.

Evan, my love. Why didn't I tell you how I felt?

The realization he might never know made her want to weep. Filled with profound sadness, she ducked her head and blinked back a rush of tears. She couldn't let Fitzgerald see her weakness. It would only make things harder for her.

Too bad she couldn't change the past. If only she'd thought to put the gun belt on that morning. If only she'd told Evan about her strange experience yesterday afternoon. If only—

A voice calling in the distance split the silence. She whipped up her head. *Thomas,* she thought, *the hired man.* He'd no doubt come to the cabin for something and found the mess in the kitchen. What would he do when he couldn't find her? Would he go to Luke Harrison's place or wait around for her to come back?

Her captor glared at her over his shoulder. Angry red welts marked his face where she'd burned him. "Looks like loverboy came back. Good. I didn't want to wait around here much longer."

Juliana gave a quick prayer, asking God to protect the unsuspecting Thomas.

The voice grew closer. He was calling her name over and over again. Odd. She wouldn't have thought he'd be all that frantic. After all, he didn't know her. Maybe he was afraid Evan or Luke would blame him if something happened to her. She hoped that wouldn't be the case.

"There he is!" he growled.

Her captor leapt up, startling her. Before she could react, he seized her arm in a bruising grip and, hauling her up, began dragging her away from the dense stand of trees. Without her bonnet to shade her eyes, the sun's rays temporarily blinded her.

Ignoring her whimpers of protest, he forced her to stand in front of him. Repulsed at being held against his foul body, she tried to inch away. He bit out a curse and wrapped his beefy arm around her neck, nearly cutting off her air supply. She started to struggle once more, but instantly stilled when she felt the tip of a gun barrel pressed against her temple.

Icy shards of fear skittered down her back. *Oh, God, no! Not like this!*

"Harrison!" he bellowed, jarring her eardrum. "Is this what you're looking for?"

Was Fitzgerald blind? Thomas Latham was shorter than Evan, not to mention a whole lot leaner. He didn't have the muscular frame Evan did. Juliana squinted, trying to get a better view.

"Let her go, Fitz," an achingly familiar voice carried across the field. "This is between you and me."

Juliana stiffened in alarm. It couldn't be. Evan was long gone by now! Wasn't he?

Gun aimed in their direction, his long, confident strides ate up the distance. The clothing told her that it was indeed Evan—he'd been dressed all in black. But what was he doing here? Hope and fear warred with one another. What if Fitzgerald shot and killed him before her very eyes?

Fitzgerald snorted. "Nope. I've been watching the two of you long enough. This girl's caught your fancy, and I'm gonna enjoy watching your face as I put a bullet through her skull."

His words chilled her to the bone. This was a man who'd killed before and wouldn't hesitate to do it again. She meant less than nothing to him.

"Besides," he growled in a voice filled with hatred, "she scarred me for life. I owe her."

He jammed the barrel hard against her temple and spots danced before her eyes. She blinked hard, trying to clear her vision. Her heart was racing like a runaway wagon.

There was no doubt in her mind her very life was on the line. There was a gun pointed to her head, and the man with the finger on the trigger was not in possession of a conscience.

"You have to admit you weren't that good-looking to begin with," Evan drawled, goading him. "I doubt a few scars are gonna make that much difference."

"You always were so sure of yourself, Harrison. But I told Cliff I didn't trust you. Something was off from the beginning. Looks like I was right." He slid the hammer back with a click.

Juliana moaned through the gag in her mouth. Evan's hard gaze flew to her, and he faltered. Alarm flashed across his face.

Fitzgerald caught the look. He let out a cruel laugh. "Not so sure of yourself now, huh? How does it feel now that I've got the upper hand?" He jerked her roughly to one side. "Throw down your weapon."

Evan fought for control. Loathing and rage churned in his gut. His sole desire in that instant was to blow a hole through Fitzgerald's chest.

This man had already stolen his brother away from him. And now Juliana was a hairsbreadth away from death. One false move could prove disastrous.

Her eyes begged him not to do it. He had no choice. Every muscle in his body tense and ready to spring into action, he warily tossed the gun on the ground.

Please, God. Help us save her. I wasn't there to save James. But there's still a chance here. Were Luke and Thomas in position? He couldn't make his move until they were. He'd have to keep him talking.

"Kick it over here," Fitz commanded.

Again, Evan did as he was told.

"Get down on your knees."

A muscle twitched in his jaw, and his mouth hardened to a grim line. His movements slow and calculated, he eased down onto his knees, palms up. "Okay, you have me where you want me. Let her go."

His mouth contorted into a sneer. "Why would I do that? She's my ace."

"What are you going to do?" Evan said, his eyes cold as a winter snow. "Kill us both? What will that get you besides more time in a jail cell?"

"If I'm going down, I'm bringin' you with me," he spat. "You and me are on the same side of the law."

"Yeah, about that…" He cocked his head to one side, his eyes narrowing.

"Stop!"

Evan jerked his head to the left and spotted Art jogging across the field, his gun aimed at Fitzgerald. Dread curled through his bones. The boy was likely to get himself killed.

"Don't do this, Fitz!" Art pleaded. "Miss O'Malley doesn't deserve this! And Roberts will kill you if you shoot Harrison!"

"Go back to your post, you idiot." Fitzgerald dismissed him. "This is my business, not yours."

Art stiffened. "I may be young, but I'm not an idiot. And, unlike you, I have a heart. Now let her go."

"I don't think so." Fitz trained his gun on Art.

Juliana cried out. Evan's gaze flew to her. She struggled against Fitz's tight hold, her fingers clawing the arm he held around her neck. *What was she doing?* He stiffened, ready to hurl himself at the other man.

Chapter Twenty-One

Juliana couldn't breathe. His arm tightened around her throat, choking her. She fought against him, unmindful of the gun. She needed air!

"Juliana, don't!"

Evan's plea reached her ears seconds before the loud crack of a weapon. Eyes squeezed tight, she hunched down and braced against the explosion of pain that never came.

Someone shoved her to the side. She landed hard. Gritting her teeth at the jarring discomfort, Juliana scrambled to get out of the way. The ropes dug painfully into her wrists. Her heel caught the edge of her dress, ripping it.

Voices volleyed all around her, as did the sounds of scuffling and muttered oaths.

Frenzied thoughts bounced around in her mind. Had Evan been shot? Was Art okay?

When she felt she was at a safe distance, she craned her neck, searching for Evan. Her hair fell in her eyes, and she shook her head to dislodge it. She recognized Luke. He was scrambling to hold down Fitzgerald. Thomas was there, too, doing his best to pull Evan off the outlaw.

Tears of relief clogged her throat at the sight of Evan unharmed. He was safe, thank God!

She wanted to scream at Evan to stop, to let the authorities mete out Fitzgerald's punishment, but the gag silenced her. Gone was the control of a few minutes ago. Fury marked his features. She'd never seen that expression on his face. Anxious over what he might do, she prayed Thomas would be able to hold him.

A movement to the side of her vision caught her attention. It was Art, and he was lying on his side cradling his shoulder. Blood trickled onto the ground from the gaping wound in his arm. No! The gag muffled her cry of distress.

Slowly, Luke's voice penetrated the haze of fury clouding Evan's brain. Staring down into his enemy's unrepentant face, he slackened his grip on his neck. He wouldn't lower himself to the other man's level.

Twisting out of Thomas's hold, Evan stumbled back, chest heaving with exertion. Sweat poured off his face. He watched as the two men tied Fitzgerald's hands and feet. Foul language spewed from the outlaw's mouth.

Satisfied Fitz was no longer a threat, Evan sprinted to Juliana's side. He dropped to his knees and eased her up into a sitting position. "Are you hurt?" He made quick work of the knot at the back of her head and removed the gag.

"Evan," she gasped. She fell against him, her head heavy on his chest.

"Everything's all right now, my darling." He lightly stroked her hair, smoothing the damp tendrils from her face. Tears burned his eyes. Overwhelming gratitude made him want to shout for joy. He held her close, hardly daring to believe she was safe in his arms. For a few minutes back there, he'd feared the worst. "You're safe. I promise that as long as I'm around to protect you, nothing like this will ever happen again."

"Evan, please." She sucked in air, her eyes pleading, "Art's been shot."

"What?" He glanced over his shoulder. "I'll see to him." He sliced through the thick rope binding her hands and helped her up. "Are you all right to walk?"

"I'm fine."

When they reached Art, Evan noticed the young man's pallor. "Art, I'm gonna check the wound. I'll be as easy as I can, buddy."

With a curt nod and a grimace, Art braced himself. Juliana moved to sit on his other side and took his hand in hers. "I'm praying for you."

He eased his eyes opened. "If it eases your mind any, ma'am, I asked Jesus to be Lord of my life. To forgive me for my sins."

The emotion on Juliana's face mirrored the feelings in Evan's heart. This was amazing news!

"Oh, Art, I'm so happy for you."

"I'm proud of you," Evan added. He squeezed Art's good shoulder before turning to tend to his injury. Luke walked up and assisted him. They were able to stop the flow of blood. It appeared that the bullet had gone straight through. There'd be no need for surgery, other than stitching up the opening.

Luke helped Evan load Art into the back of the wagon where a bound-and-gagged Fitzgerald awaited his trip to jail. Ignoring the outlaw, Evan patted Art's leg. "Juliana and I will stop by the doc's office shortly to check on you."

Humble gratitude shone in his eyes. "I'd be mighty

grateful if you'd send my ma a telegram for me. Tell her where I am."

"I'll get the information from you and send it today. How's that?"

"Thanks, Harrison. For everything."

"Watch that shoulder."

Evan turned to his cousin and Thomas and shook both their hands. "I owe you both."

"You go take care of that young lady," Luke advised. "Remember, no fear."

Evan smiled. "I remember."

He waited until the wagon started rolling down the drive to turn his attention to Juliana. She was sitting on the porch steps, watching him. He eased down beside her, his hungry gaze freely roaming her uplifted face. "Are you all right?"

Her luminous green eyes seemed just as eager to drink him in. "I'm fine. The Lord kept me safe, and He sent you to rescue me." As if a thought struck her, she tilted her head to one side. "Why did you come back?"

"I'll explain later. Right now, all I want is to look at you. Maybe the fact that you're safe and sound will start to sink in."

Summoning courage, Juliana lifted a trembling hand to caress his face. "I love you, Evan." Ignoring his sharp intake of breath, she rushed on. "And if your offer of marriage still stands, I—I accept. I understand it will be a union based on friendship alone. I know you don't return my feelings—"

"You're wrong." He suddenly gripped her shoulders. "I *do* love you, Juliana. My heart belongs to you. Has for a long time."

Juliana stared at him in disbelief. Had she heard right? His eyes were soft with emotion. "I don't blame you for not believing me. I've been an utter fool. I thought if I ignored my feelings long enough they would go away. I was wrong." He stroked her cheek with the back of his hand. "I realized that I've been letting fear rule my life. I don't want to worry anymore about what ifs. I want to focus on the here and now."

"Oh, Evan," she breathed, her heart bursting with joy, "I think I've loved you since that first day. You were so furious when Fitzgerald hurt me, you took it personally even though you didn't know me. And you were protective, so careful in your treatment of me. Deep down, I knew you were a good man."

His mouth parted in surprise. "Are you saying you cared for me all along? Before you knew the truth?"

She laughed softly. "I kept telling myself all the reasons I shouldn't fall in love with an outlaw, but my heart wouldn't listen."

"Juliana," he breathed her name with awe, lowering his head to kiss her. He held her as if she were a rare treasure, the movement of his lips against hers achingly tender. Easing away, he sent her an earnest smile. "Remember you said you wanted a man who was desperate to marry you?"

Her heart skipped a beat. The love shining in his eyes made her feel so special. "Yes, I remember."

"You're lookin' at him," he claimed softly, his hands framing her face. "You bring me such joy, Juliana. I don't want to imagine my life without you in it. Please say you'll marry me."

"I want nothing more than to be your wife. To share the rest of my days with you." She beamed, blinking back tears of joy.

"Let's start with today." He grinned, his expression more serene than she'd ever seen it.

"What do you mean?"

"I want to marry you today. We can have the pastor here perform a simple ceremony with Luke as our witness. Then we could have a fancy one in Gatlinburg for all your friends and family. What do you think of that idea?"

The dress and cake and decorations didn't matter to her. The most important thing was the joining of their lives.

Juliana wrapped her arms around his neck and lifted her face for a kiss. "Brilliant. How soon can you be ready?"

Evan held her tight against him and kissed her thoroughly. "One hour?" he whispered, his forehead resting against hers.

At this point, she would agree to anything he suggested. He *loved* her. She was still working to understand that fact. "You've got yourself a deal."

"I love you, Juliana. I always will."

His tender vow touched her deep inside. "And I you."

Epilogue

Flanked on either side by her twin sisters, Juliana waited near the cake table for her husband to join her. Dusk was fast approaching. Already lanterns were being lit and placed on the tables. Lightning bugs flitted about, their flashes of light illuminating the darkening sky. Their guests, dressed in all their finery, mixed and mingled under the trees in her mother's front yard. A month had passed since their wedding in Cades Cove. Tonight was all about celebrating their union, a way for family and friends to share in their happiness.

"You are so lucky, Juliana," Jessica gushed, her youthful face alight with happiness.

Jane, older by three minutes, declared, "It's all so romantic! And Evan is the most handsome man I've ever seen." She sighed, a dreamy look in her eyes.

Evan stood talking with his cousin Luke across the yard, and when she caught his gaze he held up a finger to indicate one more minute. Grinning, he winked at her. Her heart skipped a beat, and she grinned back.

Seeing her husband relaxed and happy thrilled her. He'd endured much loss in his life. During the last two weeks, she'd witnessed her family slowly filling the void left by the loss of his loved ones.

"What do you think, Megan?" Dark-haired Nicole, wearing an elaborate robin's-egg blue creation in the latest style and shipped straight from New York City, addressed their book-loving sister. "Would their story be a best seller?"

Juliana locked gazes with Megan and waited for her answer. "I'm not sure. All I can say is that I'm thankful this one has a happy ending." With a sweet smile and moisture in her eyes, Megan hugged her close. "I'm happy for you, sis. You finally have your very own hero."

Juliana whispered, "One day your hero will come."

Laughing softly, Megan shot back, "I hope his arrival is not quite as dramatic as Evan's."

"Juliana, my dear."

Releasing Megan, Juliana turned to her mother, radiant in her lavender brocade jacket and full skirt and looking much younger than her fifty years. Of all her family members, Alice O'Malley had handled the news of Juliana's marriage with the most grace and restraint.

"Do you have a moment? Joshua would like a word with you."

Glancing beyond Alice, Juliana spotted her cousin standing apart from the guests. He gave her a brief wave. "Of course." To her sisters, she teased, "No one lay a finger on that cake! I'll be right back."

As she approached, she noted his slumped shoulders and pursed lips. He appeared deep in thought. "Hey you." She tugged on his jacket sleeve. "Penny for your thoughts."

Joshua's smile couldn't mask the sadness in his blue eyes. "I got you something."

She looked down at the neatly wrapped package he placed in her hands. "What's this?"

"Open it."

Carefully untying the pink ribbon and peeling back the material, she admired the elegant stationery and small book with blank pages—a journal to record her experiences in her new home. "Thanks, Josh." She smiled up at him, tears springing to her eyes. She would miss his good-natured teasing and ready smile. "I can't think of a better gift."

Slipping his hands in his pockets, his expression turned solemn. "I'm gonna miss you, Jules. Who am I supposed to go fishing with once you're gone? And what about our shooting contests? It won't be the same without you here to make Caleb hoppin' mad."

She gave him a lop-sided smile. "Soon your fiancée will arrive. You can teach her all the things you taught me."

"Francesca is a city girl," he protested, "more suited to fine drawing rooms and needlework than outdoor pursuits. I doubt she'd be interested."

Juliana had never met the oil heiress, but she couldn't help but wonder if Francesca was a good fit for Joshua. "I don't mean to question your judgment, but are you certain she's the one for you?"

"I could ask the same of you," he responded.

At first, Joshua hadn't been at all happy about her decision to marry Evan. The initial confrontation between the two men had nearly ended in blows. Joshua was only being protective, of course. He wanted the best for her, just as she wanted the best for him.

"Evan is a good man."

Joshua nodded. "I have to admit he's growing on me."

To her relief, the men had formed a tenuous friendship over the last few weeks.

"Ah, here comes your husband now."

Juliana turned to see Evan, darkly handsome in his black suit, crossing the lawn with determined strides. Reaching her side, he slipped his arm around her waist and tugged her close. "Sorry to keep you waiting, sweetheart." He nodded to Joshua. "Josh. Everything all right?" His gaze drifted from one to the other.

"Fine," Joshua said. "I'm thirsty. Think I'll go grab a glass of punch."

"Josh, wait."

Stepping in front of him, she placed her hand over his heart. He'd been her dearest confidant all through childhood. They shared a lifetime of memories. "I love you, my friend. Remember we're just a few days' ride over the mountains. You're welcome anytime."

His eyes brimming with affection, he covered her hand. "I love you, too, Jules. We'll visit often. And I may even write from time to time."

"I'll hold you to that."

His voice gruff, he said to Evan, "Take care of her, Harrison."

"I love her, too," Evan said gently. "You don't have to worry."

With a curt nod, he walked away.

Evan stepped up behind her. "Are you okay?"

"I'm fine."

"Did I mention how stunning you look today, Mrs. Harrison?" he whispered near her ear, his warm breath scattering goose bumps along her neck and shoulders. Juliana relaxed back against him and gazed contentedly at the festive scene before her.

Juliana smiled. "I'm glad you approve of my dress."

"It's not the dress. It's you *in* the dress." His deep voice was a caress. "And I like all the sparkly things in your hair. You look like a fairy princess."

Her hands tightened on his.

Evan had meant it when he'd said he didn't want to wait to make her his bride. Within hours of his proposal, they'd stood before the minister in the valley's quaint white church and said their vows, their only witness Luke Harrison. The ceremony's beauty was in its simplicity, the focus solely on their love for each other. Juliana was grateful for that intimate, private ceremony and the wonderful days that had followed.

Evan had only one meeting with Sheriff Tate to discuss the case. After that, the sheriff had arranged for the transportation of Lenny Fitzgerald to Knoxville where James's murder trial would eventually be held. Thanks to Evan's tip, Cliff Roberts and his gang had been captured during their attempt to rob the Gatlinburg Bank. They were already in Knoxville awaiting trial.

As soon as a court date was set, Evan and Juliana would travel there as well. He was eager for justice. And at long last, he was allowing himself to grieve for his brother. The process was slow and at times painful, but he was relying on the Lord to help him through.

Gazing at the guests, she spotted Art and his mother talking quietly. The experiences of the last few weeks had changed him. He was more mature. There was a confidence about him now that hadn't been there before.

Sheriff Tate had agreed to let Art go free in exchange for his testimony. Juliana would forever be grateful for the sheriff's leniency.

Evan pressed a kiss on her cheek. "As long as I live, I don't want to ever spend another night without you."

She turned in his embrace and slid her arms up and around his neck. "I missed you last night, too."

His hold tightened. "Whose idea was it to consign me to your cousins' house, anyway?"

Juliana smiled. "I don't remember. Megan, perhaps. She'd think it was romantic. Was it that bad?"

"So bad I was tempted to sneak over here and kidnap you a second time."

"I'm disappointed that you didn't."

His blue eyes heated. "I love you, Juliana Harrison."

Looking over at her husband, the man she adored, she was overcome with emotion. Juliana was in awe of God's mercy and grace. His ways were indeed above her ways, His thoughts above her thoughts. On that morning in the mercantile, she never could've imagined what lay in store for her. He had taken a seemingly impossible situation and turned it around for good. God had blessed her beyond measure.

* * * * *

Dear Reader,

Thank you for choosing *The Reluctant Outlaw*. I hope you enjoyed reading about Evan and Juliana's journey to love. My favorite heroes are like Evan—tough, determined and loyal—with a measure of tenderness thrown in. Like Evan, many of us struggle with fear in different seasons of our lives. We can find comfort in the fact that God is in control. Nothing surprises Him. I admire Juliana's ability to cling to God's promises even in the midst of her ordeal. As His children, we must learn to do the same when trials come our way.

East Tennessee is near and dear to my heart. Born and raised about an hour from Gatlinburg and Cades Cove, I visited the mountains quite often and worked in Gatlinburg for a time. The majestic beauty of the Great Smoky Mountains, as well as the abundance of animal and plant life, draws millions of visitors each year. It was a pleasure to write about such a special place and envision what it must've been like over a hundred years ago.

I would love to hear from you! You can write to me at Love Inspired Books, 233 Broadway, Suite 1001, New York, NY 10279, email me at karenkirst@live.com, or visit my website at: www.karenkirst.com.

Best wishes,
Karen Kirst

Questions for Discussion

1. When Juliana is kidnapped, her faith in God's protection remains firm. Have you ever been in a situation where you've questioned His plan for your life? Were you ultimately able to trust Him? What was the outcome?

2. When we first meet Evan, he's struggling with grief and consumed with the need for revenge. When tragedy strikes, why do you think some people turn to God for comfort while others blame Him in anger?

3. How does Juliana's arrival in Evan's life change his priorities?

4. Understandably, Juliana doesn't trust Evan when he vows to take her home. Do you think she acted foolishly when she stole his horse and took off on her own? Why or why not?

5. How do Juliana's upbringing and personality aid her during her ordeal?

6. Evan feels that he failed his brother, James. How does this fuel his drive to protect Juliana?

7. Evan and Juliana allow the Talbots to believe they are man and wife. Is it okay to let someone believe something about you that's untrue if it's for a good reason?

8. How do Evan's illness and recovery affect his relationship with God?

9. How does Evan's illness test Juliana's faith?

10. Why does Juliana refuse Evan's offer of marriage of convenience? Keeping in mind the social customs of the period, is she right to turn him down? Why or why not?

11. Evan doesn't want to risk loving Juliana for fear of getting hurt. How does fear limit us? What does the Bible say about how we should handle fear?

12. Even in the midst of her ordeal, Juliana is sensitive to Art's turmoil. What are some ways we can reach out to those around us who are hurting?

13. Evan admits that forgiving the men responsible for his brother's death will take time. Is forgiveness instantaneous or a process?

14. What's the difference between revenge and justice?

15. How does each character change by the end of the story?

INSPIRATIONAL

Inspirational romances to warm your heart & soul.

Love Inspired.
HISTORICAL

TITLES AVAILABLE NEXT MONTH

Available October 11, 2011

MARRYING THE MAJOR
Victoria Bylin

FAMILY BLESSINGS
Amish Brides of Celery Fields
Anna Schmidt

ONCE UPON A THANKSGIVING
Linda Ford & Winnie Griggs

UNLAWFULLY WEDDED BRIDE
Noelle Marchand

REQUEST YOUR FREE BOOKS!

2 FREE INSPIRATIONAL NOVELS
PLUS 2
FREE
MYSTERY GIFTS

Love Inspired
HISTORICAL
INSPIRATIONAL HISTORICAL ROMANCE

YES! Please send me 2 FREE Love Inspired® Historical novels and my 2 FREE mystery gifts (gifts are worth about $10). After receiving them, if I don't wish to receive any more books, I can return the shipping statement marked "cancel." If I don't cancel, I will receive 4 brand-new novels every month and be billed just $4.49 per book in the U.S. or $4.99 per book in Canada. That's a saving of at least 22% off the cover price. It's quite a bargain! Shipping and handling is just 50¢ per book in the U.S. and 75¢ per book in Canada.* I understand that accepting the 2 free books and gifts places me under no obligation to buy anything. I can always return a shipment and cancel at any time. Even if I never buy another book, the two free books and gifts are mine to keep forever.

102/302 IDN FEHF

Name	(PLEASE PRINT)	
Address		Apt. #
City	State/Prov.	Zip/Postal Code

Signature (if under 18, a parent or guardian must sign)

Mail to the **Reader Service:**
IN U.S.A.: P.O. Box 1867, Buffalo, NY 14240-1867
IN CANADA: P.O. Box 609, Fort Erie, Ontario L2A 5X3

Not valid for current subscribers to Love Inspired Historical books.

Want to try two free books from another series?
Call 1-800-873-8635 or visit www.ReaderService.com.

* Terms and prices subject to change without notice. Prices do not include applicable taxes. Sales tax applicable in N.Y. Canadian residents will be charged applicable taxes. Offer not valid in Quebec. This offer is limited to one order per household. All orders subject to credit approval. Credit or debit balances in a customer's account(s) may be offset by any other outstanding balance owed by or to the customer. Please allow 4 to 6 weeks for delivery. Offer available while quantities last.

Your Privacy—The Reader Service is committed to protecting your privacy. Our Privacy Policy is available online at www.ReaderService.com or upon request from the Reader Service.

We make a portion of our mailing list available to reputable third parties that offer products we believe may interest you. If you prefer that we not exchange your name with third parties, or if you wish to clarify or modify your communication preferences, please visit us at www.ReaderService.com/consumerschoice or write to us at Reader Service Preference Service, P.O. Box 9062, Buffalo, NY 14269. Include your complete name and address.

LIHI1B

Sophie Bartholomew loves all things Christmas.
Caring for an orphaned little boy
makes this season even more special.
And so does helping a scarred cop move past his pain
and see the bright future that lies ahead...

Since the moment Kade had appeared at Ida June's wreath-laden door behind a spotless, eager Davey, Sophie had had butterflies in her stomach. A few hours ago, they'd been having pizza and getting better acquainted, but she felt as though she'd known him much longer than a few jam-packed days. In reality, she didn't know him at all, but there was something, some indefinable pull between them.

Maybe their mutual love for a little lost boy had connected their hearts.

"Christmas is about a child," she said. "Maybe God sent him."

One corner of Kade's mouth twisted. "Now you sound like my great-aunt."

"She's a very smart lady."

"More than I realized," he said softly, a hint of humor and mystery in the words. "A good woman is worth more than rubies."

"What?" Sophie tilted her head, puzzled. Though she recognized the proverb, she wasn't quite sure where it fit into the conversation.

"Something Ida June said."

"Ida June and her proverbs." Sophie smiled up at him. "What brought that one on?"

Kade was quiet for a moment, his gaze steady on hers. He gently brushed a strand of hair from the shoulder of her sweater, an innocent gesture that, like a cupid's arrow, went straight to her heart.

"You," he said at last.

Sophie's heart stuttered. Though she didn't quite get what he meant or why he was looking at her so strangely, a mood, strong and fascinating, shimmered in the air.

Their eyes held, both of them seeking for answers neither of them had. All Sophie had were questions she couldn't ask. So far, every time she'd approached the topic of his life in Chicago, Kade had closed himself in and locked her out.

A woman above rubies, he'd said. Had he meant her?

Sophie senses Kade's eagerness to connect. But can she convince him to open his heart to love—and to God? Don't miss THE CHRISTMAS CHILD by Rita® Award-winning author, Linda Goodnight, on sale October 2011 wherever Love Inspired books are sold!

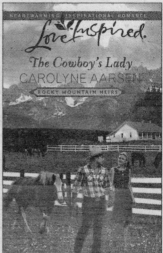